CROWN OF FIRE AND WRATH

BY

SLOANE MURPHY

A Crown of Fire and Wrath
The Shadow Walkers Saga #5
Part of The Seven Realms Saga

Published by Hudson Indie Ink
www.hudsonindieink.com

A Crown of Fire and Wrath/Sloane Murphy – 2nd ed.
ISBN-13 - 978-1-915118-02-8

And once the storm is over, you won't remember how you made it through, how you managed to survive. You won't even be sure whether the storm is really over.
But one thing is certain.
When you come out of the store, you won't be the same person who walked in.
Thats what the storm is all about.

- HARUKI MURAKAMI

ONE

LEVI

I'm going to fucking kill him.

It takes less than a split second for a riot to start behind me, just another reason I'm going to fucking kill him.

"What the actual fuck just happened?" Colt yells taking a step towards me as I turn to face them all. I level him with a look and Caleb places a hand on his shoulder, holding him in place. I'm sure it's more for Colt's safety than my own. As good of a Hunter as Colt is, he's not fought an Angel before. Even if I held back for Remy's sake, he could end up like his brother, and that isn't something I want to do.

"Why the hell did you let him take her?" Creek grinds

out, his eyes are black and his fists clenched as he keeps a tight leash on the Demon inside of him. I take a deep breath, because they are going to like this about as much as I do. Fuck, I really am going to kill him.

"First of all, I didn't let him do a damn thing. Stopping Michael is about as simple and easy as stopping a goddamn hurricane." I massage my temples, closing my eyes for a brief reprieve before looking back at everyone. I'm not sure exactly who the biggest threat is here right now, but Morgan looks like she wants my head. Between her and her Horsemen, I'm pretty sure they could probably take it too. "But, much as I hate to admit it, she is safe with him. Probably safer than she is here right now."

Shouts start up all over again, and it takes every ounce of willpower not to lose my shit at them. I'm not exactly spitting fucking rainbows about Remy being taken from us once more either, but are they forgetting that she very nearly just fucking died on us? *Again.*

"Why, pray tell, is she safe with him?" Kain asks, his sarcasm overriding his anger, but it's still there, flashing in his eyes and in his descended fangs.

"Because he's in love with her." The words leave my mouth and silence descends across them all. It's as if time pauses momentarily as they take it in.

"Of course he fucking is," Caleb mutters. I barely get chance to open my mouth when pain rips through me and

I'm flying backwards through the air. The sound of tree trunks snapping as I fly backwards is all I can hear as I crash through the tree line on the edge of the field, leaving destruction in my wake. I groan as I finally hit the ground. I lift my head, trying not to let my anger overrule the logic of the fact that they deserve to be angry, because they don't know the whole story yet, but I'll be fucked if I'm just going to stand here and take it. It's not like I fucking asked Bauer to try and kill her right in front of us, or invited Michael down here to take her away from us.

I climb to my feet, take a deep breath, and brace myself as I spot the three of them barreling towards me. Roman reaches me first and tackles me, his shoulder to my gut taking me down before his fists start flying, first at my ribs, then my face. I keep my arms up as much as I can to protect myself from the angry Lycan. There's only so much of this I'm going to allow before I start fighting back, regardless of what Remy would think. Everything I do, I do for her. Case in point, the beat down I'm currently being handed without fighting back.

I keep blocking as many fists as I can before throwing Roman off of me, and I get to my feet. I groan as the pain in my ribs hits me when I'm on my feet, then Creek and Kain attack me at once. Becoming a Demon certainly seems to suit Creek, but fuck I wish he hadn't been such a good student with learning his powers. Every punch of his is like ten with the weight of his power behind it. He isn't enough to hurt me properly alone, but the three of them, with their anger, who fucking knows.

A whistle pierces the air followed by a loud bang, startling us all. "As much fun as this is boys," Morgan drawls. "This isn't going to bring her back, and I'm pretty sure she'll be pissed as fuck if you break each other."

She pauses for a minute, levelling each of us with a look that makes me feel like a naughty fucking kid—even though I did nothing wrong—before she looks directly at me again. "You fix it, or I will. We both know which is going to cause less bloodshed."

"And you wondered why *we* were the protective ones," Bryce mutters, looking towards Colt who rolls his eyes. I wait for the other three to start heading back towards the others before I make my way over. I'm not getting caught off guard by those assholes attacking from behind.

The Horsemen are all glaring at me, despite Caleb and Bryce's flippant comments. Fallon hasn't said a word, but I can see Marie talking to her quietly as the glow around her flickers. Her lips are pressed together, and if looks could kill… well, I'd be saying goodnight for sure. Colt moves over towards her and Marie, I guess trying to help talk her down. Between the two of them, they seem to have her covered.

I temper down the storm inside me that still threatens to

break through, remembering that these people are Remy's family. Our family. I reach the edge of the crown when Nonnie heads towards me, wooden spoon in hand, waving it at me like she's going to use it to break me in two. Kain intercepts her with the help of Luc, who is also still just glaring at me.

"Stupid Angel boy, letting my Remy get taken. Go and get her. Right now," Nonnie insists, but I shake my head. "I said right now! Stupid boy."

"It's not that simple," I sigh, and suddenly all eyes are on me again. I mean, I knew this wasn't going to go down well, but fuck. When I get my hands on Michael, he is going to have a lot to fucking answer for. I take a deep breath before vowing to kill him again.

"What the fuck does that mean?" Malik asks, and I flinch a little at the venom in his voice. He and Killian might be the quieter two of that quartet but that doesn't mean they're not just as dangerous, if not more so. Never underestimate a Horseman. Too many people have died doing exactly that. There's a reason they became a legend, even in the human realm.

I take a deep breath and run a hand through my too long hair. "It means, that I'm still banished from Avalon. I can't just walk in there and carry her away."

"The fuck you can't!" Roman growls.

"I really can't, not without declaring war. And unless

any of you have secret wings, you aren't getting in either. Plus, like I said before. She's probably safer there right now." I wave to the bloody remains of Bauer to prove my point. "Until we know exactly who the fuck is behind all of this, Avalon might just be a safe haven for her. No factions can get there. And if she's with Michael, well, he's the head of the Archangels for a reason. Though we can't take too long deciding what the fuck we're going to do, because like the Shadow Realm, time moves quicker in Avalon than it does here."

"And he loves her?" Roman growls, his eyes flashing silver.

"Yeah. He has for a long time," I sigh.

"Then she isn't fucking safe with him," Creek adds. "If he lays a hand on her…"

"He won't," I tell him.

"I don't understand," Kain mutters. "You said he loved her."

"Safe haven or not, you need to get into Avalon and make sure she's okay." Morgan looks at me, her tone brokering no argument. Not that I'd try, like I say, the five of them might be able to take me, and I didn't want to hurt them, for Remy's sake. Plus, I don't disagree with her.

"And I will. I'll head there tomorrow, I think, for tonight we should let her rest. Michael will have been able to heal her, Angel glass or no. She'll still need time to recover from that."

"He can heal damage by Angel glass?" Morgan asks, her eyes wide and I nod.

"He's a Shadow Walker. Same as Remy. Their healing powers are like no other. They just can't heal that sort of damage on themselves. Nature's balancing act. He just doesn't advertise it, and he doesn't tell many people because so many people fear the true power of a Walker. Plus, he has other powers too, so it's never really questioned. I only know because Amantara knew. Like I said, he loves her." The words are like razors on my tongue. Admitting that he loves her, that he's probably better for her right now, it shreds every part of me, but I refuse to focus on that. My only focus is making sure everyone here is okay, and then getting my girl back.

With that thought, I look over to Colt who has moved back near the horsemen, and staring at what's left of his brother. His death wasn't pretty, but he didn't deserve anything less. I acted without thought, and while I'm sure Remy will have something to say about it later, I did what needed to be done. I won't ever be sorry for that. Even if she hates me for it, I'll know I did it for her.

More than being upset about Bauer, she'll likely be pissed that Colt is essentially alone now. Especially if Hunters aren't cycling. Again, wasn't exactly at the forefront of my mind, but I can't say the world isn't a better place without Bauer. Though, knowing Michael and his meddling, Bauer is likely in a line in the Shadow Realm right now rather than being given the option to cycle, if it's even still possible. I can only hope a few others landed down there too.

I'm sure Caleb and the guys will treat them right if they do.

"Shall we head back inside?" I offer, clasping Colt's shoulder, pulling his attention from his brother. Muttering ensues, but everyone eventually heads back into the house while I try to put a plan together in my mind about how the hell I'm going to tear Avalon's defenses apart to get my girl back, because if that's what it takes, I have no issues tearing apart the entire world.

Everyone else has gone to their designated rooms for the night, resigned to the fact that there's nothing they can do right now, and that tearing my head off isn't going to achieve anything. Hell, there's not much I can do right now, and if that doesn't piss me off beyond belief…

Fucking Michael. Of course, he was watching, just waiting for that moment to quite fucking literally swoop in and take her from me. I clench my fists again, only the memory of how much Everly loved this fucking kitchen, hell the whole fucking house, stops me from tearing shit apart. Instead I take a deep breath and look to the ceiling, counting back from a hundred trying to calm myself, and failing.

"Good to see you're not as calm as you seemed earlier." Morgan's drawl brings my head up and my focus back to the here and now, rather than picturing how many ways I can fuck up all the people who ever thought it was a good idea to mess with my Angel.

"A good general never shows his true emotion, you rally the troops and feel later," I tell her, my voice stilted as I try to push the rage back down.

"Maybe so, but you're not just a good general. You've always been more than that. It was why she loved you in the first place. Even back then, when neither of you could get your shit together enough to admit it fully. She loved that you trusted her to be just as good of a soldier as you were, that you believed in her. That you believed in all of them. I knew more about you back then than I ever could have dreamt of knowing." She winks at me before she perches on one of the stools at the island and eyes me. "So, what's the plan, General?"

I snort at my old title, but answer her, nonetheless. "What makes you think I have a plan?"

"You're a general first and foremost, even before you're her lover. You always have a plan, it's practically a part of your DNA." She rolls her eyes, like my question was preposterous. I mean, she's not entirely wrong, but fucking still.

"Beyond hitting Avalon's weak spots that I know they have and tearing their defenses to the ground until Michael relents? Plus, I trained the Death Dealers well. Even with Serafina at the helm, they're not going to just roll over. Though, I mean they might, it's me." I ponder it for a minute then shrug. It's not the worst idea anyway. "Other than that, not much just yet. Well, except trying to work out who the fuck is pulling the strings on all of this so we can actually just live in peace for a while."

"Well, since Caleb has Jack nice and shackled back home, maybe we can get some answers for you." She smirks, and I try not to look as shocked as I feel. "Caleb only told Remy earlier, I'm not surprised you don't know yet. He swore the others to secrecy until he could tell her, he was practically giddy at the prospect of repaying some kindness back to Remy's old beau. It would seem that shot to the head landed him right back in our territory, and since we had an alert out on him, we got him practically as he appeared. He won't be back and doing any damage to our girl. Oooh, and Bryce caught himself a special little soul too, Ferry brought him Archer just before we came here. If anyone was going to make people tell their secrets it will be those two."

"I hope they fuck them up. Nice and slow." I grin,

and it's almost feral, but I don't give a shit. They deserve every piece of monster I have no doubt lives inside of the Horsemen.

"Oh, they will. And if anyone else pops up, we'll get them too. Malik called dibs on Bauer when we went upstairs, so if he shows up, he'll be… questioned also. Anything for our girl. Fuck knows how much we owe her, even after everything lately. Some debts can never be paid."

I nod, because I know exactly what she means. While I might not know everything about how she and Amantara became friends, or everything that happened with the six of them, the more time we spend with them, the more I've learned. It never fails to shock me just how pure Remy's soul is, despite everything. She'll happily give every single part of herself for the ones she loves, which is exactly why I need to do a better job protecting her, so she doesn't have to keep giving everything. She's died for each of us at one point or another, and it's not right or fair that she keeps being asked to give more.

Enough is e-fucking-nough. Thankfully, she has more people in her corner watching her back now, which reminds me…

"Thank you. For earlier. For stepping in. You didn't have to."

"It was nothing." She waves her hand to dismiss me.

"Them beating the crap out of you, while potentially entertaining, wasn't useful to anyone, and it would've just upset Remy if she found out. Especially since you all only just started playing nice together."

I rub the back of my neck, swallowing the shame and embarrassment that threatens to rise, even though I didn't really do anything. She's not wrong. Remy would be pissed if she found out we were fighting amongst ourselves, but then, I don't blame the guys at all. In their shoes, I'd have attacked me too. It's not like it was me they really wanted to hit. Michael was the intended target. Another line in my tally of reasons to kill that asshole.

"Don't worry, Leviathan. They'll all realize at some point that you quite literally breathe to keep her happy, that everything you do is for her. It might not be obvious to everyone, but I see it. All of it. It's why I didn't let my guys beat the crap out of you too. But I wasn't fucking about earlier. You sort this shit with Michael, or I will. And if we march on Avalon, it won't be pretty." The hard set of her face leaves me with no illusion that they'd raze the place if that's what it took.

"Understood," I say, nodding.

"That being said, we'll do whatever we can to help. That includes helping you find out who the fuck has it out for Remy so bad they're willing a war of this size. Considering the people they pulled to their side, it could've been catastrophic. It still could be, we don't know how many others there are that we don't know about. You know what they say about cutting off a hydra's head. I don't need to tell you to keep your guard up. I'm heading up to bed, but remember, if you need anything, anything at all, just let me know. If it's in my power, it'll be done."

And just like that, she stands and saunters from the room, every inch the queen she is. It's easy to see what her guys see in her, but she doesn't have a thing on Remy. Not a fucking one.

TWO

REMY

"What do you mean, Avalon?" I try to climb out of his arms, but his hold is firm, keeping me where I am. "Please tell me you're joking?"

He frowns down at me, and I squirm under his intense gaze. This all just feels way too familiar considering I met him like ten minutes ago, regardless of the fact I must have known him before, and the fact that he just saved my life—though I still have no idea how he did that. I thought Angel glass was a death sentence.

"I don't joke about your safety, little bird. Never have. Never will." He walks further into the room, and puts me down so that I'm lying on one of the two plush soft grey sofas in here. I sigh as the buttery soft material cradles my still aching body. Whatever Michael did to heal me has definitely helped, but a bone deep ache remains in place of the fiery pain. I try to sit up, and pain flares through my shoulder where I put weight on that arm. I wince and lay the fuck back down. Much as I hate feeling vulnerable, he seems to be worried about my wellbeing, so I'm reasonably confident he isn't going to try and kill me.

Then again, I've thought that before and been wrong. Bauer's face as he loomed above me flashes into my mind, but I shake it off and stuff it the fuck down. Now is not the time to deal with that. I just add it to the almost overwhelmingly full box of shit that I have yet to process properly.

"How are you feeling?" he asks as he crouches beside me, scanning over me. I close my eyes and catalogue the truth of my answer before I speak.

"I hurt, pretty much everywhere, but the burning from the Angel glass has gone. I just ache, all over." I sigh, and open my eyes to find his intense brown eyes still studying me. The depth of emotion almost suffocates me, but he pulls back and stands. It helps me breathe a little easier, because I'm pretty sure I have enough to deal with, without facing the truth behind that look.

"Wait here. I'll go get some stuff sorted for your stay here, and I'll bring something to help with the pain. Then we can talk."

I nod at his words, though I have a dozen questions as well as more than a small objection about staying here when I barely know him, even if he did save my life. However, getting rid of the pain will help clear my head, so I don't object. He literally pops out of sight, the flash of light making me wince. My eyes start to water, and I try to blink it away. My head really didn't need that. Man, I just want to go home, back to my guys.

Oh fates, I bet my guys are losing their fucking shit. I massage my temples as I groan just thinking about the potential fallout back home with the way I ended up here. Especially because if I am in Avalon, none of them can get here. At least not without starting a fucking war.

That can be next on my list, after getting rid of this crippling body ache. That and trying to work out why it is Michael seems to be helping me, and treating me with such reverence. Especially when everything I've heard about him made me think he would be beyond pissed that I was an Angel again, and worst-case scenario, wanted me dead.

My mind feels so fuzzy from everything that's happened, I haven't even started to process the fact that Bauer tried to kill me yet and that he's dead. I am in no way prepared to deal with the emotions that come with that right now, or the fact that Colt is practically alone now. He's the only one of us left. My heart aches for him, but that's also not something I can let myself focus on either.

Not until I know that I'm actually safe here.

Levi let Caleb hand me over to Michael, but since Michael could apparently heal the Angel glass wound, which I'm still reeling from too, then I don't suppose he had much other choice. But that doesn't help me know whether or not he can be trusted. Levi certainly hasn't made him out to be a guy that's on our side.

Except, the way Michael looked at me when he first took me in his arms seems so at odds with everything I've heard about him. The weighted looks from him, even everything he's said tells me maybe I've got him wrong. I huff, because having all of my memories back properly would be really fucking useful right now, but for now, I guess I'm playing it safe. Well as much as I can since I'm essentially trapped here.

Fates, I'm driving myself nuts, going in circles inside my own mind. Maybe it's just the shock of everything that happened fucking with me.

Michael flashes back into the room with that blinding white light of his and is at my side in seconds. I blink as my eyes water again, that warm smile of his back on his face as he sits on the edge of the sofa next to me. "You need to drink this."

He helps me sit up, since I can't manage it on my own, and raises a glass vial to my lips. I contemplate not drinking it, I don't know him, but his actions so far don't tell me he wants to hurt me. Though, I've been wrong before. The pain is almost overwhelming, so I drink down the clear fluid, trying not to gag as the sour concoction hits my tastebuds. I swallow and stick out my tongue, trying not to shiver at the sensation.

"Yeah, sorry, it tastes awful, I should have warned you, I forget that you don't remember everything about, well everything, but it should help." He smiles sadly at me, brushing my hair from my forehead as his eyes soften. "You should try to sleep now, little bird. I know you'll have a million questions; you always do." He smiles as if he knows me on a way deeper level that I have any recollection of, and the way he speaks to me, that soothing deep voice of his, makes me feel like I'm almost safe.

As he finishes speaking, as a yawn tears through me, and I wonder what exactly it was I just drank to make me so sleepy so quickly, but the thought is lost as darkness seeps in and I fall unconscious.

I wake as light filters in through the windows and I stretch out in bed. It takes me a second to remember everything that happened yesterday and realize where the hell I am. It all hits me, and I feel like I might drown if I think on it too much, so I put it back in its box, and refocus on my surroundings. The room is similar to the room I was in yesterday, it's big and airy, full of glass, whites and greys, with touches of navy blue.

Wherever it is that Michael lives, it's pretty beautiful in here. It reminds me of some sort of beautiful, clean beach house. No idea why, it just has that sort of tranquil feeling to it.

It hits me that I'm in bed, when I fell asleep on the couch. I panic for a minute and I lift the comforter, letting out a deep breath because I'm still fully clothed. Well, that would've been more than a little creepy. Even if he did save my life.

"Oh good, you're awake." Michael is in the doorway, leaning against the doorframe, a mug of what smells like coffee in his hands. He chuckles as he watches me and brings me the mug. "I see not much has changed when it comes to you and coffee."

I take the mug without a second thought and sip the java goodness. It occurs to me I should be more cautious, but something inside me feels settled here. Maybe it's because I'm an Angel, in the city of Angels, or maybe it's because Michael just isn't registering as a threat to me. I don't know, but the coffee tastes like a little piece of heaven, and I can't help but groan. My eyes dart to Michael after I realize quite how that sounded, his eyes sparkle with laughter, and I can see he's trying not to laugh out loud.

"Sorry." I shrug and take another sip, trying to control myself at how good this tastes. "What exactly, is in this?"

"It's just coffee. But it's a blend we created here with Angel senses in mind, since they're so heightened." His amusement at my happiness is more than apparent, and he just looks at me like he did yesterday. Like he knows me in a much deeper sense that I have any memory of.

"Why did you help me?" I can't help but blurt out the words, and his expression softens as he comes and sits on the end of the bed, facing me. He runs a hand down his face and looks the ceiling, as if trying to find the right words to answer my question.

"The answer to that isn't as simple as it should be," he tells me, looking conflicted. "But the bigger picture, is that I couldn't not help you, little bird."

He seems almost pained at the thought, which just confuses me more. "Okay, first, what is with the nickname? And second why bring me here? If I was healed, why was it necessary?"

At my question he almost looks bashful, which makes me double take. Is he blushing? What the actual fuck.

"It's safer here for you, little bird. Avalon is your home. Your *real* home," he tells me, sounding almost sad. "As for the nickname. I've called you it for longer than I care to remember, from when you first learned to fly."

"I am so confused." I groan and pinch the bridge of

my nose.

"I can only imagine, but I can maybe help you finally unlock all of your memories, if you'd let me help you?" He sounds hopeful, and that makes me wary. Apparently being betrayed as much as I have recently has left me a little jaded.

"Why would you do that?" I watch him closely as I ask the question, and he flinches a little at my accusing tone.

"For the same reason I helped you yesterday. I can't not." He shrugs a little, but pins me with an intense stare, as if he's searching for something inside of my very soul. His face falls a little, so I guess he doesn't find what he was looking for.

"You really don't remember me at all, do you?" The pain in those words slices through me, cutting me as sure as any blade would. I shake my head, unable to speak. Emotion clogs my throat and I have no idea why. I try to swallow, to push it down, just like always, because breaking down right now is not something I can do. Even if I am safe here, with him, there is no way I'm going to break right now.

"I guess that makes more sense." He sighs and stands. "You're safe here, and it makes sense for you to stay here until you're fully healed. Just, please, stay until then, and I'll unlock your memories, all of them. Then I'll answer any other questions you have too." The crinkles at the edges of his eyes are the only outward sign of his sadness, but there's something deep inside of me that tells me to trust him. That makes me feel sad that he's so sad right now.

"Okay, just until I'm healed, and my memories are unlocked."

"Thank you." He lets out a deep breath, like he expected a fight. I probably should have put up more of a fight, and I squirm under his gaze as I realize it. Something about him is just so fucking disarming. He sighs again and walks towards me.

"Let me show you something, it might make you feel at ease." He offers me his hand, to help me get up from the bed. Considering how I felt yesterday, I accept his offer and ease from the bed carefully, checking the pain in my shoulder as I do. It's practically gone, but the bone ache still hasn't completely gone, which just makes me feel tired even though I just woke up.

He puts an arm around my waist, steadying me as I stand. He holds on a little longer than necessary, then I realize he's planning to help me to whatever it is he wants to show me. I step out of his hold, a stab of guilt hits me as his face falls, but I stuff it down. I don't know him, even if he seemingly knows me, and if someone who wasn't my family had their hands on my guys, I'd be taking heads, so with them in mind, I put distance between us. Whatever this is feels like more than it should be. He smiles at me tightly before leaving the room, motioning for me to follow him.

I follow him, albeit slowly, because fucking ow, into the main room, where I fell asleep last night. I sit on the sofa as directed, and try not to look as relieved. Apparently even having been healed, Angel glass is an absolute bitch of an injury. Not that I didn't know that, but I've never known myself feel so shit after being healed. Then again, I've never nearly died from Angel glass before either.

He sits beside me, and I realize that above the fireplace opposite us is what looks like a concave mirror. The surface ripples at the wave of Michael's hand. Holy crap, it's Angel glass. I blink, and then Levi fills the image.

"What is this?" I look to Michael who still looks so fucking sad it makes my heart hurt.

"This is what is happening at the manor right now. Things move faster here, so it's only been minutes there since you were taken. I thought you'd want to see for yourself." He goes quiet as Levi starts speaking, and my heart stutters at the pain and frustration in his voice.

"First of all, I didn't let him do a damn thing. Stopping Michael is about as simple and easy as stopping a goddamn hurricane." Levi massages his temples, and my heart sinks a little at how stressed he is, though Michael snorts softly at his words, but I can't stop watching Levi. "But, much as I hate to admit it, she is safe with him. Probably safer than she is here right now."

The glass fades after his words, and I look back at Michael skeptically. "That's a pretty convenient clip for you to show me."

"I can show you more, but you looked so sad watching him. The last thing I want to do is make you sad."

I sigh as I lean back on the sofa and settle into the soft cushions. Does Levi not want me to go home? Why would he agree that I'm safer here if he didn't believe it? He had no way of knowing I could see him. My heart sinks further. I just want to go home, but if I am safer here, does that make it safer for everyone else? Or is being here putting them at more risk?

"I can practically see the cogs in your mind spinning out of control. How about I get you another tonic, one less potent, but one that will help with the pain, and I can show you more than just this sky loft? Avalon is a beautiful place."

After drinking another gag inducing tonic, I feel better. The ache is dulled, not wholly gone, but it's enough that I can walk normally again now. I follow Michael to the far end of the main room, which seems to be just huge panels of glass, covered in a white tulle. He pushes a button on the wall, and I realize the glass is one very long door as it starts to retract. The tulle curtain shifts in the breeze that comes through the now open wall, and Michael leads me out to a balcony I hadn't realized was out there.

I gasp as I step out onto the glass-walled balcony. Michael wasn't wrong. Avalon really is beautiful. We seem to be in a ridiculously tall, white tower, which when I look around the edge of the balcony, seems to be one of four. They all jut up into spiked points at the top, but they all seem to have the same lower floors from what I can see up here. I look out across the city.

The buildings are laid out to circle this tower, and in the distance, the sparkle of light glinting off of water greets me. A huge white stone bridge goes across it, to what looks like another circular island almost identical to this one. I focus, straining my eyes in a way I haven't before, and as the other island comes into focus, I realize it is exactly the same. At least, it has the same tower at its center. It has another bridge about a quarter of the way round the island, but mist stops me being able to see where it goes to.

A giddiness I didn't expect fills me at the possibility of exploring. Especially when it hits me that the figures darting around the skies aren't birds, but Angels. Comprehension stuns me, because I have no memory of ever seeing anything so amazing. It's quite literally another world here.

My still somewhat human mind is pretty blown. I mean, I know Angels exist, I am one, I've been around them, but actually seeing this place. It just feels different.

"It's beautiful huh?" Michael says, watching me as I try to take it all in. I nod, still unable to look away from the gleaming city. "Levi taught you how to fly again, right?"

"He did." I nod while I bite my lip. "I've not done it much though."

"Well, time to sink or swim, little bird." He extends his wings behind him, I still can't get over just how white they are when he climbs up onto the glass perch and steps off the ledge. He drops and my heart practically stops, but then he laughs as he shoots towards the sky, like a shining beacon. It's as if the whole city pauses to watch him as he climbs higher before swooping back down to hover in front of me.

"Show off," I mumble as I unfurl my wings, hoping like fuck I remember what the hell I'm doing. I really should have practiced this more, and now I feel like an idiot for not. The ache in my bones extends through my wings, and I pray to anyone that might be listening not to let me die from this flight after everything I've been through to survive up to this point. I try not to pay attention to how Michael is studying my wings. I get it, they're different too. It seems everything about me is.

I take a deep breath, stretch out my wings, and step from the ledge. My wings catch the air drift, and I float for a minute, before Michael appears at my side, a smile back on his face. He seems happy to fly at my pace, which makes me feel better, because trying to fly while I ache, plus trying to take it everything around me is a lot.

Most people avoid us as he shows me around from the skies, and I don't know if that's because of me, or him, but I try not to pay much mind to it. Levi told me how unpopular Shadow Walkers are among Angels, so it's not all that surprising.

We fly around this island, not venturing towards the bridge, and Michael points out to me different sectors the island is split into. The white central spires are the Archangel Towers. They also have cells beneath them that link to tunnels running throughout the entire island. There's the residential quarter, the industrial quarter, the commercial quarter, and then finally, the enforcement quarter. Where the Angels who police everyday life here live and work.

There's so much to take in, and I'm pretty sure not everything sticks, but since Michael is going to unravel the mystery that is my memories, hopefully it will all make more sense soon. It's about time, I need my memories back. They could hold the answers I've been searching for, the clues to what the hell has happened to my life this last year.

I nearly miss Michael speaking to me, lost in my own thoughts as we head back to his sky loft. The Archangel Towers are something of beauty. They're so very different to anything I've ever seen, but then, that doesn't surprise me considering where we are.

"Are you ready to get back? You look tired," Michael asks, looking me over. His brow is furrowed like he's worried about me, but he's right, I am tired. I haven't ever flown this much. Even though he's taken it easy on me speed wise, it's been a lot.

"Yeah, it's so beautiful out here, but I am tired." My stomach rumbles as I speak, and I blush as he chuckles.

"We'll get you some food too. Unless you'd rather go out to eat?" He sounds so hopeful, but I don't want to blur any lines here. He's helping me, I get that, and Levi said himself I'm safer here, which is the only reason I'm not protesting healing here right now, but the second I feel better, I'm going home and I don't need any more complications in my life. Fates knows I have enough of those. Much as this place feels like a missing part of me, it's not home for me, not anymore.

"No, I think I'm too tired for that. If we could just grab something small and then I can sleep for a bit?" I try to be as friendly as I can, because he really has been nothing but nice, and he's still Michael. A guy doesn't have that many stories flying around about him without some reason for it.

"Of course." He smiles at me, though some of the light in his eyes has dimmed. "Let's head back." I follow him as he leads back towards the towers, and he helps me down from the glass perch once I land. As soon as my I tuck my wings away, tiredness practically knocks me on my ass. I might have just pushed it a little too hard.

"You curl up on the couch, I'll sort food and bring it over." Michael smiles at me as we enter the loft, and he hits the button to close the giant glass panel. I don't argue with him, mainly because I don't have the energy to. I stumble over to the sofa, and flop down onto the cushions. I curl my legs under me and get comfortable, this sofa might be comfier than the bed. I snort a laugh at the thought, but shake my head. Fates I'm an idiot when I'm tired.

I close my eyes, just for a second, while Michael is sorting food, but the darkness claims me and carries me away.

THREE

We spent most of yesterday exploring with Michael showing me places I used to haunt, my favorite spots. It's becoming increasingly clear to me that Levi chose to omit that Michael and I were close. Because there is no way he could know all of this if we weren't. And the way he looks at me… I can't help but wonder if there's history there, but I also don't want to say anything and make it more awkward than it already is. Fate knows it wouldn't be the first time I've met someone who knew more about me than I do myself.

He's already said he can unlock my memories, which is why I'm sitting here in his kitchen trying not to fidget while I wait for him to wake up. At least, I think he's asleep. I haven't really dared to explore his loft beyond the room I've stayed in and this main room. I'm just assuming I'm in the guest room, because, well, awkward.

"Morning," he practically sings the word as he enters the loft, and I try not to startle. "Did you sleep okay? I popped out and got us some pastries. My cooking skills are about as good as yours, so I figured I'd save my poor kitchen being punished today."

He puts the brown cardboard box down on the island I'm sitting at, and I try not to drool at the buttery smell that fills my senses.

"Coffee?" He moves towards the machine on the opposite side of the room and I nod. I tried to use it earlier, but it's so fucking complicated, too many options, so I just left it alone and hoped he wouldn't take long to wake up. Even if apparently he was already up and out by the time I made it in here.

"Thank you." I smile at him as I raise the mug he hands me to my lips, trying not to groan as the sweet nectar passes my lips. It really is better than any coffee I've ever drank. "So, I was wondering…"

"You want me to help you get your memories back before you face the council?"

I blink slowly because it's like he's in my head, and it occurs to me that he genuinely could be. He laughs at me and my eyes go wide.

"I'm not in your mind. The look on your face. You

always were an open book." He shakes his head as he leans on the counter opposite to where I'm sitting. "But yeah, we can do that. I'd probably rather wait until after you go in front of the council, but I also understand why you'd rather go in there armed. It's not going to be easy though."

"What do you mean?"

"I mean reconciling everything and everyone you've been. It's a gift that something has kept your memories locked away. The emotional impact of it all is going to be a huge hit. Like Tsunami levels." His brow furrows as he speaks, and I get the feeling he's regretting offering to help me, but I also get the feeling that even though he might not be fully on board with my plan, he won't try to talk me out of it. He doesn't seem the type. At least not with me. I've only seen him alone with me, and he's been a very different Michael to the one I've heard so much about. "But if that's what you want, we'll do it."

I feel the heat rise up my neck at the way he says those words, and the way he looks at me when he does.

"Okay." I swallow trying to move past how awkward I feel. "How do we do this?"

"Well, from what I've gathered you've managed to put a block of some sort on your memories. Luckily, the mind is my specialty. We just need to remove the block, and it will all come flooding back. I just need to peer into your mind."

"I thought you said you couldn't read my mind?" I ask, skeptically.

"I said I wasn't in your head. I wouldn't enter your mind without permission, little bird." He smiles at me, and I relax. He's so open, so warm, it's hard not to trust him, even when everyone keeps proving to me I shouldn't trust so easily. I don't ever want to be so cynical that I don't give people a chance. Even if that makes me an idiot. "But I know you better than you realize, because we're the same, you and I."

"What does that even mean?"

"It means, I'm a Shadow Walker too. And that means, you can do what I do. It's why I don't advertise what I am, but it's also why so many people dislike our kind. It means that I can enter your mind, even without your permission, though I wouldn't, but it means that you can do it too. Along with a whole host of other fun, including the other stuff that makes people more than a little terrified of us. And that's without us just being total badasses." He winks, as if he didn't just completely blow my mind. I open my mouth, but I'm pretty much speechless.

"Don't worry, little bird. After you get your memories back, you should remember everything you could do before, and we'll make sure you have every possible thing in your arsenal before we're done. I won't leave you defenseless. I've more than learned my lesson."

"I don't know what that means."

"It means that I gave you up once, and you died. Now, let's finish eating before I dive into your mind, shall we?" He reaches for the pastry box and pulls one out before pushing the box over to me. If he thinks I can eat right now, he is sorely mistaken.

Also, what the fuck is it with Angels and their talking in fucking riddles? He just said so much, but none of it really made any sense. What does he mean he gave me up? I'd ask, but I'm not sure I'd even get a real answer. So, I finish my coffee and wait for my lives to finally be unlocked, fully.

At least this way, there's no more surprises. Right?

"Come lay down, little bird." Michael pats the bed in the room I've been staying in, and I approach him slowly. Yes, I want this, I know it's going to be for the best in the long run, but fear spikes inside of me. What if I can't handle whatever it is that I've blocked myself from remembering? What if past me knew I wouldn't survive if I knew whatever it was that I've suppressed?

I take a deep breath and climb onto the bed.

"Are you sure about this?" he asks as he looks down at me with concern. He looks at me like he's seeing inside of me. Like he can see more of me than I've ever let anyone see.

"I'm sure." My voice shakes a little with the words, but I mean them. No matter how much it might hurt to remember everything, no matter how much it might change who I fundamentally am, I need this. It's more than a want. I am tired of the surprises, of not having every facet of myself available in my arsenal, it might even give me the answer about who the fuck it is that wants me dead.

I lie down and he moves to sit beside me. "I'll make this as painless as I can, little bird."

He smiles at me, but his eyes are sad as he moves his hands to my face. He caresses my cheek softly, startling me, but he moves his hands to hover on my temples and smiles. "Close your eyes, Remy. I'll see you soon."

I close my eyes at his request, and for a minute nothing happens. Then, a bright white light fills my mind until I can't see or think about anything else. It intensifies and I feel tears streaming down my face when the pain starts. Like pins on every inch of my skin, under my nails, and inside my mind.

Michael cries out beside me, and then the light increases further until the memories wash over me like a tidal wave, and I get swept away.

"You can do this, little bird. You can do anything you put

your mind to." I look up at him, the man that everyone fears so much, but who has always been on my side, in my corner, pushing me to be the best version of myself, and never making me feel less because of what I am. Which can't be said for most of the people in Avalon.

I can't help what I am, but that doesn't make their fear any less. I suppose it doesn't help that I've always lived to the beat of my own drum, but if they don't like it, they can, quite frankly, get fucked.

"I know I can. I just need a minute. Entering your mind is a little scary. Hell, being in my own head is all kinds of terrifying most of the time." He grins from where he's sitting opposite me, completely unafraid of the possibility of me getting inside his head. It could be because he has nothing to hide, but it's more likely that his mental shields are so fucking insane that I won't get anything he doesn't want me to get. Even if I tried. But I wouldn't. I already know that I could ask him anything and he'll be honest with me.

Some might think our relationship is a little strange, but then, Michael is so feared, and yet respected, that no one would dare say a thing with him around anyway. Except, maybe, for Leviathan. He's never had any issues challenging Michael. About anything. Including me.

I close my eyes and focus on picturing the path from my mind to Michael's, and I feel the difference between the shields he has up now, and the ones he has usually. These ones are squishy. Pliable. Normally it's an immovable force, just like the man himself. He's letting me in, but he's only made it a little easier. He still wants me to have to struggle. Always the teacher, and the warrior in him makes him a hard ass teacher.

"Come on, little bird. Try harder."

I groan, because this particular power scares the crap out of me. I don't want to be what everyone thinks I am. I don't mind being a pariah so much, I've always been okay in my own company. I don't need people. But ever since my powers manifested, this is the one I've avoided learning. Centuries have passed since then, but I focused on becoming a warrior. Learning to fight without my powers, which is why Leviathan and I became as close as we are, and how I ended up being the right hand to the General of the Death Dealers.

My parents looked proud that day. Not that they spoke to me. They haven't since my powers manifested, but it sucks to be them, because I learned really quickly that I'm more than capable of looking after myself. Plus, the few people I have, that I now consider practically family, they're more than I could ever need. I made something of myself without their help.

I focus again and try to breach Michael's shields, pushing harder than I did before, and with an almost audible pop, the shield around his mind shatters and I'm overcome by his thoughts, his emotions. Holy shit. There's so much that I retreat, hoping the heat I can feel on my neck isn't too obvious. I open my eyes and find him smiling at me, all the warmth and love I felt in his mind showing on his face.

I don't know what to say. What to think.

I had no idea.

I mean, maybe a suspicion, but not really.

"Amantara, stop." His words are soft as he caresses my cheek. "This changes nothing. Though, it shows me you're stronger than we thought. You got through more shields than I intended for you to."

"I'm sorry," I whisper, trying to process everything I just learned.

"Don't be, little bird. I am sorry for underestimating you." His palm is warm against my cheek, and I can't help but find comfort in it. In him. But I don't feel that way. At least, I've never thought about him, at least not like that.

"Well isn't this cozy." Leviathan's drawl breaks the spell I'm under as he leans against the stone arch in the gardens we're sitting in. It's quiet down here, I've always felt at peace, which is why we chose to try this here.

Michael's hand withdraws from my cheek, taking the heat with him, but my cheeks burn plenty on their own at Leviathan's insinuation.

"Leviathan," Michael growls as he stands and offers

me a hand to help me up. Leviathan's glare zeroes in on the hand, like it's his worst enemy. "What brings you here?"

"I came to find Amantara. We're patrolling tonight. Demons keep breaching the tear between the Shadow Realm and the human realm. I see I interrupted." He looks like he'd happily take Michael's head from his shoulders, and the tension increases between the two of them. Practically sparking as I stand. I don't take Michael's hand but I do hug him.

"Thank you for today, we can keep working tomorrow?" I ask softly with a smile.

"Of course, little bird." Leviathan scoffs at Michael's words but doesn't say a thing. I don't understand the dislike between the two of them, I'm just glad that they try to at least be amicable when they're with me. They both mean so much to me, I don't know what I'd do if they made me try to take sides. "I'll see you in the morning."

Michael unfurls his wings, and with a beat disappears from sight, leaving me with an extremely surly Leviathan. He's standing there, looking at me with his arms crossed, the leather straps from his arm braces strain against his muscles, and I can't help but roll my eyes at him. "What crawled up your ass today?"

"The way he looks at you is creepy. He's old enough to be our dad."

"Age is just a number, especially when you're immortal.

I don't get why you two hate each other so much."

"You wouldn't." It's his turn to roll his eyes at me and mutters something I can't make out.

"Are we going?" I walk towards him and unfurl my wings, the wings that make me so different to everyone else in Avalon, and prepare to do the only part of my life I have figured out. I pull my hood up and pick up my bow that I propped up against a tree when I came down here with Michael, before patting myself down, making sure my karambit knives are still secure, along with my throwing knives. A good Death Dealer never leaves home without their weapons. A lesson I learned early on.

Leviathan watches me, without saying a word, and unfurls his wings. They're pure darkness and I think they're beautiful. Not that I'd ever tell him that. Close as we might be, I don't think he'd take it as a compliment.

"We're just waiting on you. Nevin is already geared up." He tilts his head up, and I notice Nevin hovering in the skies above us. It always shocks me that he's a Death Dealer, that he comes with us on excursions like this. His skills definitely lean towards the studious part of our way of life, but I guess, having his knowledge on hand when we're in the thick of it has helped us more than once.

"Then let's go."

FOUR

I stretch out in bed, yawning as I wake. It takes a second to orientate myself when everything hits me at once. What happened yesterday. My memories being unlocked. I open my eyes and look around frantically for Michael, who I find passed out beside me.

Shit.

I move to wake him when the tidal wave of emotion inside me from seeing him there threatens to take me. The memories of every moment with him, as if triggered at the sight of him. Tears stream down my face as my heart races to the point I panic.

My hands shake and I try to clench my fists to stop the attack coming over me as flashes assault my mind. Memories of him, us together, everything he taught me.

He has to be okay. He can't be fucked up because he helped me. I won't survive it.

I shake him, and he stirs, groaning but alive.

Fuck.

I can't control everything inside of me when it comes to him apparently. This is not good.

I take a deep breath and hold it as I stuff every last drop of emotion currently threatening to overwhelm me down. Bottling emotion is something I've always excelled at, it's not something that's going to fail me now. Later me can try to process this. I am not in a position to deal with it right now.

I flicker through my mind, the memories that come to the forefront, most of which are from my life as Amantara. She and I are so different, and yet, the same. It's like watching a movie of someone else's life, and while I know I'm going to need to reconcile with my memories at some point—and figure out where the fuck I go from here, who the fuck I am now—that is not my focus right now.

I push it all back, glad that whatever Michael did worked, but also still kind of terrified it broke him. I try to rouse him again and his eyes flutter, it takes a second, but his eyes open and focus on my face.

"Little bird? Are you okay?" His voice is gravelly with sleep, as he rubs his temple and pushes himself to sit up and face me. He scours every inch of me with a look, as if searching for some sort of wound or injury. I'm sure it won't take him long to realize the only place I'm broken right now are the places he can't see.

"I'm…" I shake my head. I can't bring myself to lie and say I'm okay. Because I'm not. Even without looking inside myself too far, I know I'm not okay. But I'm also not about to deal with that right now when he might be hurt. I swallow the lump in my throat and attempt to speak again. "Are you okay?"

"I'm fine, little bird. That block you put on your memories just took a lot out of me to shatter. Whoever built it, they knew what they were doing. I almost thought I wouldn't be able to get through." He runs a hand through his hair and then down his face, as if trying to wake himself back up. Looking out of the window he sighs. "We've only been out about an hour or so. We haven't lost much time, which is surprising. How are you doing? Really."

He looks at me like he can see inside of me again. And I guess he kind of can. I don't know how much he saw when he lifted the block, and I don't want to ask. Vulnerable isn't a setting I work well in.

"I'll be okay," I tell him with a small shrug, and tuck my hair behind my ear.

"You always used to do that when you lied to me." He smiles sadly at me, and I look down at my hands in my lap. "But you will be okay. If I can help, I will. You know that, little bird. I will always be here for you. No matter what the others might think."

"Thank you," I whisper, a stray tear running down my face. "I'm glad you're okay."

He shifts towards me and pulls me into his lap, as he's done so many times before. He wraps his arms around me and just holds me, being a safe space, a space of no judgment, where I can break a little.

I don't let it go on too long. Just long enough that I can get myself together, then push my emotions all the fucking way down until I'm ready to deal with them. Which is not right now. My memories are there, but the emotions that come with them, they're going the fuck back away. Right now, I just need the facts of my past. The information that comes from remembering. Everything else can wait.

"So, what time are the council expecting us?" I ask him as I move myself back beside him, trying not to feel guilty about taking comfort from him, when my guys are probably still losing their shit back home. "And when can I go home?"

I ask the question, more from respect than anything. I know I need to see the council, face some of my past, but I'm going home after. They can try to keep me here, but they have no real idea of what I can do. Even Michael has no real idea, and that's without the extra pit of darkness I can feel inside myself from when I awoke in the Shadow

Realm. It feels unnatural, like a black oily slick inside of myself, but it still feels like me.

My mind whirs at everything it's trying to take back in, as Michael watches me, pondering his own words. I take a deep breath and slow my mind as I wait for him to speak.

"They're expecting us tonight. I wanted to give you more time."

"Okay, so after that, I can leave?" I put it to him as a question, because I know he can physically keep me here, but I also know he won't stop me leaving.

"This is your home, little bird," he says softly, and I feel my heart crack again.

"My home is on Earth now. Having my memories back doesn't change that. It doesn't change how I feel about the others. My home is where they are. I won't hide here while everyone else tries to find out who is trying to kill me. You should know that better than anyone."

He sighs at my words and shakes his head. "I do. We'll talk about this later, after we meet with the council."

"I'm not going to change my mind about this," I tell him firmly. I owe him a lot. Everything really. But that doesn't mean I'll stay here from some sense of duty.

"You never do."

The rest of the morning passes simply enough. I stay in

bed, my body not feeling as happy about the shit we've put it through. Apparently, undoing the block took more out of me than I thought, plus, still a baby Angel, which I'm remembering comes with more restrictions than I'm happy about. So, I rest.

Until the skies turn dark outside. The skies here never go dark.

Lightning cracks across the clouds as thunder rolls throughout Avalon. Loud enough to make the walls shake.

"What the hell is going on?" I ask as I walk into the main room and find Michael on the balcony.

"What do you think? He was never going to let me have you for long."

"Levi." I sigh, rubbing my eyes. "You lifted his banishment once. Just let him in."

"I lifted his banishment to help you." He doesn't even look at me as he says the words, but his shoulders tense, his whole body is on alert.

"Keeping him out isn't going to help anyone. I don't understand why you banished him in the first time."

"I banished him, because he broke the rules when he saved you," he growls, turning to face me. "I banished him, because he got to do what I couldn't. Like he always does."

My heart about stops in my chest. I am not ready for this conversation right now. "Michael…"

Thunder cracks across the skies again, shaking the sky loft, and I try to find the right words, but I don't have them so I try to appeal to the warrior I know he is. The man who loves his people. "He won't give up."

"I know." He turns away from me again. "But just letting him in will hurt Avalon more than it will help it. It makes me look weak. That, that would hurt Avalon, and I'm not prepared to do that. I already let him back in once, if I do it again…"

"If you do it again, Avalon's defenses won't be shredded. He built them, he knows the weak spots. It's his people protecting the city. If you think that they won't bow to him. Even with Serafina in charge, he will always be their general. It's who he is, it's who they are. Even she will bow to him eventually. Better that it comes from you, than to have him make you have to give in. He was always going to come. You had to know that."

"I thought I'd have longer. But you're right. He'll always come for you. And I always end up letting you go." He unfurls his wings and pushes off of the balcony, shooting off into the distance towards where Levi would have appeared when he reached Avalon. Outside the walls that aren't visible from here, the walls that the Death Dealers protect with their lives. Outside the magical barrier the helps to protect everything that Avalon is. Outside and locked out from getting to me.

I just hope they don't kill each other before they realize how much it would hurt me to lose either of them.

What a fucking mess.

And I thought getting my memories back would make things easier. Instead, it just makes things more complicated than ever. That's before I even dive into everything.

Fucking awesome.

Lightning and thunder continue to batter the defenses of Avalon, but I know that Levi is taking it easy. He has much more in his arsenal than that. This is his warning shot. He knew we'd know it was him. No one else can do what he does with such flare. He knew that Michael would have no choice but to go to him. I just have to hope that they can put aside whatever it is that was between them long before I came along, to at least try to not tear Avalon to the ground.

I move back into the kitchen and pour myself more coffee. The dull ache of healing from the Angel glass along with the aches from unlocking my memories merge, but the coffee helps. It always does. I try not to let my anxiety about what the hell they're doing wash over me, but sitting here, doing nothing, doesn't make it that easy. There isn't even a TV or a stray book around here for me to distract myself. Michael gives minimalism a whole new meaning.

I sit, and I snack on the pastries, eating my anxiety, while I wait for them to sort their shit out.

Hours pass before the sky brightens again. To say I'm a caffeinated wreck is probably an understatement, but I'm also so very excited to see Levi. I nearly died. Again. But this time, something happened. It hit me that this could've been it for me, there isn't another loophole for us to find. If I die, that's it. And I'm leaving so much behind if I die.

I feel almost human again in my new found appreciation for death and the finality of it all. To think it's been just less than a year since I was human is a little staggering.

A crash sounds and I look back to the balcony. The yin and yang that are Michael and Levi. The light to the darkness. It's a sight to behold. Them both there, wings out, the tension and anger between them crackling like a live wire.

"Remy..." Levi's voice cracks as he takes a step towards me. I fly across the room and fling myself into his waiting arms. He holds me so tight that I think I might break down, but I just enjoy the feel of him. I nearly lost him, and that's not something I'm willing to do. Ever again. Bauer might be one of the biggest betrayals of my life times, and there's been a good amount of them, but he gave me this at least. A greater appreciation for everything I have, everything I could, and never want to lose.

I let him hold me, until he's ready to let go. I want to

be mindful of Michael's feelings, but he kind of kidnapped me, so I'm giving Levi this time. Just like I'll give the others when I get back.

"Thank god you're okay," he says as he pulls back from me. He keeps a hold on my arms as he looks me over. He searches my eyes for something, and his face falls a little. "You unlocked it all, didn't you?"

"Of course, she did. Leaving her blind was dangerous," Michael answers for me with a snort.

"You did this," Levi growls, and moves me behind him. I sigh, because I do not need protecting, especially not from Michael, but this pissing contest is older than I am. And I don't even really want to look at how old that is too closely.

"You guys…" I start with a sigh. "Can we just not?"

They both turn to look at me, Michael at least has the recompense to look a little guilty. Levi however, just looks pissed still.

"Whatever this is…" I wave my hands between them, trying like fuck not to roll my eyes. "Can we just leave it? We have way more important things to think about than whatever you two can't put behind you." I turn to Michael, and Levi growls lowly under his breath. "When are we due before the council? You were gone for a while, so I assume it's soon."

"You're taking her before the council? Are you fucking

insane? They've been trying to put her down for a fucking millennia!" Levi roars, and gets in Michael's face. Michael pushes him away, but he barely moves an inch. I move and get between them, destroying the sky loft isn't on my to do list today.

"Okay, so this, whatever this is, isn't going to help anyone," I say, putting my hands on Levi's chest. "You're here now, so you can come with me, I'm pretty sure no one is going to put me down, especially since I do remember why most of them dislike me now. But if they try, you and I can leave and never come back." I take a deep breath, waiting for the static coming from him that tickles against my skin to withdraw. He stares down into my eyes, warring with himself. His love for me, his need to protect me against the knowledge that I'm not going to just back down. He looks almost sad as he accepts that fact, which hurts, but I am not, nor have I ever been a damsel that needs saving. I'm not going to start being that person right now.

The static recedes and the air becomes less thick around us as he backs down. I feel Michael soften behind me, and I move before the fact that I'm wedged between them becomes our next issue. Levi might not be the jealous, possessive type with the other guys, but here, with Michael, that's exactly what he is.

"When are we going?" Levi asks Michael, though his

gaze remains on me.

"We're due there in an hour," Michael tells us both, and Levi wraps his hand around mine, pulling me closer to him.

"Good, then I have time to go to my own loft," Levi snarls, and walks with his hand still wrapped around mine, out of the front door, and leads me away from Michael. It takes a second to remember that Levi's loft is in this same tower. Not on this level, because there's only one loft per level this high up, so I move with him to the stairwell and go down a few flights of stairs, to where the four peaks of the towers join, and then head back up towards his place. He doesn't say a word as we move through the building, even with all of the looks we get. Each one more terrified or horrified than the last.

Apparently, our arrival here wasn't exactly known, despite my flight with Michael. Won't take long for everyone to know now, Avalon has that small-town mentality, and gossip spreads like wildfire around here. We reach the loft without a word, and I follow him in.

I take in the area, and it's like being in a time capsule. Nothing has changed since the last time I was here, well, I mean, it's been updated a little, but it's essentially the same. The dark grey walls, with hints of white, and the odd shock of purple, it's just as dark and welcoming as ever. The huge black sofas look so welcoming, like a cloud you could just sink into.

"Are you really okay?" Levi asks as he wraps his arms around me, softening for the first time since he arrived here. I sink into the feel of him, the comfort of him, it's exactly what I need. The turmoil inside of me quiets a little with him here.

"I will be. It's just a lot of deal with, having everything back in my head. I'm trying not to focus on it too much right now. I want to get through seeing the council and then go home. Then, then I'll examine what's going on inside of me properly." His arms tighten around me as I speak, and I wonder, just for a minute, if he'll just take me home, regardless of what I want. Council be damned.

"You don't have to see them, Remy. You owe them nothing." His voice is soft as his breath whispers across my neck, before he turns me and kisses me.

"I know I don't, but I feel like I should. This was our home. Yours for much longer than mine. We shouldn't be cut off from it because they're a giant bag of dicks."

His chest shakes as he chuckles at me.

"If it's what you want, I'll be there right beside you, but you should know that they could banish me forever and I wouldn't care. All I need in this life, Remy, is you."

FIVE

We walk into the Archangel council chambers, me in the middle of them, looking like a force to be reckoned with. Not that the egos on the council give a fuck. Their sneers and looks of disgust are impossible to miss. Though they're mainly directed at me. Those that dare to try and meet Levi's eyes keep a healthy dose of fear, most just don't try to look at him directly.

"Leviathan, you son of a bitch, fancy finding you back here." The thick twang from Gabe as his cheery voice booms across the space makes me smile. I didn't know if he'd be here, but he was always one to side with us. The Archangel of Chaos. He always did love how much Levi and I being in a room together fucked with everyone.

"Gabriel. I didn't know if you'd be here." Levi's smile

is genuine as he embraces our old friend.

"Well, look at you, Amantara. Causing such a fuss even after you died. Only you could cause more chaos than I can." He winks at me, making me smile before wrapping me up in a bear hug.

"It's good to see you, old friend," I say quietly before he releases me. I'm one of the very few people who he used to let call him Gabe. He might seem mischievous and laid back, but the Archangel of Chaos tends to see the worst of people, so he doesn't tend to trust many. Even fewer does he let get close. I make a mental note to talk to him about my current issues back on Earth. He might have a singular style of looking at things that the rest of us haven't thought about.

Michael walks straight past us to the head of the very long table that holds the council. It's the one part of him we always fought about. That his role, his job, it comes above all else. On the one hand, I get it, he is a leader, and he didn't get to where he is by prioritizing other things, but it's exactly why he and I could never work. Despite what my memories might suggest.

He would never put anything above his sense of duty. It's what makes him the perfect leader of Avalon, but it means that whoever he is with, is always second fiddle. I might not need to be the sun of your world, but I want to at least be a factor in your decision process. That isn't something that would happen with him. He knew it as well as I did, which is why nothing ever happened with us. It's also why we never speak of it.

Michael sits, and the chatter in the room dies down. Levi's seat at the table remains empty as he stands by my side. His banishment was lifted, so he can take his chair again, but this is his way of showing every person in the room where his loyalties lie. Not that they weren't already aware, but he's never been the guy who kisses the ring. In his mind, he won't care that his banishment is lifted. They were going to let me die, and that doesn't work for him.

Hell, they're probably pissed that Michael didn't let the Angel glass take me. Not that any one of them would dare to say it to his face.

Gabe remains standing beside us too, it's not something I expected, but his support is always welcome. Even if it is half because he loves making the others uncomfortable.

"You all know why we're here. If news hadn't reached you before now, the proof is obvious." Michael's voice booms across the room, and every person's gaze bounces from him to me, and the very angry Archangel of War beside me, before going back to their leader. I'm pretty sure they'd rather follow his orders to lick his boots than accept me back into the fold. Luckily for them, I have no interest in being part of the fold, I just don't want to be hunted for merely existing.

"Amantara, reborn as Remington Bennett, is miraculously an Angel once more. While I am still looking into how this was possible, it does appear to be a one off, a loophole in the Hunter's curse, purely because she was an Angel first. We are still looking into what this means in regards to the Hunters. I am aware that some of you work with the Hunters in some capacity, but I ask you to keep the possibilities of the changes to their life cycles to yourself until we have more solid information." He pauses, letting his words impact as he intended before looking at me and then back to his council. "Leviathan's banishment has been lifted, and will therefore, be reinstated as General of the Death Dealers. Amantara's position as his second will be returned to her, should she want it. She *will* be accepted back into the community, and any attempts on her life will be punished in the same fashion. Do I make myself clear?"

The room erupts at his declaration. Levi looks at Michael, eyebrows raised, he obviously had no idea of Michael's plans. Which makes me feel a little better, because I had no idea either. I don't want to be a part of the Death Dealers, and Michael knows that. I already made my wishes about returning home very clear. I have no idea what this might mean for Levi. If he'll even accept his position back.

The noise grows to a roaring level when Levi unleashes a crack of thunder and the rooms instantly goes silent.

"I do not want to reclaim my place as a Death Dealer." I tell them all clearly. "I have a life on Earth that I do not wish to give up. Considering most of you don't want me here, I don't see why this would be a problem to grant. All I want is to live in peace."

"Want to live on Earth, but want to be able to call on us when you get in trouble you mean. Shadow Walkers always end up in trouble." Lucinda, a blonde Angel on the council, who is as cold as her icy hair color suggests sneers at me. "With the Archangel of War on your side, what's to stop you dragging us into your problems. It's no secret where his loyalties lie."

I roll my eyes, she's always been a cold-hearted bitch, and I've never really given a fuck about her opinions.

"I ask nothing of Leviathan that he isn't willing to do," I tell her, while Levi practically shakes with anger beside me. She looks to him, and her eyes go wide as she takes him in. I'm not sure she's seen him lose his shit before, but he's really close right now. I put a hand on his arm practically willing him to calm. Him going nuclear isn't going to help anyone right now.

"I don't remember asking, or making this as an optional thing," Michael says as he stands, crossing his arms. "Any issues with my decision can be brought directly to me. Are there any other issues of business today?"

He looks at each person at the table individually, they

each shake their head, and a small weight lifts. While some of them might not be happy about what he's said, I don't think any of them would go against a direct order from him. No matter how much they hate it. There are worse things than death, and the punishment for disobeying him is one of those things.

Michael finishes his round of the table before nodding and glancing over to where we're standing. "Then we're done here."

"Did she really need to be there for that?" Levi grunts as he speaks to Michael once everyone else has left.

"She did, they needed to see her. That she's not a threat. Hiding wouldn't have helped anyone. Now everyone is aware that neither of you are to be fucked with, and there's no ambiguity in the message that went out." Michael smiles at me which just seems to piss Levi off more. "If you'll excuse me, I need to get a few things sorted. Come and see me later, little bird? I have something for you."

"Of course, thank you." He hugs me and I return it, savoring the feel of him, because I get the feeling that once I leave here this time, it might just be the last time I see my old friend and mentor.

"There's someone else here who would like to see you too," Michael says, his gaze bouncing between us. "Your mother requested some time with you."

My heart just about stops in my chest. There's so much unresolved with my mom, but with everything else going on, my need to settle everything seems almost insignificant. I nod, regardless, because I'm not just going to leave her hanging.

"Thank you. I'll seek her out." At my words he nods and leaves the room, leaving Levi and I alone in the council chambers. The high vaulted ceilings in here have always left me breathless, it truly is a place of wonder.

"Well, that was all very—"

"Don't," I interrupt, I'm not ready or interested in listening to how much they dislike each other.

"You're right. I'm sorry." He looks down at me and rubs the back of his neck. "I'll try to keep a lid on it. He just rubs me the wrong way. That's no secret, but you're right."

"Thank you." I stretch up on my tiptoes and kiss his cheek, but he captures me by the waist and kisses me until I'm breathless. My eyes flutter open when he finally pulls back and he smirks down at me.

"I have something I want to show you," he murmurs as he holds me close. "Then we can go see your mom, but then, I'm getting you home. Luckily time moves a lot faster here, so the guys won't kick my ass for not just coming back instantly. They're not exactly my biggest fans right now."

"Do I even want to know?" I ask, raising an eyebrow.

"Probably not," he laughs. "Come on, let's get going, the sooner we do, the sooner I can get you home."

I sigh at the word. Home. I never thought of it before, but home isn't a place. Not exactly. It's where they are, all of them. I try not to focus on that niggling inside of me that tells me it's not going to be as simple as I want it to be now that I have my memories back. I love them, each of them, with every piece of myself, the problem is, that there are now so many versions of myself inside my head, different versions of how I loved them in the past. I'm not the person they fell in love with anymore, well I mean, I am, but I'm also irrevocably changed.

I worry my lip as I stuff the thought back down. That's a problem for future me. Though I have a feeling it's going to be something I need to resolve sooner rather than later.

"Where are we going?" I ask Levi as he takes my hand and leads me from the council chamber. He picks me up as if I'm nothing and spreads his wings, before soaring into the skies.

"You'll see," he teases and I can't help but roll my eyes. I've had enough surprises for a lifetime, and I'm not exactly a fan of them, but I indulge him, because it's so very rare he's this carefree. Especially here in Avalon. I like to think that part of that is because of me, but I'm also aware I've caused him more than a little pain.

The mark on my arm is proof of that. The bond between us from my last life before this one as a Hunter. The one where I loved him, and another. Where I saved him, or thought I did, without even knowing him. He bound us together, granting me his protection. The Angel runes on my arm a manifestation of everything he blessed me with when I awoke last as a Hunter. The protection, the ability to remember more than I should have, so that I could remember him. It's almost as if that mark lead to everything that's happened, but I wouldn't change a thing. Not when it led me to all of them, and gave us the ability to build the life we're working towards. I'm also a little convinced the mark was part of the reason my magic was available in this last life as a Hunter, it was why I was able to become an Angel once more.

But that's a conversation for another time. Another place.

It takes me a moment to pull myself from my internal monologue to realize where he's brought me.

"My old house," I gasp as we land, on the very outskirts of Avalon, the best place for an outcast like to me live in peace. I'd almost forgotten about this place. I might have all of my memories back, but there is a lot to sift through.

"I kept it sealed after… but I came here after each life of yours, and added pieces of you, just hoping that one day,

I might get to show you this place again. But it was also a place I could come between your lives and remember that you weren't completely gone." My heart aches at his words. My emotions are running a gauntlet inside of me at the minute, but I extinguish the majority of it so as not to be overwhelmed, and kiss his cheek before he places my feet on the ground.

"Levi… I don't know what to say. Thank you just doesn't seem like enough."

"You never have to thank me, angel. I told you, everything I do, I do for you, for us. Let's go in, there's something I think you're going to want back." He pushes the wooden door open, the musty smell hits me first, it's obviously been a while since he was here last.

He turns the light on and opens up the windows while I debate whether or not going inside is a good idea. I already have enough inside of me that I'm bottling up right now, and I'm not sure how much more I can take before I break. I know it's coming, I just don't really want to do it here in Avalon, where I spent my entire life as an outcast.

"Are you coming?" he asks as he pokes his head out of the door. I take a deep breath, mentally preparing myself for whatever he might have in here, and step across the threshold. It's like being hurtled back in time. My house was never the biggest, or the grandest, but it was enough for me. One open living space, with a bathroom off to the side. My bed in the far corner, not too far from the kitchen and coffee pot, of course. Then the main living space to the front. There's more clutter in here than I remember, though considering Levi has been adding to this place for a couple of centuries, that's not too much of a shock I guess.

I stand just inside the doorway, taking in the changes he's made, when he heads over to the far side of the living space to my old weapons cabinet. He fusses for a minute before turning back to face me with two boxes in his hands.

Oh shit.

I remember those boxes.

Even with all the dust in the house, the wood practically shines as he places them on the table and waits for me to approach.

"You kept them?" I ask, a lump in my throat.

"Of course I did. I had them made for you, I remember the first time I gave them to you, I wasn't just going to let them get lost in the aftermath of the war." He smiles sadly at me, and the pain etched on his face makes me want to cry. I sacrificed myself for him, and I'd do it again, but I hate how much it hurt him anyway.

I move towards the table, a slight tremor in my hands. It's silly, being so scared of opening those boxes when I know what's inside, but the fact that he had them made, that he kept them, it's almost overwhelming right now.

I open the first box, and smile down at my old friends.

Two black karambit blades nestled in velvet, with my Angel sigil, the archer constellation, just like the birthmark I had before I reawoke as an Angel, engraved into the metal on one side, and the crown wrapped in thorns on the other. His sigil. I brush my fingers across the cold dark blades and sigh. These blades got me through a lot of tight spots.

I move to the bigger rectangular box and smile up at Levi. "Thank you. Thank you for finding them, and for keeping them." I open the second box and find the bow he had crafted for me. Black wood with purple details, with both of our sigils on again. It amazes me that I could ever have forgotten the beauty of the gifts he once gave me.

"You have nothing to thank me for," he says softly as he moves to stand behind me, wrapping his arms around my waist as I brush my fingers along the bow.

"I have so much to thank you for, that thank you isn't ever going to be enough, but it's all that I have."

"I have you, Remy. That's all I'll ever need."

We spent most of the night at the house, just going through all of the bits he'd added, and enjoying being in each other's company. We laid in the bed for a while, while Levi just held me. I think nearly losing me again, in a very permanent way, is hitting him, so I just lay there and enjoyed the peace it brought me.

"We should probably head to Michael's soon, we also need to find your mother, then we can get home," Levi mumbles. I lift my head from his chest and smile.

"Can we go to the markets first? I always loved the markets in the early morning, before they got too busy." My words make him smile and groan all at the same time. The markets are on the edges of the city, near the water, and are really not easily defensible because it's so open, but we have nothing to fear here. Not for now at least. It's so peaceful, knowing that someone isn't going to try and kill us while we're here, but I will not hide, even if I am safer in Avalon.

"We can go, but not for long."

"Thank you, but yes, not for long. I want to get home too. Though, I'm not looking forward to the whole, putting myself in danger speech I know I'm going to get. I half expected it from you."

"Oh yeah, that's definitely coming." He chuckles. "But I'm just glad you're alive and safe. That can wait till we're home and have more privacy than Avalon affords." He swats my ass, as if giving a preview of what's to come, and I can't be sorry about that.

"I'm going to grab a quick shower, and then we can go!" I jump up from the bed and sway my hips as I walk away from him, feeling his stare on my ass. It's been way too long since I've been with any of my men. I miss the feel of them on my skin, inside of me. I also really need to connect with them all again, especially with everything inside my head now. I bite my lip and look back at him over my shoulder, hoping he picks up at what I'm asking without saying a word.

"Maybe you could use some company!"

I don't answer, I just wink and smile before turning away, stripping away my last piece of clothing and stepping into the Italian-style shower. It's more than big enough for the two of us and I'm eager to see just how sturdy the walls are in Avalon when it comes to Levi's endless hunger.

The air changes when he steps into the bathroom. He's not yet behind me but the electric charge in the atmosphere makes my skin ripple with anticipation.

I need him, more than I'm willing to admit out loud, but the fact that I nearly lost all of this. Him. It makes me need him more than he'll ever know.

"You realize that this will make us late to the markets, right?" His hands are on my hips, fingers squeezing my flesh tentatively like he's making sure he won't hurt me.

"I'm okay, Levi. I promise." I reach my hand up and stroke his cheek. He needs that reassurance, I know him. His brand of hunger is always on the rough side and he would tone it down for me any day of the week, but I don't want him to. I don't want a watered-down version of him, I want the full force of everything that he is. I want to see the bright red desire that burns in his eyes every time he touches me. Without it, he wouldn't be him.

And I need… him.

"I couldn't live with myself if I hurt you after everything…" his words trail off as he turns me, so my back is against his chest as his mouth glides along the column of my neck. His erection pushing into my lower back, his hands sliding up to cup my breasts, he burns a trail of kisses up to my jaw and then back down. I haven't even turned the water on yet, but I don't have to worry, Levi takes care of it for me.

With one hand massaging my flesh, his fingers pinching my nipples, his other is adjusting the water temperature until it's the perfect heat without burning my skin.

My body automatically relaxes into his chest, as his hands make their way down to my eagerly awaiting pussy. With the back of my head resting at the crook of his shoulder, I close my eyes and let him take complete control. That's his forte. Control. It's how he makes me feel alive, by controlling my pleasure and his. I can sense how much he needs it after everything we've been through the last few days.

"Every time you put yourself in danger, you're killing a small part of me, Remy. But, my god, every time I touch you, it breathes life back into me." He clutches at my throat and with fingers, gentle but firm, he tilts my head at the perfect angle for his mouth.

Our kiss starts out sweet almost. Like tentative teenagers learning the feel of the other. But it only lasts a fragment of a second before his tongue is sweeping into my mouth and devouring me as if he's scared he'll never have chance to again.

My breathing picks up, my chest heaving with each breath that I take. His fingers tighten at my throat, while his other hand is exploring my most sensitive spot as though it's our first time. One finger sweeps over my clit, another gliding inside me.

We never part as he brings his finger to our joined mouths and smears my juices across our lips. I can taste myself and it's heady. More so is the fact that he can taste me too, and it's making him harder than I could have ever imagined.

"The nectar of life is you, Remy."

His words do something to me. They ignite something inside of me, making me react without the slightest thought to anything or anyone else.

Ripping myself away from him, I turn on my heel and slam back against him, my chest against his, my hands in his wet hair, pulling him down so I can show him exactly what he does to me.

Levi pushes me against the shower wall, kicks my feet apart, and steps inside my parted thighs before clamping his hands under them and pulling me up and onto his rigid cock. He's not playing anymore. There is no hesitancy about him, now. No holds barred. No guilt or what ifs.

There is only me, him, and the fucking we both deserve.

With the water beating across his back, the droplets splash across my face but as his mouth slams down on mine, his cock fills me to the hilt, and everything else is completely forgotten.

My arms wrap around his neck, our mouths dancing to the rhythm of our fucking, and my body is humming with need.

I need harder.

I need faster.

I need… more.

"God, yes," he responds, and I realize that I've spoken aloud. I'm so completely lost in him, in the feel of him that I'm not even coherent enough to realize when I'm speaking.

With his every thrust inside me, I slide up and down the tiled wall. I can feel every vein and every velvety inch of his cock as he fucks the Angelic right out of me.

"My dirty girl likes it when I fuck her raw, doesn't she?"

"Levi, yes, please. More." Phrases are no longer possible. Soon, I'll just be gasping at his every word.

"Did you miss my dick, Remy? Did you miss what it

can do for you?"

"Ah, gah…" I'm unable to form words, even if just to answer him.

Our bodies slap together every time he fills me to the hilt, and each time, I feel the power of him. The utter strength that lives inside every muscle and every tendon. Opening my eyes to admire his beauty, the veins at his neck pulse with his ravaging need for me.

"Come inside me, Levi. Mark me, please."

Shifting slightly, he pushes me harder against the wall and strategically places his hands on my ass. He's not moving, his dick is fully seated inside me as his fingers separate my cheeks and his middle finger breaches my opening, through the ring of muscles, adding to the fullness that consumes my every cell.

"Hang on, angel. And don't forget to scream as loud as you want. Avalon needs to know who you belong to."

I don't have time to fully grasp his meaning as his cock slides out at the same time as his finger and then they plunge back in at the same time as he invades my mouth with his tongue.

I see stars. He's fucking me everywhere. My mouth, my pussy, my ass. He's everywhere and I'm nowhere in particular.

I'm afraid we'll break the wall, afraid it won't resist the force with which he is pummeling me to my orgasmic death.

“Come all over my cock, angel. Do it, now.”

His words unhinge me. They give me the permission I didn’t realize I needed, to let go of everything. My fears, my guilt, my doubts.

I let it all go, let it fly out of me like they don’t belong. Only he does. Right now, the only thing I need inside of me is him as I come undone around him. His thrusts don’t relent, not letting me come down until he comes inside of me with a roar. He slows to a stop, his forehead on mine before he kisses me softly.

“That’s my girl,” he hums into my ear, bringing me back to earth with tender kisses and dirty words. “I love it when you come all over my dick, angel. It’s like finding my favorite blanket.”

“Levi?” I feel drunk as he pulls his finger out of my ass and slowly pulls me off of his cock.

“Yes, angel?”

“I love your cock.”

“Oh Angel, it loves you, too.”

SIX

I finish strapping my knives to my thighs and recount the salt-crafted, iron-tipped arrows in my quiver. Not all Demons get put down by salt or iron, but that's why I have my knives and my sword. My power simmers inside of me, I've barely touched it recently, other than working with Morganna to seal the portal between the two realms.

We've been fighting this war for longer than any of us imagined, but with the seal closed, my deal with Morganna and her men, and the battle plans we have for today, I'm feeling confident that we'll be back home again soon. Finally, Leviathan and I can start something real together, rather than the stolen moments we have right now.

I look around the small house I call home—I came back briefly to stock up on arrows, because the ones we make in the human realm just don't seem to pack as much of a punch—and I smile. My own piece of the city, carved out for myself, not tainted by the outside worlds.

I have more than enough crazy to deal with outside of these walls, fates know I cherish this place. It's my safe haven. The knock at the door stops my movements. Leviathan and Nevin are with Serafina and Amelia in the human realm. No one else comes here. I should have paid more attention, been more alert.

I put on hand on the sword hilt at my hip and move cautiously towards the door. I take a deep breath and hold it, to quiet myself as much as I can. This might be Avalon, but nowhere is safe for someone like me.

"Little bird, your shields are down," the voice calls out, laughing, and I relax, but put my shields up. "That's better," Michael says as he opens the door and peers inside to where I'm standing.

"I wasn't expecting you. Is everything okay?" I ask as he enters and closes the door behind him. The last time I saw him, we left things… well, it was awkward as fuck.

"Everything's fine, I just thought we should talk, and since you're so rarely alone these days…"

I shift from one foot to the other while trying not to wring out my hands. Give me a battle any single day and I'll jump at it. Ask me to talk about feelings and stuff… nope. No Siree. No thank you. I'm out.

"I know that this isn't as simple as I'd like it to be, and I never meant to kiss you."

Heat climbs up my neck at his words. He kissed me just before I left at the start of the war. Just after I told him that Leviathan had confessed his feelings for me, and I wasn't sure what to do. Michael has always been the guy I could talk to about anything, but apparently, I'm blind as hell, because I missed the fact that Michael, as well as Leviathan, seemed to want to kiss me.

"I…" I try to find the right words, but he shakes his head, stopping me.

"I am not asking anything of you, Amantara. I can't be what you need, not with everything else I have going on, and especially not now. I love you, I've made no secret of that, at least I thought not." His voice catches as he speaks, seeing him like this hurts me, but I don't know how to fix it. He takes a breath and continues. "But I also know I can't be what you need. What I'm trying to tell you is that I love you. But I know Leviathan loves you too. He can be what you need. Far better than I ever can. I'm not asking you to pick, I want you to follow your heart wherever it leads you, but I will live with whatever you choose and be here for you no matter what happens."

I let out a sigh of relief. I never want to lose him, but I also know I don't love him, at least not in the same way that he loves me, and that's not fair to him. But his words comfort me, because I don't know how to choose without someone getting hurt.

"Michael…" I start, but he cuts me off again, engulfing me in a hug.

"Just be safe, Amantara. I don't know what I'd do if something happened to you."

We walk through the markets, and I can't remember the last time I smiled so hard. The smells that fill the air, the hubbub of people moving about their lives. It just all reminds me of a much easier time in my life. A much more peaceful one. This was the little sliver of peace that I needed. Especially since after I showered, and sat down to sort my hair, I got lost down the rabbit hole of the memories now available to me.

So many different versions of myself, none of which feel like me, and I feel disjointed. Like I almost don't know who I am anymore now that I know everything. I didn't examine it too deeply before I shut it down and pulled myself from that dark place.

I pull my focus back to where we are when Levi stiffens beside me. I look up at him and follow his line of sight when I see my mom. I've been so desperate to connect with her, even more so since dad died and she told us about how grandfather had a hand in her death but the thought of wading through everything inside of me, going through the emotional rollercoaster that is finally having time with her, fills me with panic.

I grasp Levi's hand, pulling his gaze down to me, and I know in an instant he knows I need to get out of here. There's so much that is unresolved with my mom, and as much as it pains me to dodge her, the thought of facing her, of having to dig through everything inside of myself to do that, to talk the way we once did. I'm not ready for that. I might be a pro at leaving stuff for future Remy to deal with, but that box is getting real close to overflowing.

Levi pulls me in the opposite direction, and I go with him, without struggle. I don't even turn back, because I know if I see her face again right now, I won't be able to hold it together, and breaking right now isn't an option. I take in deep breaths as Levi moves us through the crowds, to the thick of all the people, so we can be anonymous. Well, as much as you can be in Avalon anyway. Levi's isn't exactly a face people forget.

I follow as he leads us through the other side of the crowd and towards the sky loft where Michael will be waiting for us. I can't just leave without saying goodbye. Especially after how things went the last time I left here. My stomach flips just thinking about it. I should have known something was coming. I still don't know if they ever found out who shot that arrow. Or if it's all linked to everything now.

Now isn't the time to worry about that. God knows my to do list is more than long enough. I know seeing my mom is going to be on there, but first… first I need to go home and reassure my guys I'm okay. Just a few more hurdles to jump through before I do. Levi could have us out of here in a heartbeat, but I'd rather not have him be banished again. This place never meant as much to me as it did to him.

Levi pulls me to him and lifts me up into his arms, making me squeak in surprise. I wrap my arms around his neck, looking up at him with a smile on my face. The way he looks at me makes me breathless, my whole body shivers as he stretches his wings and shoots us into the skies.

"I wondered if you'd actually come here, or if you'd just try to leave," Michael says, as he looks up from the dining table where he's studying a dozen texts with maps spread across it.

"Don't tempt me," Levi grumbles as he puts me on the floor. I roll my eyes so hard I swear I see the inside of my skull.

"Can we please just not?" This constant piggy in the middle thing is exhausting.

"Sorry," Levi says, sheepishly as he rubs the back of

his neck. I look over to Michael who almost looks smug.

"I meant you too," I say with a pointed stare. The smile falls from his face, and he has the decency to look a little shamed.

"Sorry," he says, shaking his head. "You're right. Thank you for coming to see me, I know you didn't technically have to, but it will make things easier. I also have something to run past you." Levi's interest looks peaked, and I let out a deep breath. Being here felt peaceful to start with, but the more I'm here, the more suffocated I feel. Especially now that I have access to my memories. The soothing feeling this place gave me, is like how I felt here before my powers manifested, after that, well that's when it all went to hell.

Thankfully, I had a few people happy to look out for me. I wonder briefly where Amantara's parents—my parents—are now. After they abandoned me so spectacularly, did they feel any guilt?

I shake my head and pull myself back to the present and the issues I have to deal with in the here and now.

"What was it you wanted to tell us about?" I ask Michael, and head towards the table he's sitting at, with Levi close behind.

"Like I said to you before, I've been watching what's been going on as much as I can since Levi was here last. I've been trying to piece the puzzle together, with what I'd seen even before then, though I can't see everything in the human realm, it's just not that simple. But, as I said in my letter, I think this all leads back to Amelia."

I think back trying to work out who he means, when it hits me. She was a Death Dealer. I was never close with her, but she was always around. Never too far from us. Just, in the background. If I remember rightly, her and Serafina were pretty close. Both born as female warriors, destined to join the Death Dealers. They had a lot in common.

"There is no way," Levi protests, but then it's as if something in his mind clicks and his face pales a little. "The Archiver…"

"That was her nickname for a while, Nevin adopted it after he took up the role at your side, but she was a bookish type, despite her skill with a bow and arrow," Michael reminds him, and I nod as it comes back to me. "She was also never a fan of Amantara's."

He looks at me, but it's still strange to be called that, despite my memories. My name has been Remy for so long now, that despite the fact it was probably Amantara longer, Remy is what feels natural to me.

"You're not wrong," Levi says, his eyes narrowed as he takes in the maps on the table. "You really think she could be behind all of what's happened? What reason could she possibly have? This is a very long time to hold a grudge." His skeptical tone makes me laugh.

"She hated me. She hated me because I was at your side," I tell him. "She hated me because I had Michael's ear. Think of the family she's from. The presumptive thought that she should be where I was, that a Shadow Walker didn't deserve what I had. Think of how much that would have driven her insane considering how she thought of Shadow Walkers. It's not implausible. I wouldn't put it past her to be the one who fired the arrow that day. But to hold a grudge this long…"

"It was a man who fired the arrow that day. We never found them, but I saw the outline clear enough," Levi counters and Michael nods.

"And I've never disguised myself to look like a man to get in and out of somewhere unnoticed either," I say, rolling my eyes. "If you didn't catch the person, do not presume anything. It could be that you never found anyone *because* you were looking for a man."

"You forget that arrow was meant for me," Levi says softly, his eyes looking down at me, the guilt there threatens to break in two.

"Or was it?" I shrug. "Michael is the only other person who can heal those wounds. Everyone knew he couldn't go to the human realm back then, it was too risky. Especially since the King had only just fallen. Anyone that knew us, knew I'd never let you take that arrow, because I didn't trust my abilities enough to trust that I could save you."

My voice catches, remembering the feeling of the arrow breaching my heart. The look on his face as he realized what I'd done.

I take a deep breath to keep the tears at bay. My emotions have been haywire since Michael unlocked my memories. Yes, he warned me, but I thought that like always, I could be a master of my emotions. That I could compartmentalize it all. I keep trying, but it keeps catching me off guard.

"She's right," Michael says, his voice croaking. He clears it and looks up. "Everyone knew about what was between the two of you. They knew that she doubted her healing ability, despite being so well versed in the others. It was no secret how selfless she is, even if people used it against her." The weight of both of their stares slams into me, but I roll my shoulders and press forward.

"So, it definitely could have been her, but we have no proof. I also have no idea why she'd hold the grudge for so long."

"Well, she kind of disappeared from the face of the universe after you died. No one has seen or heard from her since. She never returned with the other Death Dealers. No one knew where she went," Michael tells me, before shooting Levi a look. "Leviathan was too busy sorting out the mess he'd created with the Hunter's curse and dealing with the fall out of what he did for you to be much use in the first few months after your death."

"Don't pretend like I was the only one who was distracted," Levi snarls, and I sigh.

"Please?" is all I say and they both nod. At least they're trying, that's more than I've gotten from either of them before.

"Thank you. Since you think it's Amelia, do you have any idea where she could be? Any idea why she'd still be attacking after so long?" I ask Michael.

"Some grudges burn so deep, that they're impossible to move past." His gaze darts over my shoulder towards Levi but looks back at me quickly. "I can't say for sure as to why, but she's definitely someone of interest. Just with everything going on here right now, I don't have people to spare to search for her."

"What does that mean?" Levi asks.

"There is a reason there was not a vote about the two of you coming back on board. Things here are unsettled. I'm still looking into the why of it, but dissension is crawling through the ranks here. Whispers questioning our alliances." His words crash into me like a wave. It's because of me. Because he's been helping me.

"I'm sorry," I whisper.

"It is not your fault, little bird. I have been distracted since Levi saved you a year ago. It's amazing how petty immortals can be, considering that amount of time is but a drop in the ocean for us. But regardless, I have it under control for now."

"We have numbers, in the human realm and in the Shadow Realm. We can put out feelers, see if anyone knows anything about the missing Angel," Levi tells him.

"I've done some research, you can take it with you. Hopefully it will help. If I can help more I will, but if you both refuse to stay here, there isn't much I can do to keep her safe." Michael looks directly at Levi.

"Of course we're not staying. She'll be safe with us."

"You mean like she was safe before? She would be safe here. Protected in the way all of Avalon is. With me," Michael counters, and my anger rises. Are they seriously talking about me like I'm not standing right fucking here?

"She will be safe at home," Levi growls.

"This is her home!" Michael booms, and I lose my shit.

"Are you seriously fucking trying to make this decision for me, as if I'm not standing right the fuck here?" I glare at them both, but they're both so fucking stubborn and bone headed that they don't back down. You could cut the tension in the room with a knife.

"The decision of my safety does not belong to either one of you. You can give me your opinions, hell, I welcome them, but if either of you think you are going to dictate to me, you can jog the fuck on." I am so angry I can barely see straight. I am sick of being treated like I'm less. At the crackle in the room, I look to Levi, worried his anger has gotten away from him, and find his wide-eyed stare at me.

A sort of black lighting curls around my hands and forearms. What the actual fuck is that?

"Remy, take a deep breath," Levi says lowly, his voice soothing, but the anger inside of me reacts, as if he's just trying to dictate another fucking order to me. I push at the rage, the logical voice in the back of my mind reaching me amongst the swirling of emotion inside of myself. I shake my head and take a deep breath. That's when I feel that tether inside of me, flying around like a live wire. I clench my fists and pull on the tether, pulling the power back inside of myself.

"Morgan really wasn't messing around when she said there was something dark inside of you," Levi says, as the electricity leaves the air. Michael is just standing there, blinking at me.

"What was that?" I ask, to no one in particular, but hoping one of them has an answer.

"That… that was shadow fire," Michael says with an audible gulp. "That is not something I have seen in a very, very long time."

Awesome. That seems about right.

"Can it hurt her?" Levi asks him, but Michael shakes his head.

"It doesn't hurt the bearer, but this is definitely

something no one outside of this room should know about. If you thought the Angels would be on edge with your presence here little bird, this will not help.

"I don't understand?" I say, confused.

"Shadow fire is something of myth. At least, these days. I've only seen one person bear it before, and that was in a time when I was a boy, when Shadow Walkers were more in number. The strongest of them, Azekial, the leader of Archangels back then, could wield shadow fire… it is the only substance known to be able to kill an Angel other than Angel glass."

Well fuck.

SEVEN

I crouch behind the marble table, the barrage of fire from the Demons inside the room is almost overwhelming. I got separated from Leviathan and the guys when I chased one of them this way. I should've known better. Now I'm trapped, pinned down, and I can practically hear the maniacal laughter of the Demons as I throw some fire of my own back at them. One Angel might not have as much power as a dozen Demons, but I'm a Shadow Walker, and that means I can hurt them more than most Angels. The links I have with Demons is unlike any other Angels. It makes us closer, but it also means that they're less likely to heal from my power.

I might not have a huge arsenal up my sleeve, not like Michael, my healing skills are seriously lacking, but my shadows and my fire. They're my strongest weapons. I blanket the room in shadows, straining as I try to make sure I cover everyone in here. I can feel each of them, their power reaching for the weird familiarity of my own, and once I can sense them, and they can't see me fully, I gather my fire in my hand, a ball of blue flame dancing.

I feel the sweat trickle down my spine at the amount of power I'm using. I can hear shouts from down the hall, but I don't have time to pay attention to that. My entire focus has to be on getting myself out of this room, and back to the guys. I grow the ball of fire, but the shadows start to recede as I reach the limit of my power well. Their attack never stops, and as the shadows start to fade, their attack increases. I take a deep breath and close my eyes before popping up, and sending my giant ball of flame into multiple smaller ones, one for each Demon in here.

"Amantara!" Tobin's voice echoes down the hall, as I drop back into a crouch, hoping that the flames hit their targets. He strides into the room, bow drawn and fires off arrow after arrow, taking cover behind a pillar to the right of me. I look up to him, but I'm depleted. We were led into a trap, this supposedly almost empty hideout was a nest of all forms of Demons. I know Morganna has been having an issue with the power play over in the Shadow Realm, but I don't think I've ever seen this many Demons on Earth before.

I tuck it away to check in with her, if and when I get out of this mess, and look back at Tobin. His worried gaze keeps darting back to me as more Demons fill the space opposite us. There must be another entrance on that side of the room.

Fuck.

'I'm sorry,' I mouth to Tobin who shakes his head. The four of us, Tobin, Nevin, Leviathan and I have been working as a four for as long as I can remember. This probably isn't the worst situation we've found ourselves in, but it sure is fucking close.

A roar from down the hall reaches my ears as the entire building shakes. I guess Leviathan is getting pissed off. I take a deep breath and put myself together. I refuse to be the weak link here. I send a tendril of my power out into the room, searching for someone briming with power, and once I latch on, I drain them. I won't incapacitate them, but it will give me enough juice to help us get the hell out of here. Hopefully unscathed.

The screech from the Demon as I drain his power pierces my eardrums, and Tobin winces at the sound. Thank the fates for rapid healing, because I'm pretty sure my ear drums just burst. I nod at Tobin as he takes a deep breath and pulls another arrow from his quiver. I try not to be envious of his blessed quiver, the one that never runs out of arrows, but I fail most of the time.

I push the shadows out of me again and dart over to Tobin who fires into the darkness as we make a run back into the hall.

"We need to get the fuck out of here," he breathes as we run back towards where Leviathan and Nevin were when I saw them last. I nod, not wasting precious air on words. The air around us is filling with smoke, we might be able to handle it, but it's not exactly comfortable.

"Tobin!" Nevin's voice shouts from behind us, I spin on my heel just as he darts towards the Demon between us. The Demon unleashes his power, but Nevin is a shield, he's impervious to pretty much all powers, and he can share it, just with a limited range. His shield reaches me first, and Tobin takes the majority of the blow from the Demon.

"No!" Nevin's pained cry swallows all other noise. I shoot a ball of blue flame at the Demon, and he disintegrates, before turning to Tobin who is bleeding on the floor beside me. "How, how is he bleeding? He's an Angel. This isn't meant to be fatal!"

Nevin's cries hurt me, he just saved my life. And now his brother might not survive. He's right, this shouldn't hurt him. At least not this bad. I don't understand. Nevin lifts Tobin's head as he coughs, blood trickling from his mouth.

"Heal him!" Nevin screams at me, but Tobin reaches up and touches his arm, shaking his head.

"She can't big brother, you know it." He coughs again and I fall to my knees. "It's not her fault. That Demon, whatever that was, it's something I've never felt before."

"Please, just try," Nevin pleads with me, and so I reach my hands over to Tobin, willing the supposed healing power inside of me to my hands. The power leaves my hands and I feel it flow into him. He sighs, like he's at peace, but then his breathing stops, as a tear runs down my face.

"I am so, so, sorry," I choke out as I look up to Nevin's tear stained face.

"This isn't your fault, Amantara," he says softly. "It's mine. I wasn't strong enough to protect you both. He would've wanted me to save you first. It's who he is."

"But…"

"I won't ever regret saving you, just the fact I couldn't save him too." He stands, lifting Tobin's body. "We need to get back to Leviathan, and get the fuck out of here. Then we need to find out how the fuck this happened."

After the bombshell Michael dropped on me earlier, he left Levi and I. The thought of my safety on Earth set aside in wake of my new power. I left Levi at his loft to prepare everything he wanted to take home with us, and I went to my house to do the same. I've been here about an hour, longer than I thought I would be, but there was something about going through my stuff here that felt cathartic. I don't have much to take home. Small keepsakes, and weapons mostly, which I've got packed up and mainly in the bag I sling over my shoulder. It feels heavier than I expected, but I've carried worse. I close the door to the house and lock the door. I don't know if or when I'll be back here, but it's nice to know it's here if I should choose to come back.

"Remy." I freeze at the voice calling my name and close my eyes, key still in the door. "Remy?"

I turn at the second use of my name to face my mom. She looks hesitant, and I'm guessing the look of horror on my face isn't helping.

"I wanted… I wanted to speak to you. We didn't have much time before, and there is so much that I didn't get to speak to you about," she says hesitantly.

"Did you know?" I ask her, my voice cracking. She knows what I'm talking about. My deaths at the hands of my family from my time as a Hunter. Her eyes flash with tears but she swipes at them before they fall.

"Not at first. But when they wouldn't take you through the ritual, or even tell you about what we were, I suspected. I fought them, but it was a different time. I was a different person." She looks at the floor, wringing her hands. I recognize the movement, it's one of my own, and that somehow makes what she did worse.

"You could have told me," I say quietly. "You could have told me the truth, rather than let me go on unaware. You could have told me the truth in any of my lives, but you left me, left us all, unaware. You let us all believe the hate and vitriol that Dad and Grandfather spouted. You let me think that you were on my side, keeping my secrets, being my closest confidant, but really, you betrayed me worst of all. Because you just sat there and let it happen. You didn't step in. You didn't stop them."

"Remy…"

"I had a son," I tell her, cutting her off and her hand flies to her mouth as her tears finally spill. "Everly, she was one of my descendants. I know you knew her. Levi watched out for them, because he loved me. That is what you do for the ones you love. You… you just lied and acted like a coward." The words cut like the knives strapped to my thighs would.

"I am so sorry, Remy." She sobs, but I can't comfort her. I hadn't known how angry I was at her for what she did, or didn't do, but right now, right now, she doesn't deserve my sympathy.

"I don't accept it," I tell her. "You might have saved me this time, and for that I'm thankful. But for the rest…" My words trail off as she wraps her arms around herself.

"I understand. I didn't… there isn't ever going to be anything I can do that shows you just how sorry I am, for all of it. But I will be there, whenever you need it, whether you want me to be or not. I love you, Remington Bennett. Every piece of you, and I'm sorry I wasn't courageous enough before to show you that."

She finishes her sentence and takes a deep breath. I stay still, unsure if she's finished, but I'm not sure I can stay and hear anything else she has to say. She turns and walks away from me, and I watch her go until she disappears over the horizon, then I drop to the floor in a crouch, hugging my knees as I try to catch my breath.

My wings unfurl and wrap around me, blanketing me in shadow, and I almost feel safe. I need to go home. I need to be around my guys, because until then, I'm not going to be able to feel like myself again.

I take a deep breath and stand, picking up the other boxes I had put out here with the things I wanted to take home, and push off of the ground to fly back to Levi's loft.

Levi braces as we land, me in his arms. Apparently, me coming home of my own accord was out of the question, but considering everything that's happened of late, I decided to let him have this. Especially because after seeing my mom, I really just wanted to lean on him for a minute. It might seem foolish or weak to want to lean on him, but fuck anyone that wants to judge. A girl can only be so strong, some of the time.

He squeezes me tight against his chest before moving so my feet can touch the ground. I blink, letting my eyes adjust to the dusky evening, much darker than the bright Avalon that we left.

"Remy," he says softly, his arm still banded around my back, and he moves the other to encircle me as I look up at him. "I love you. I need you to know that, before I ask you to stop throwing yourself in dangerous situations. I know you trusted Bauer, but I also know that you've taken a death shot for the people you love without hesitation in the past. I need you to hear me, because if something happens to you, we won't survive without you. *I* won't survive without you." He reaches up, his hand cupping my cheek before he kisses me softly. He pulls back, and the fear in his eyes hits me. I don't think I've ever seen him truly afraid.

"I will try," I whisper, and lean my head against his chest, listening to his heartbeat as he holds me tightly. I won't promise him anything, because I don't want to break it, but I mean what I say. I really will try to be mindful. I saw his face after Bauer stabbed me, before Michael arrived. He looked broken. Like he might tear the world apart.

"What happened to Bauer?" I ask quietly, not sure how I feel about him right now.

"He's gone," he says, his body tenses beneath me, but I don't lift my head from his chest.

"Good," I sigh, and sink into his embrace a little more, not willing to dwell on exactly how gone he is regardless.

"We should let the others know you're back, angel. It will only have been a day here since I left, but they'll be anxious to make sure you're okay." His lips move against my hair as he murmurs the words to me softly.

"I know the feeling. Are you sure they're here?" I ask, pulling back from his arms, half-surprised they haven't realized we're back. Levi tilts his head to gesture behind me. I turn and see my other guys waiting at the threshold to the manor, Roman seeming to be being held back by the other two. I step out of Levi's embrace fully and move towards my guys with a smile, and that's when they move, Roman pushing past Creek and Kain to get to me.

He always has been the most impatient of them all. He wraps his arms around me and lifts me from the ground when he reaches me, spinning us around. He squeezes me so tight, I'm thankful I don't need to breathe so much anymore, because if I were human, I'd be very broken right now. I chuckle softly, and he pulls back a little.

"You're okay?" he sighs, questioning me, as much as reassuring himself as he looks me over.

"I'm fine. I was sore for a day or two, but I'm okay now," I tell him, before he crushes me against him again. I let him take his time, take the comfort he needs from me, all while being very aware of the others standing, waiting.

He pulls back again, the glow of his eyes bright. As if his wolf is telling me he's glad I'm back too.

"Ready to share yet, man?" Creek laughs softly, and Roman growls softly.

"No," he says gruffly, but I laugh and pat his chest.

"I'm not going anywhere. I'm okay. You can let me go for a minute."

"I am not letting you out of my sight again!" he declares, before begrudgingly letting me go, and Creek sweeps me up in his own hug.

"I was so worried about you, beautiful. Please, don't ever make me have to live through that fear again," he says softly against my ear as he holds me.

"I'll try," I tell him, the same as I did Levi.

Creek being more considerate, pulls back and kisses me hard, showing me just how much he missed me, before pulling back and handing me over to Kain.

"Mon amour," he sighs, as his fingers caress my cheek. As if making sure I'm really here.

"Hi," I whisper, not sure what else to say. Plus, he too hugs me, so tight as if I might disappear if he lets me go.

"I thought we'd lost you for good." His voice is thick as he clings to me, and I hold him tight, to let him know I'm here.

"You can't get rid of me that easily," I murmur, trying to lighten the mood a little. Levi laughs from behind me, and I can feel Kain shake beneath me as he laughs too. I smile, glad the somber mood has lifted a little.

"Is everyone else gone?" I ask them as I pull back slightly, but he entwines his fingers with mine, not yet ready to let me go. I get it, and I missed them all too, so I don't object.

"Pretty much," Creek says, his eyes wandering up and down my body, checking for injury.

"Where is she? Is she home? My Remy girl?" Nonnie's voice makes me smile, and I turn to see her as she reaches the door. "You're here! Oh my goodness."

She rushes towards me and hugs me tighter than any of the guys did, and I try not to cry. She peppers my face with kisses as she holds my cheeks and I can't escape her fussing. "Come, you need to eat. You nearly died, and you nearly took my heart with you Remy girl. Come, come."

Taking my hand, she pulls me, and in doing so tugs Kain along with us, who is just smiling at me still. The others filter in behind us, no one taking their eyes from me.

We spent the evening together in the kitchen, just talking about everything that happened in Avalon. The boxes we brought back with us are just littered in a corner. I've been passed from lap to chair more times than I care to count, but I let them. I know they need this. Need me.

I shut my mind off before we came here, so I could focus on my guys, make sure they were okay, because it might be me that nearly died, but I know that if it were the other way around, I'd be a fucking mess.

They're all just talking about the loose ends we still have. Including the potential traitor amongst the Lycans, and Lizzie, the rogue Witch and her coven. I stay quiet for the most part, just listening to everything they've been working on while I've been training with Serafina. Here was me thinking most of the stuff we were worried about was done, but no, they were just handling stuff themselves. I don't have the energy or the want to chastise them for keeping stuff from me yet again, but you better believe that it's a conversation we're going to have real soon.

I stifle another yawn, I'm really looking forward to this part of everything ebbing away, though, when I think about it, I haven't slept in a few days, so maybe I'm due to be tired. I'm too tired to think about it too deeply.

"We should get you to bed, precious," Kain murmurs. I'm currently in his lap, my head resting on his shoulder. I nod and move to stand, but his arms tighten around me. He loops one arm under my legs, and stands, lifting me effortlessly.

"We still need to talk about this whole Michael thing,"

Roman grumbles, looking at me, his jealous and possessive nature very much on show.

"We can talk about that when she's not exhausted. We'll see you guys tomorrow," Kain tells them firmly. Creek and Roman start to protest, but as I lift my head their objections stop. Kain's face is set, and brokers no argument.

I tap Kain's chest, and he lets me down. I move to each of my guys, kissing them goodnight, before moving back to Kain's side. He lifts me again, and I think for a second about objecting, but I can't find it in me. I think this is more for him, than it is for me, so I allow him to carry me to his room here.

He places me on the edge of the bed, and lifts his t-shirt, his eyes barely leaving me, as if he's scared I'll disappear if he does. My breath hitches as I take in the smooth, lean planes of his chest. He really is beautiful. I sigh as he lifts the hem of my sweater and takes it off of me. He looks at me, his eyes darting to my shoulder. I brush over the faint line there, amongst Levi's mark, trying not to think about what happened.

"Remy…" Kain says, the anguish in his voice as he steps towards me and cups my face in his hands.

"I remember… I remember everything," I tell him, and his eyes go wide.

"Are you okay?" he asks, his eyes not leaving mine, his gaze so intense, it's like he can see inside of me. I shake my head a little, and take a deep breath.

"I don't know who I am right now," I tell him quietly, my gaze dropping to the floor. He crouches in front of me, and uses his finger to tip my chin up so that I'm looking at him again.

"Remy, it doesn't matter to me. Any of it. I love you. No matter what you've done, what you are. There is nothing in this universe that could change that. You are mine, as I am yours. You've been through so very much. We can talk, and I'll listen to everything you choose to tell me without any judgment, or you can take a minute, and we'll talk another time. You don't have to deal with it all right now."

His words settle the racing emotions inside me, and I manage to stuff most of it back down, focusing on just him. I lean forward and capture his lips with my own, pouring every ounce of love I feel for him into the kiss.

His reaction is immediate. Strong hands cup my face as his kiss transports me to a place where worries are nothingness and the present moment is everything.

His nimble fingers quickly unbutton my pants, pushing them down over my ass. I kick and wiggle right out of them before launching them somewhere in the corner of the room. I interrupt our kiss just long enough to undress him, so that he's just as naked as I am and then his lips are back on mine, like a starving man finding what he's been looking for. Fingers threading through hair and moans echoing off the walls.

I feel so small in his arms when he's lying on top of me. His need to protect me is so ingrained in his very being that feeling the sheer weight of him is a comfort in and of itself.

"Kain?" His name pours from my lips like warm honey.

"Yes, precious?"

"Make love to me."

Kain freezes for a beat, his vibrant eyes staring into my soul as though he can still see us as we were many lifetimes ago. And maybe he can.

We lie there without moving, just enjoying each other's warmth. His naked body rocking back and forth on my heated skin. His cock is leisurely sliding up and down my increasingly wet pussy bringing a smile to his face, so bright my entire life lights up.

"You're getting wetter by the second. It's so fucking hot." I don't even blush at his words, I just push my hips up and beg him for more without uttering a single word.

On his stroke downward, he pushes inside me in one smooth thrust, filling me completely. Making me feel whole, again.

My moan sparks some kind of fire in his eyes and in a split second, he's boxing me in between his forearms, biting and sucking on my mouth, his fingers curling in my hair as he makes sweet love to me.

Just like I asked.

Just like I needed.

With every thrust, he's more frantic. More demanding. More desperate to have me.

And my body is aching for him to own me, to reassure me. I need to remember that I'm alive and he's here. They all are. Even if I'm currently under his spell, my men are always present in my mind and soul, no matter whose cock is making me feel perfection.

"I've missed you so fucking much, precious. Don't ever do this to me again. To us."

I don't answer. What could I possibly say?

But I react with my own desperate kisses, my own nails digging into his scalp. My blunt teeth trying to break the skin of his neck. I want to drink him and eat him as he fucks the love right into me.

With Kain, it's the perfect balance between fucking and lovemaking.

Slow, hard thrusts change the tempo of our rhythm. From leisurely to impatient, Kain squeezes me a little harder, kisses me a little more fervently, rubs on me a little more desperately. He's close but he will never come before me, it goes against everything he believes.

But I won't come unless he drinks from me, I need him to take that essence from me, proving to the both of us that I'm still alive.

Nipping at my lip, he slams into me once, then twice.

On the third thrust, he licks a path across my lips before turning my head and sinking his teeth into my thrumming vein.

The sensation is unequaled.

I think I scream but I can't be sure. All I know is that my orgasm starts at the tip of my toes and renders me blind for a few seconds as all of my emotions crash together like a tornado in the Midwest.

It's only when I come back down from my high that I realize that Kain is the one crying out from his own pleasure. His neck is strained from the effort, his face a mask of utter pleasure. His mouth deliciously open like he's unable to control himself.

He's beautiful when he comes.

He's beautiful because he only comes for me.

EIGHT

I wake up and stretch out, finding the bed empty beside me. I have no idea what time it is, but I am surprised to find myself alone. I pull myself up to sit as the door opens and Kain appears, half dressed, and maybe the most casual I've ever seen him with just his suit pants and shirt, the sleeves rolled up. Hot damn those forearms. I shake my head, and refocus. He has a tray in his hands, the smell of bacon wafting in the room with him. I can't stop the grin spreading across my face as he moves towards me, and graces with me a smile of his own.

"Morning precious," he murmurs as he sets the tray on my lap and kisses my forehead. His gaze run the length of my body, as if making sure that I'm here, and I'm whole. I take his hand and squeeze it, trying to reassure him as best

I can.

“Morning,” I sigh happily. “Are you okay?”

The worry in his eyes is obvious, it was there last night, but I guess I’d hoped that after last night, he’d feel better.

“As long as you are okay, mon amour, then I am fine. Nearly losing you like that, for good…” his voice croaks and it’s like a dagger to the heart.

“I’m sorry.”

“It was not your fault. Your brother… I am just glad you’re okay, that you’re here, and that I haven’t lost you for good.”

“Me too,” I tell him softly, and he perches on the bed next to me.

“Now, enough of that. I had to basically battle to the death to be able to keep you to myself for an extra few minutes, so how about you eat your breakfast in peace, compliments of Nonnie, and then we can talk with the others.” He squeezes my hand again before releasing it, and letting me dig in.

He’s not wrong, we need to talk. And I’m not sure they’re all going to exactly like what I have to say, but better that it’s out there.

I groan as the bacon hits my tongue. Damn I missed bacon, real bacon. Some things in Avalon might be better, but bacon isn’t one of them, though I will miss that coffee, unless I can sweet talk Levi into smuggling me some beans.

It doesn't take me long to eat and freshen up. I sneak back to my own room to get dressed, I really want to wear one of my snarky t-shirts today, but considering the conversation I'm about to have, I pull on a plain black, long sleeved shirt and a pair of jeans, with my boots. I throw on an oversized sweater with the words '*savage love'* scrawled across it, and braid my hair, which is so long now that even braided it falls to my waist. I leave the closet and find Kain sitting, waiting for me on my bed, now fully dressed, in his trademark black on black suit and tie, not a wrinkle in sight. His eyes practically glow as he looks at me. I will never get bored of him looking at me like that, as if I'm the only thing he needs to survive.

His eyes move to the column of my throat, and my breathing hitches. It's been a while since he fed properly, last night was barely a touch. I tilt my head exposing my neck for him and he's in front of me in the blink of an eye. His gaze pierces mine, and I nod softly, giving him permission to take what he needs. He holds me reverently, pulling me towards him before kissing my neck softly, making me sigh. His teeth puncture my skin with no hesitancy, and he groans as my blood spills. I hold onto him to keep myself upright, as pleasure floods my system. I'm wet again in an instant, I clench my thighs together, sighing at the sensations singing through my bloodstream.

His tongue laves at my neck as he licks up the last

drops of blood before the puncture wounds heal, and then he kisses me, the taste of me still in his mouth.

"Thank you, mon amour." His voice is practically a purr, and I feel boneless, but I smile at him, before resting my forehead on his shoulder for a moment while I compose myself. "The others will be waiting."

I smile again, even though he can't see me, because yes, I imagine they are. My guys aren't the most patient, and the way Kain claimed me last night was almost amusing. There was no arguing with him as he stalked from the kitchen with me in his arms. The look on Roman's and Creek's faces were ones to behold. Levi was the only other one amused, but I imagine that's because he practically had me to himself in Avalon.

"Of course, can't keep them waiting," I tell him, amused. He pulls the pocket square from his suit jacket and wipes my neck, making sure all traces of blood are gone. I kiss his cheek softly and head out of the room to find the others. The sound of their voices makes me smile as I turn around, realizing they're in the gym. If anyone throws me in the pool today, there will be hell to pay.

I open the door, with Kain behind me, and lean on him while I just watch them shooting the shit as they work out. Apparently, their frustration from last night didn't go anywhere if the view in front of me is anything to go by. But my heart lightens seeing how close they're getting. Who would've thought that this would ever be a possibility? That any factions could get on this well, let alone these particular guys. I sigh happily and they all notice my arrival.

"Morning," I practically sing as I spring into the area, and Roman is on me in a second, wrapping his very sweaty arms around me, but I can't find it in me to complain, even if he is a little gross.

He buries his face in my neck and takes a deep breath, then relaxes in my arms. I can't imagine how hard the wolf has been riding him since everything happened. I don't even really know what happened after Bauer stabbed me, my mind is a little fuzzy, but being fatally stabbed will do that to a girl. I meet Creek's gaze over Roman's shoulder, and he gives me a soft smile. He might be a different man now to the one I've known for so long, but deep down, he's still my big softie. He cares so deeply about everything, and everyone, and I can see that even though he's impatient to get his own reassurance again that I'm still here, he doesn't begrudge the others their time with me.

"Don't ever do that to me again," Roman grumbles lowly, his chest vibrating with his words, he doesn't pull back even an inch, if anything his arms tighten around me.

"I don't plan to," I whisper back to him as I thread my fingers through his hair. He pulls back, and looks down at me, his eyes flash, and he takes another deep breath. The glow settles, and he smiles, and I know that the wolf has finally settled.

Creek moves towards me and gets his own hug in, squeezing me tight but keeping it reasonably brief. I feel his power wash over me, a light pleasure coating my skin, and it makes me laugh softly. He winks at me and pulls back, giving me some space.

"Glad as I am to be back, I think we need to talk," I tell them all, trying to keep my voice light, despite the fact that what we're about to discuss is probably going to piss them off.

"Nothing good ever comes from those words," Creek groans, and scrubs a hand down his face.

"Ain't that the truth," Roman agrees.

"Shall we move this conversation to a more comfortable setting, with less things available to launch?" Kain chuckles, and Levi joins in.

"It's not that bad, I just… I need you guys to stop keeping things from me. Even if you think it's to protect me. I got all of my memories back, so I have access to pretty much everything, but I have no doubt that you all kept things from me in the past under the guise of protecting me, so there's likely still a ton of stuff I have no idea about. I am not some helpless girl that needs to be saved or protected, I never have been, so I need you all to put the alpha bullshit away, and include me in the conversations. Case in point,

Michael," I say, turning to Levi. "You very obviously left some crucial information out there, I half understand it, but that doesn't mean I agree with it."

He does at least look a little sorry, but only a little.

"I did what I thought was best in the moment. Michael has always been… mercurial. And obviously he's not my biggest fan, plus, there was literally a bounty on your head at one point. He didn't go against it, so I wasn't to know that he still thought you hung the moon. That being said, I'll try my best not to keep anything from you from now."

"Thank you." I move towards him and kiss his cheek.

"Was that everything?" Creek asks, smiling cheekily at me.

"Pretty much." I shrug.

"Awesome, because I have plans for us today." He rushes me and lifts me from my feet, running from the gym with me in his arms, with shouts following from behind us while I laugh.

"What's your big surprise?" I ask, as Creek tucks me into the passenger seat of his truck and puts my buckle on. He just smiles at me and closes the door before making his way around and climbing in the cab beside me. "You're not going to tell me?"

"Wouldn't be a surprise if I told you, would it?" His

grin is infectious, and I feel one of my own spread across my face.

"You know how I feel about surprises," I huff, but it doesn't quite land thanks to my smile.

"I know you pretend to not like them, because you're nosy as fuck and just want to know everything ever in the universe." He laughs as he backs up and heads out of the drive of the manor.

"Pfft."

He shakes his head, still laughing at me and my fake outrage. "Remy, I've known you way too long for you to even begin to try that. Now sit there, and be a good girl." He winks at me, and the temptation to show him just how much of a good girl I am is so fucking real, but I sit on my hands to stop them from straying. I think he needs this as much as I do, a day, just the two of us, doing random shit. Though, I don't know that it's random shit, because he won't fucking tell me what's going on!

He turns the radio up and starts singing to the Sam Hunt song playing, and my grin turns cheesy as he basically serenades me while he drives. He might usually opt out of karaoke, because my guy can be shy, but he has absolutely no reason to, because damn he can sing. I lean back in the seat and close my eyes, just listening as he sings to each song as it changes on the radio, letting the rumble of the engine soothe me along with it.

We drive for nearly an hour when the car pulls to a stop. I open my eyes, and realize we're at a gas station. I look over at Creek who is just smiling at me. "Do you want anything?"

"No, I'm good." He watches me and then shakes his head before climbing out of the truck. I have no idea where we are, I don't recognize the gas station, but I trust Creek, so I don't freak out. Though he's right, I really am nosy, and I really would like to know where the hell it is that we're going. It's not long before he climbs back into the truck, and we keep going on the very twisty road up in the mountains.

I really have no idea where it is that we're going, but Creek seems so relaxed, that I try not to overthink it. Which, for me, is an enormous task, but I lean back in the chair again and just watch the scenery pass me by, as Creek intertwines his fingers with mine. He squeezes my hand gently, and smiles when I glance over at him, but doesn't take his eyes from the road. He might have Demon reflexes now, and I might be an Angel, but I love that he never takes risks with my safety.

We drive for like another hour, up and up the mountains, until he takes a turn off down a dirt road. I open my mouth to ask him where the hell we are, but he shakes his head before I even say a word.

Men.

I roll my eyes, but smile with it because this is so him. Of course, he's not giving me even the smallest hint. He pulls the truck off to the side of the road and unbuckles himself before turning to look at me. "Good thing you've got decent shoes on."

I laugh at him and he grins wider. "Where the hell are we?"

"You'll see, come on, beautiful. Let's go on an adventure." He laughs so boyishly, so carefree, that I'm transported back to another time momentarily. A time when we didn't have the weight of worlds hanging over us. He climbs out of the truck and is opening my door before I even get my belt off. He seems so excited, and it's practically infectious. His hands take me by the waist and he lifts me from the truck, so I wrap my arms and legs around him, kissing him, letting how carefree he is wash over me, and enjoy this time with him. Fate knows I've got plenty of other time to worry about everything else in our lives.

"I could just carry you to where we're going… or I could just keep you here," he says as he pushes us up against his truck and kisses me again.

"Tempting as that is, we came all this way, I want to know where we're going!"

He smiles even as he groans at me, but kisses me again and then pops me back on my feet.

"Come on then, let's go." He winks at me as he turns and heads into the thick trees lining the road. We hike through the bush for what feels like an age, and I've never been happier about my new found Angel status because I don't get tired the entire trek, so score one in the Angel column.

Creek stops in front of me and turns to face me, his face hidden in the shadows of the forest, but his green eyes are like beacons in the night. "Close your eyes."

I just blink at him, because, is he nuts? I'll trip and break myself.

"Just close your eyes, Remy. Trust me."

"I trust you with my life," I tell him honestly, because it couldn't be more true.

"Then close your eyes," he huffs with a small laugh, and I shrug but do as he asks. A twig snap as he moves towards me. He moves behind me and put his hands on my waist. He nudges me forward. Even with unsure footing, I try to let him just direct me. I can practically feel his smile. We move like this for a few minutes, our progress slow, because despite trusting him, walking with my eyes closed in a fucking forest is still enough to make a girl hesitant. I don't care if I'm practically unbreakable, I still hurt easily enough.

As we leave the cover of the trees, the air feels cleaner, fresher, and the breeze whips through my hair.

"Few more steps," he whispers in my ear, and my skin pimples from his breath on me. I move to where he positions me, and then he puts his hands over my eyes. "Ready?"

"I think so?" I laugh softly at his words, but I'm excited to see where he's brought me.

"Okay, open your eyes." He says the words as he takes his hands from my eyes. I blink a few times against the sudden bright light, but once I can see, my breath catches.

"This is…" I have no words for the beauty in front of me. We're standing at the edge of a cliff, looking out at the stormy ocean, the sun out in the distance, the clear blue sky. It's just so… beautiful.

"I know. I found it by accident, but I've come here a few times when I've needed to get my mind together. I know you've been dealing with a lot, so I thought you might like a little slice of peace." I sigh happily at his words. He's always been so thoughtful, and I'm glad the change in him didn't change that.

"Thank you," I tell him as he wraps his arms around my waist and leans his chin on my shoulder.

"There's another reason I brought you here too." His playful tone is back, and my stomach flips. "This cliff is perfect for cliff diving."

"Holy shit. We've not done that…"

"Not since that time we lived on that island. I know.

I would've taken you there, but it's a little different there now." He squeezes me tighter, and I can practically feel the excitement radiating through him. "Think it will still be as much fun, even though we're basically indestructible?"

"Hell yes it will. We're still reasonably new to this immortal shit. And if I shut out the Amantara part of my mind, I still feel so very human. Let's do this!" I scramble from his arms and start kicking off my shoes and strip out of my clothes. It doesn't take him a second to follow suit, and once we're down to our undies, we walk to the edge.

"Ready?" I ask, almost breathless at the thought of it, as my stomach feels like the butterflies in it are rioting.

"Ready as you are." He laughs, and squeezes my hand. "Last one in cooks dinner."

He jumps off the edge as he says the words, leaving me standing watching, we both know I'm never cooking. But once he resurfaces in the water with a whoop, I take a few steps back then run to edge and jump off into a dive.

The wind rushes past me, filling my ears, so loud I barely hear my own screams just before I break the surface of the water.

"Holy fuck that's cold!" I squeal as I surface, Creek just laughs before submerging, then coming up and flicking his hair back off his face. "You belong in a shampoo commercial."

He laughs with me before splashing me. "Again?"

He doesn't even need to ask, I haven't felt this free in longer than I can remember.

"Hell fucking yes."

NINE

After an amazing day with Creek yesterday, Roman crawled into my bed with us last night, which is how I find myself tangled up in them both when I wake. Roman's hand is on my hip, my head on his chest, while my legs are intertwined with Creek's. It's not a bad place to find myself.

I untangle myself from them both without them stirring, which is a feat in itself, and get ready for the day. Today, I want to go and see Colt. I should probably have gone to see him already, and Fallon, but reassuring the guys I wasn't going anywhere has been basically a full-time thing since I got back. And Roman is still in a bit of a funk because I haven't had much one on one time with him since I got back from Avalon, but I'll make it up to him later. There's an itch inside of me that's pushing me to go and see Colt, so that's the first thing on my agenda today.

I shower quickly, washing my hair before rebraiding it to keep it out of the way, and dress as quietly as I can.

"Running off so early?" Roman rumbles as he walks into my closet in nothing but a pair of boxers, and a black t-shirt, the sight of him half asleep and still ready for me is almost enough to make me rethink my plans.

"Sorry, I didn't mean to wake you," I tell him, biting my lip.

"You're the best thing to wake up to," he says as he pulls me towards him and kisses me with so much heat I practically melt under his touch. His fingertips graze the skin where my t-shirt rides up as I wrap my arms around his neck, and I groan at the contact. Fuck I missed this.

I might not have been gone long, but it's been forever since I was with my guys properly with everything that was going on before Michael took me. I press up against him and his hands travel down to my ass, he cups it with his hands before lifting me. I wrap my legs around him, our lips never parting, and he pushes me up against the wall, his hardness obvious as he presses into me.

When he pulls back, I'm panting, and he graces me with a wolfish smile. "Good morning, princess."

"Uh-huh," is all I manage to get out, which makes him chuckle. I groan, because the shaking of his body from the chuckle rubs him against me again.

"To be continued," he says softly, taking my lips again gently before setting me back on my feet. I groan as he pulls away from me, but I know he's not wrong. I have plans, and this, this can be put on hold until tonight.

"I love you," I tell him softly, and he pulls me into him again.

"I love you too." He squeezes me tight before releasing me. "Now get out of here before I change my mind and tie you to the bed for the whole day."

"I mean… I am definitely not opposed to this idea," I say, as I run my hands up his bare chest. "I most certainly could be persuaded to move my plans from today to tomorrow."

He looks up to the ceiling as if trying to find the strength to tell me no, even though he doesn't know what my plans are. He looks back down at me, and his eyes are glowing.

"Fuck this," he mutters before picking me up and slinging me over his shoulder. I squeak, and Creek just smiles and waves at me from the bed as Roman takes me from the room and strides down the hall to his. I guess an audience isn't on his list. He pushes the door open, and locks it behind him. It's pretty pointless in this house, but then, no one is going to try and bust through a locked door either.

He drops me on the bed, evidence of how much he

wants me is very much on show, and I lick my lips.

He drags a chair from the corner of the room and drops into it, his eyes never leaving me.

"Strip," he commands, and I stand. I kick off my boots, getting them out of the way, before lifting my sweater slowly, thanking the fates I chose to put on the pretty pink underwear today. His gaze follows my fingers as I feather my touch back down to the hem of my t-shirt. I lift it over my head, and he growls lowly at the sight of the light pink lace that covers me.

My fingers trace down to the buttons on my jeans and I pop each one of them open slowly, and his eyes start to glow as the blush pink of my thong becomes visible.

"Fuck me, you're beautiful," he says, his fingers gripping the arms of the chair, as if holding himself in place. I step out of the jeans and sashay over to him. I bend forward and kiss him, running my hands down his chest and down his thighs, coming back up to brush over the hardness of him under his boxers.

He growls under the brief touch and I pull back with a smirk on my face. I hook my thumbs through the side of my thong, and he jumps from the chair, stopping me in place.

"Mine," his chest rumbles with the words, and he stops my movements. He walks us backwards until the backs of my knees hit the bed and I fall onto it. I sigh as he pushes my thighs open and drops to his knees. "So fucking beautiful."

He spreads me open, staring at me like I'm his last meal. I lean up on my elbows to watch him as he keeps one strong hand on my thigh. He groans as he feels how wet I am. I tip my head back as his fingers tease my clit, before he leans forward and tastes me. "Fuck, I will never get tired of that."

He ravages me with his tongue, before sliding two fingers inside of me, pushing me closer and closer to the edge. My pants increase and just before I fall over the edge, he stops. I cry out, and I can feel his smile against me. "Not yet, princess. I own this pussy, right now it is all mine, and I don't think you worked hard enough for that just yet."

At first, I frown, not really sure what he's planning. I mean, yes, he likes to be in control and domineering but surely he's not going to…

"You'll come when I say you come. And trust me, after that little stunt? Well, let's just say, I've got ideas."

Now, I've never been afraid of my men. I have always given them my unmitigated trust but as those words slide from between his lips, I realize that he is going to milk this control thing until I beg for forgiveness and do everything he orders.

But there is only one tiny kink in that plan, 'kink' being the opportune word…

I don't follow instructions very well.

"What if I come anyway?"

Oh shit. Now, why did I have to go and say that?

"Oh, princess, I hope you do. That way, you'll see the full extent of my control issues."

Damn it. Now, I'm curious about the extent of… My eyes drop to the bulge that clearly screams just how invested he is in this dominating game and I'm part curious and part terrified, in the best of ways.

"I guess we'll just have to wait and see, won't we?"

I'm so getting punished for that.

The sting on the inside of my thigh is immediate. Looking down, I realize he's just bitten me, leaving a light imprint of his teeth on my milky skin.

I like it.

Actually, I love seeing his mark on me. It's physical proof of his devotion to me. Of the power of our love. It's so… Roman.

"I'm going to enjoy hearing you scream, princess. Trust me, the guys are all taking bets on how loud you can get."

There's no way he's telling the truth.

Although…

No. They wouldn't dare.

Would they?

Another sting on my other thigh and I can feel my juices building, the muscles in my pussy contracting, yearning for something to hold and squeeze.

"Why did you bite me, again? I didn't even back talk you?"

"You were distracted thinking of them. Just thought I'd bring you back to the present."

Suddenly he's up and walking to the ceiling to floor drapes making me wonder if he's completely lost his mind.

"Hello? I'm spread wide open, Roman. Have you lost interest?" I know he hasn't. Roman is single minded in his desire for me which means he's got an idea, and I'm probably screwed.

Literally.

"Don't worry, princess. I couldn't forget you even if I wanted to and forgetting you is never an option."

Turning my head to follow his movements, I watch as he unties the rope holding the drapes back and pulls on the material, presumably to test its sturdiness, and he grunts his approval.

Blinking back my confusion, I follow his movements to the other pulled back drape and watch as he repeats his actions.

Untie.

Pull.

Grunt.

It's only when he's at my side, wrapping the velvety rope around my wrist that I associate the kink to his idea.

Not only is he going to make me work for my orgasm, he's making sure I don't get the job done myself.

"Don't you trust me, Roman?"

"With my life, princess. Except when it comes to coming all over my face. You tend to disobey and I'm not having that tonight."

Fates, I love this man.

Once he's finished tying me to the somewhat unbreakable headboard, he bends and drops me a kiss that promises pain and pleasure and everything in between.

With my arms crossed above my head, the plush pillow nestling my head comfortably, I follow him with my gaze until he's back at the foot and staring hungrily at my spread thighs.

"Like what you see?"

"Oh, princess, you have no idea."

Pulling his black tee over his head, leaving his hair in full-blown disarray, he stands there clothed only from the hips down, the delicious V at his hips inviting me to lick all the way down to what I truly desire.

"Like what you see?" he throws my words back at me, a devilish smirk adorning his lips.

"You have no idea," I wink and spread my legs just a bit wider, enough to pry a groan from him.

Kneeling on the bed, Roman places both of his middle fingers on each of my ankles, right above the inside bones, and then proceeds to glide up my calves with a feather touch until he reaches my bent knees. His eyes dart from one leg to the other but then focuses on my pussy. I grow wetter by the second, with every touch, every look, and every breath he takes.

"I'm going to eat your pussy, Remy. In fact…" he pauses, his fingers tortuously sliding up my thighs leaving goosebumps in their wake, "I'm going to push my tongue inside you and lick you until you can't take it anymore."

He pauses again, and I can't help but whimper as his hands tease me.

"And just when you're going to come all over my face, I'm going to stop."

His fingers halt abruptly as though following the course of his words. Torturing me with his dirty mouth.

"I want you panting. Screaming at me. I want to hear your need in every threat you throw at me."

He knows me so well.

"I would gag you but…" His fingers resume their slow pace up to the crease between thigh and crotch and just as he grazes my lower lip, he finishes his thought, "hearing you beg is almost, almost, the best part."

"That's… quite the visual." I'm panting already, practically feeling the heat of his tongue pushing inside me. I want to lean up and watch him as he opens my pussy and licks his lips as he stares at me open and vulnerable.

I can only guess at what he's thinking but I'm sure it's something at the corners of Dirty Street and Filthy Avenue.

As I'm imagining all of the crazy ways he's going to make me beg to come, I feel lips on me. They're soft and barely touching me. A feather-like caress across my clit and down my slit.

Then it's his breath.

A tender gust blowing from bottom to top leaving me trembling between hot and cold.

I'm so focused on the sensations that I cry out as his two fingers slowly slide inside me, turning and twisting the further they go.

Grabbing onto the headboard, I'm equal parts pushing for more and pulling away from the abundance of it all. It's almost too much. Yet, I know that the tenderness is just a ploy. He's buttering me up so I can fall even harder.

As his fingers reach the hilt, he curls them and suddenly my back arches off the bed, my eyes wide open and my mouth dropping in a silent cry of need.

"That's it, princess, feel that secret spot? I can hit that… Every. Single. Time. I can make you feel like you're going to fly and crash all at the same time. I will take you to the edge and bring you back without even breaking a sweat."

I know he can.

That simple caress to the deepest part of me is almost bringing tears to my eyes.

My pussy is so wet, I can hear every movement from his fingers and his palm as he rubs against my sensitive skin.

My fingers are gripping the wood, aching from the effort all the while I'm almost desperate to rip the rope off and just rub my clit until I come completely undone.

But I won't. Because he won't let me.

It's a beautiful kind of torture.

Then his fingers are gone, replaced instantly by his hot tongue and soft lips. Licking one side then another, the top then the bottom. Twisting this way and that.

I'm writhing under his touch, my conflicting emotions at war, my need to come and my desire to follow his commands.

"Don't do it, Remy. Do. Not. Come."

My hips shoot off the bed, seeking out any kind of reprieve from the onslaught of pleasure his mouth is bestowing upon me.

"Roman." I'm out of breath, my thoughts one continuous stream of, "please, please, please," but nothing comes out.

Roman slows down then stops all together, his eyes fixated on my face until I feel his stare and look right back at him.

Blinking away my haze of need, I try to yell at him to get back to what he was doing but my muscles are too tired from fighting away the orgasm.

The worst part is that I know for a fact that he's just getting started. He's barely touched my clit for more than two seconds.

"What do you need, princess?"

"Come."

"No."

That's all he says before he winks, throws me a smirk and then kisses my pussy like he's been deprived of me for far longer than he'd ever want.

My hips are simultaneously fighting him off and pushing for more contact. More tongue, more teeth, more sucking. And then, his fingers that were once inside my pussy, are pushing inside my ass, breaching the tightness of my muscles and owning me completely.

"Oh fates, please, please." One of my wrists comes free from the velvety contraption and without even thinking about the consequences, it flies to my clit, having a split-second moment to rub my engorged nub before Roman tsks like an annoyed professor and slaps it away.

"Touch yourself again and I stop everything."

I can't be sure he's bluffing. I mean, I know for a fact he gets off on fucking my pussy with his mouth but then he also gets off on making me wait for it. Beg for it, even.

And I will.

Bringing my hand back to the headboard, I pretend to

be a good girl and let him do his damage.

But when his tongue plunges inside me and his thumb starts light circles around my clit, I truly believe I'm about to explode and become one with utter nothingness.

I'm going to come.

It's inevitable.

I can't control this and it's going to be amazing. I can see the stars, the universe flying towards me at the speed of light, my nerve endings lighting up at the tip of my toes and my pussy pulsing with the rhythm of his tongue.

There it is…

And then it all stops.

The stars, the universe, the tingling.

Gone. All I have left is the contractions of my muscles seeking out something to hold on to as my juices flow freely from my opening.

"I told you not to come, princess. You almost did."

"You're evil."

"You love it." I do. I can't deny it and really, I don't want to.

My breaths are coming in sporadically and I can faintly register the sound of fabric flying across the room.

When I open my eyes, Roman is completely naked except for a smirk firmly planted on the side of his mouth.

"I promise I'll be a good girl, Roman. Please. Please, please, please, let me come."

He closes his eyes as though absorbing the sound of my pleas, feeding from them, before he directs his hungry gaze right back at me.

"Spread wide open, princess. Invite me inside you."

And I do. I bring my knees up as far as they'll go and open my pussy up for him to lovingly assault.

With his steel hardness in hand and his gaze firmly fixated on my eyes, he inches forward, pointing the head of his dick at my opening, and he announces, "You come when I say you come."

Then his cock is inside me, pushing deep in one swift thrust.

"You come because I allow it."

His hands are clutching my open thighs, fingers digging in my flesh and nails biting into my skin.

"You scream because I cause it."

He pulls out slowly and then slams back inside me, making my breath catch.

"You coat my dick with your cum because I demand it."

He continues to fuck me like a crazed animal, a beast demanding control. A wolf led by his instincts.

My voice is losing power, the screams scratching away at its volume. I'm mouthing, "please," hoping he can read my lips.

Then he stops and my world comes to screeching halt.

Again.

His breaths are just as erratic and heavy as mine. He's close. I know it, I can see it in the rise and fall of his chest, in the bright shine of his eyes, in the tense line of his jaw. He's warring with himself.

To come or not to come?

It's never really a question, is it?

Leaning in, chest to chest, he whispers against my lips, "Come for me, princess."

And just as the last "s" leaves his breath, he thrusts inside me. The head of his cock pummels the walls of my pussy and his groin rubs against my aching clit, until my entire body gives in and every single nerve ending in my body lights up like the Rockefeller Christmas tree sending me in a frenzy of shakes and screams.

The stars are back, the universe engulfing me once again, the electric zapping from my toes to the ends of my hairs is short-circuiting my brain cells as my mind and body shut down from the power of my orgasm.

It's glorious. It's everything.

It's… Roman.

TEN

Roman was true to his word, and he really did tie me to his bed for most of the day, only letting up once dinner rolled around and his stomach growled at him. So now I'm sore, but in the best way, because it has been an *intense* few days with my guys. Not that I'm complaining, because holy hell, not a chance, but I think me and my body need a day of rest to recover a little.

So today, I plan to train, since Creek told me that Colt isn't available today. I want to go running. Do something that makes me feel like me again. Because with everything going on around us, and inside of me, I've never felt less like myself in all of my lives.

I pull on my sneakers, tie my hair up, and rather than heading into the gym, I decide to run outside. The way I used to. I stretch out on the patio, taking in the chirping of birds as the sun rises over the horizon spilling oranges and pinks into the dawning sky. It's beautiful, all of it. I lose myself to it for a few moments, just letting myself be, before I start off towards the edge of the property. Today, I run using no powers, just pushing myself until I can't go anymore. Pushing until I puke. Just like before.

So I start at a jog, picking up my pace once I reach the edge of the stream and then kick it up a notch as I head towards the back of the property. I try to clear my mind of all of the craziness swirling around inside of me, as hard as it is, I push every little fucking thing aside and just exist. Taking note of how small I am in the universe, and accept that not everything is in my control. I lap the property four times before my breathing starts to struggle, so I push harder. Needing to feel something, anything, that makes me feel like myself.

Other than the touch of my guys, everything just feels a little… off.

Well, not off. Just, different.

I know I need to take the time to go through everything in my head, in my heart. I have literally a millennia of information locked up inside myself, for when I want it, but my biggest problem right now, is there are so many different versions of me, that I don't know which one is right.

I let out a deep breath and keep pushing, clearing my mind of the insanity that threatens to spill over, and locking it back up until I feel lighter. I don't know how much time passes while I run, but the sun is high in the sky by the time I drag myself inside, still not feeling even close to as exhausted as I once would have been. Angel benefits I guess. I head to the gym, and strip down before diving into the pool. No one else is in here, and they sure as hell aren't going to mind me swimming naked if they do stumble across me.

So I swim. Doing laps until my arms and legs finally start to feel like jelly, and I enjoy it. It's not a surprise the battles during the War of the Fallen went on for so long. No one got fucking tired.

Immortals.

My internal eye roll makes me snort with laughter as I pull myself up out of the pool, and head for the towel rack. I get it wrapped around me, just as the door opens and I find Levi staring at me, his face unreadable.

"Are you finished punishing yourself yet?" he says, leaning against the doorjamb with his arms crossed. He looks pissed off, and I have no idea why, I've barely seen him since I got home. Though I guess that in itself could be reasoning enough for Mr. Grumpy himself. The thought makes me think of Everly, and I smile sadly, before turning back to look at him.

"I'm not punishing myself. I just wanted to work out," I tell him as I swoop down and pick up my discarded clothing.

"Remy, you've been working out for roughly twelve hours. Now, let's try this again. Are you finished punishing yourself?"

I roll my eyes at him, and bundle the clothes in my arms. "I wasn't punishing myself, you don't have to believe me. I was just trying to clear my mind, so I could think clearly. Maybe you should nearly die and see what it does to you."

I regret the words the minute I say them, but they're out there and I can't take them back. He looks like I just kicked his puppy. "You're not the only one who has to live with that."

"I know," I sigh. "But, I am the one with a dozen personalities in my head right now, it's never been this hard to just kind of merge them, maybe it's because of the Amantara stuff now too, but I don't feel like myself."

"I can understand that, but you need to talk to us Remy. Just like you don't want us to hide stuff from you, you need to talk to us too. It goes both ways."

"Fine. I'm sorry, I'll try. It's just… not that easy."

"Which I can also understand. But there's healthier ways to deal with it all too. Are you feeling better now?"

"I am." I smile at him, trying not to feel as self-conscious as I do. I have no idea why I do.

"Good, then get dressed and meet us in the kitchen, we've got theories to discuss, and plans to draw up to settle this bullshit once and for all. Then maybe we can all find a little peace.

I drop my head onto the table, because we've been going in circles for about an hour, and we've not even spoken about Michael's theories yet. They've just been bickering about pretty much nothing, and it's driving me insane.

"I'm telling you, we need to focus on this first," Roman says, exasperated, while Levi just stands there, arms crossed, not saying a word as he stares him down.

Men.

"Guys, much fun as all this is, we're getting nowhere. Can I suggest we take a break, eat something and reduce the hangry in the room, and then try again please?" I say, but it comes out mumbled with my head still on the table. I look up and find each of them looking at me. Roman and Levi have the decency to look a little guilty while Kain and Creek just smirk at me.

So what if I'm the only hangry one here for real, those two certainly have their panties in a twist about something, and I'm going to stab someone if I have to keep listening to it without some food. The sun has officially set, and I've not eaten all day, which I'm fully aware is my own fault.

"We should have fed you before we even started speaking," Creek laughs.

"I can whip something up," Levi says, heading over to the fridge.

"That Angel boy better not be in my fridge!" Nonnie's voice echoes into the room, reaching us less than a minute before she appears. Levi steps back from the fridge with his hands up in the air in surrender.

"Wouldn't dream of making food in my own kitchen." I can tell that he tries not to smile as he says the words and heads back towards us, dodging Nonnie as she shakes her fist at him. All the while I'm trying not to laugh at it all.

"What would you like to eat, Remy girl?" she asks me with a soft smile on her face. Kain scoffs quietly, because she's not that nice to any of them, which makes me laugh all on its own.

"I don't mind, Nonnie. Whatever you fancy whipping up is good with me."

"Such a precious girl. You sit tight and Nonnie will get you sorted." She claps her hands and heads to the pantry while Levi sits back down with the rest of us.

"How do you do that?" he asks, laughing quietly.

"I have no idea what you mean." I flutter my lashes as him, taking the piss.

"Our girl captures the hearts of everyone she meets," Creek says cheesily, making everyone else laugh, and I shake my head.

"Apparently not everyone," I say, waving my arm across the books strewn over the table to make my point. "Someone, very much wants me dead."

I look to Levi who is watching me closely. "Do you think Nevin or Serafina might know where Amelia is?"

"I doubt it," he answers, shaking his head.

"Who is Amelia?" Kain asks from beside me.

"Amelia used to be a Death Dealer. She's not been seen or heard from since the war, according to Michael. He thinks she could be the root cause of all of this. I'm not as confident as he is, but it's another thing to think about," I tell them, while Levi pulls out his phone.

"I've dropped Nevin a message. When he comes to Earth next, he'll get it. Hopefully it's not too long till he pops up."

We switch topics, and discuss lighter things until Nonnie feeds us, though Creek, Roman, and Kain all look pretty eager to discuss Amelia again. I try not to think about it, and just enjoy the stupid stories that they tell about their pasts, things that happened in-between my times with them. We've got forever together, so I no longer feel that twang of sadness when thinking about the time we spent apart in the past.

I finish the Shakshuka Nonnie made for us, and lean back in my chair, more than a little contented. I pat my stomach and pull my legs up to sit cross legged on the chair. A knock on the glass door startles me. I turn and see Nevin opening the door and entering the room.

"You summoned?" he says with a tight smile, looking at Levi.

"I didn't expect you so soon," Levi tells him, standing. Nevin moves towards us and sits at the end of the table, opposite where Levi is sitting.

"Since Michael re-instated you as general, he's had me stationed here just in case you needed anything from Avalon, since no one would suspect anything at me being gone, and Remy is here already." He huffs, and crosses his arms. I look at him concerned. He looks tired, like he's overworking himself, and I wonder what it is Michael and Levi have him doing.

"Do you want some food? Nonnie always cooks way more than we need," I offer, and he gives me a tight smile.

"Thank you, that would be amazing." I move to stand and Kain puts a hand on my arm.

"I'll sort it," he says as he stands.

"Thanks," I say at the same time as Nevin.

"So, what brings me here this late in the day?" Nevin asks again as Kain places a plate in front of him, and pours him a glass of whiskey like the rest of us.

"Amelia," I tell him. He looks bewildered at the name before pushing his glasses further up his nose. I've decided they must just be for show, because Angels don't need glasses, and I have no memory of him having them before this life. Unless something happened to him, but I'm not rude enough to just ask him, despite how curious I am about it.

"Amelia hasn't been seen or heard from in forever," he says as his gaze bounces between Levi and I. "What on earth does she have to do with anything? For all we know, she could be dead." He takes a bite of the food in front of him, but he doesn't seem all that interested in it.

"That's what we're trying to find out. Archer's journals mention something briefly that could point to her, and Michael seems pretty convinced, even though he hasn't been able to track her," I tell him pointedly.

"This seems like a pretty out there lead, you sure this is what you want me to focus on?" he says, looking straight to Levi. I guess it makes sense, Levi is his general, but it still rankles me that he dismisses me so easily, when it's me everyone's trying to kill. Fuck it, a millennia of routine is going to be a hard habit to break, so I'm not going to take it personally. At least I'm going to try and not take it personally.

Levi goes through everything he and Michael discussed with me about Amelia when we were in Avalon, filling the guys in as well as Nevin, while I add anything he misses, albeit it isn't much.

“You really think she could be behind all of this?” Creek asks.

“It’s possible, she really did hate me once upon a time,” I tell him with a shrug.

“She is also very good at being single-minded. It is very possible for her to hold onto something this long, though I’m not sure why she would’ve waited this long to strike,” Levi adds.

“If, and I mean *if* it’s her, she could have Clara with her. She’s not been seen since then either. Plus she’s a seer. It could explain the why now, if it’s her at all.”

“I forgot about Clara!” She was a quiet, tiny little thing. Wouldn’t say boo to a goose. A real wallflower type. She was nice enough when I spoke to her, but she was rarely around me in Avalon. I guess being around someone that can potentially see into your mind, when you’re a seer, could be a little daunting.

“You really think they’d be together after all this time?” Levi asks Nevin.

“It’s possible, I can look into it. Was there anything else?” Nevin asks, standing, looking around at each of us at the table. I press my lips together to stop something falling out of my mouth. He’s being rude, even for him. The only reason I’m holding my tongue is because he seems stressed enough, but if he doesn’t rein in his big dick attitude, I’ll reel it the fuck in for him.

“No, and thank you for coming so quickly,” Levi says with a tight smile. Apparently, he noticed it too.

“I’ll let you know if I find anything.” He turns and leaves as abruptly as he appeared, while I just shake my head.

“Wonder who pissed in his cornflakes,” Creek says, shaking his head as he takes a sip of his whiskey.

“What a waste,” I sigh, taking his plate and clearing it. I might not have ever struggled to find food, but the waste of it frustrates me greatly.

“He did seem strAngely high strung. Maybe it has to do with the unrest Michael hinted about in Avalon.” Levi offers.

“Maybe,” I mutter, as I sit back down at the table.

“Now that’s sorted, we need to work out what our next moves are. There are still too many unknowns on our chess board. While Nevin is hunting down the potential Queen, we need to find the remaining pawns,” Kain says, and Roman rolls his eyes.

“We’ve got two players left at least that we know of that pose the biggest threats,” Roman adds, and Levi nods.

“The Witch and her coven, and the unknown Lycan pack,” Creek says, leaning back in his chair.

“Has there been any news from the Witches?” Kain asks, but no one answers.

“I’ll check in with Fallon and Marie. I’m not sure

what's going on with them, but I'll ask," I say, trying not to sound as tense as I feel. All of this almost feels like too much. I thought we were so close to this being over when we captured Archer. But of course, it's not. I just hope that we can work something out soon.

"Any progress with the Lycans?" Levi asks Roman who is practically grinding his teeth in frustration.

"Theron still says he has no idea. Whoever it is, has hidden themselves well enough, or at least covered their tracks. Since the death of Echo, everything has been very calm. Are you sure that journal said it was two Lycans?"

"Sorry," I say, nodding at Roman. I know how hard this is for me, but it must be harder for him. He's trusted his alphas for lifetimes. For them to betray him like this… I can't help but feel responsible.

"You have nothing to be sorry for," he sighs, running his hand through his hair. "It just means that I might have to go to the compound and interrogate myself. It's not that I don't trust Theron & Tobias to get to the bottom of it, but there's nothing quite like being interrogated by your alpha."

"I don't think we should be splitting up unless absolutely necessary," Levi says, voicing the thoughts inside my head. Even if those thoughts make me an uber needy bitch.

"I won't go unless absolutely necessary," Roman

agrees, and I smile softly at him.

"Anything else we need to catch up on tonight? I'm beat, and my mom wants to see me tomorrow," Creek says, stretching out as he stands.

No one says anything, so I stand too, and the others follow suit. Levi grabs my hand as I go to leave the room, and the others leave, giving us some time alone.

"How are you doing?" he asks, his gaze taking me in, practically piercing my soul. His hand cups my cheek and I lean into his touch.

"I'm okay, I think. Still processing a lot," I tell him softly.

"Avoiding processing you mean," he says with a smirk and I roll my eyes.

"What if I am? We have a lot going on."

"Not as much as we have had. If you need a minute to breathe, you can take it. We can take care of everything," he offers, it's sweet, but he knows as well as I do, I don't let others deal with my mess.

"Thank you, but no. This insanity is only on you all because of me. I'm not going to run away and let you just handle it. For the minute I'm okay. If that changes, I'll let you know."

"Promise?"

"I promise."

After trying to retreat to my room last night, I got picked up and carried to Levi's, where everyone ended up piling in. I can't say I'm upset about it. With everything that's been going on, being around my guys brings me a semblance of peace. Even if they're not always so happy about everyone doing the whole puppy pile thing, apparently everyone could tell that I needed each of them.

Levi was right, I'm definitely avoiding dealing with stuff, but I'm worried if I start trying, a tsunami is going to hit me, and I'm not sure I'll survive it. But being around them dulls the fear that everything inside of me is going to consume me. Let's not even start about me avoiding what it is I'm capable of with shadow fire at my disposal.

Just nope.

Today is not the day I'm going to try and unravel it all.

When I woke this morning, I was alone, but there was a note telling me that they're all off running errands of one form or the other, meaning I have some time alone. A knock breaks my train of thought before the door opens.

"My Remy girl… I brought you breakfast! Those boys went out, doing all the things, so I thought you'd enjoy a nice relaxing morning. Nothing better for that than bacon and French toast!" Nonnie's joyful voice makes me smile as she places the tray over my lap and fusses around me.

"Thank you, Nonnie. You didn't have to do this."

"Psssh," she hisses as she waves me off. "Remy girl, I've never seen Kain with more light in his eyes than when you are in his life. For that alone, you deserve the world, but the way you accept my Luc, accept all of us, despite the prejudice around you, you looked past it all. You are special, Remy girl. You deserve to be spoiled, every day of your life." Her words make my eyes prick with tears. I blink to keep them from falling as she takes my hands. "I hope whoever started all of this crazy business you're all dealing with finds a painful and lengthy death, so that you can finally find the peace you deserve."

She wipes one of the tears away, and kisses my cheek before leaving me alone with my grief, and a warmth in my heart I feared I wouldn't feel again with Everly no longer around.

I pick at the breakfast she bought me, trying to keep my Demons buried under lock and key, but the longer I'm here, the more I feel, the louder those Demons become.

"Hey Princess." I jump as Roman's voice reaches me. I guess I really was off in a world of my own. "What's wrong?"

He sits beside me, and tucks my hair behind my ear. I lean into his touch, he's always able to make me forget everything outside of him, and I could really use that right now.

"Just getting a little lost inside myself," I tell him with a sad smile.

"Well then, it's your lucky day. I have just the idea for forgetting the world." He smiles at me, and it's as if his wolf is smiling at me. Beautiful but deadly.

"What did you have in mind?" I ask.

"That, princess, would be telling," he says, bopping me on the nose with a finger like I'm a naughty pup, making me laugh. "Now come on, eat up, get dressed and let's get going. I'm excited now. Don't want to keep me waiting." He winks at me and I laugh again.

I do as he says, and hurry to get ready. Even just the anticipation of the day with him makes the darkness inside of me seem a little bit further away. It doesn't take me long, and before I know it, we're in my car and he's driving. Not quite sure how I let that happen, I rarely hand over the wheel of Betty, but I suppose I'll concede this once since I have no idea where we're going.

He looks so relaxed that I can't even find it in myself to harass him to find out where he's taking me. I sit back and enjoy the ride along the coast.

We drive for a while, before he pulls into a car lot, and my eyes go wide.

No way.

"This is your surprise?" I ask, trying not to sound as excited as I feel. I've always wanted to come here, it's like something out of the movies.

"You like?" he asks, that wolfish grin back on his face.

"This is perfect!" I squeal, hugging him while he laughs at me.

"If I'd known it would've made you this happy, I'd have done this months ago." He climbs from the car as I scramble to undo my seatbelt and follow.

Santa Monica freaking pier!

I've literally wanted to come here forever. Every movie I watched as a teenager had a scene that was set here. The Ferris wheel, the rollercoaster, the sounds, the sights, even the smells. It's perfection.

Roman takes my hand and I practically drag him onto the pier, lost in our own little corner of heaven.

ELEVEN

I take a deep breath as I clench the steering wheel and look up at my family's house. I know Colt is in there, and I know I need to see him, but I don't know that I'm ready for this. Acknowledging everything I have to once I step through that door.

I take another breath, fortifying myself against the tumultuous emotions inside of me that I still have to look at properly, and climb out of the car. I think of the day I had with Roman yesterday, our day of forgetting. It's one of the best days I remember ever having. It was like being a kid again, indulging in everything we wanted without consequence. It brings a smile to my lips before I knock on the door.

"Shit." Colt's shout reaches me alongside a crash, so

I open the door and walk in towards the stairs. The crash came from upstairs, so I take the stairs a few at a time, and follow the cursing to Bauer's room.

"Are you okay?" I ask as I enter the room, making Colt jump and he hits his head on the shelf he was bent underneath.

"Fuck," he groans, rubbing the top of his head as I try not to smile. "You're home!"

His shock at seeing me doesn't take long to pass and he kicks boxes out of the way as he rushes towards me. I meet him in the middle of the room and hug him as tight as he holds me. "I didn't know if you'd be back…"

"As if you're getting rid of me that easy," I tell him lightly, and he squeezes me tighter.

"I nearly lost you, little bit." His voice is thick and he holds on for another minute before releasing me.

"I'm too hard to kill," I tell him with a wink, trying to make light of it all.

"Fucking Bauer…" he growls, and pulls on his hair a little.

"You don't have to hate him, Colt. He was your brother."

"And you're my sister. He fucked up, beyond fucked up. I should just burn this place to the ground. The whole place feels tainted." He sighs and my heart breaks. I never meant for any of this to happen.

"I'm sorry, Colt."

"You have fuck all to be sorry for, Rem. None of this is on you, or your fault. Bauer fooled us all, he is the only one responsible for any of this bullshit. Well, him and Dad. I've found more than a few bits these few days you've been gone, hinting towards the fact that Dad was working with them. I think that's why Archer killed Dad. Wrapping up loose ends."

"Holy shit. You really think so? Surely Dad would never have worked with other factions?"

"If it meant he could rule them in the end? I sure as shit think he'd go for that." He sighs. "Enough about this craziness for now. Let's go get coffee, it's early as fuck, and I want to hear about what the shit happened to you after that batshit fucking insane Angel kidnapped you."

"Michael didn't kidnap me," I tell him, a little unsure because I have no real memory of it.

"He sure as fuck did. You should have seen the chaos that erupted once you left. I thought Morgan was going to declare war," he says over his shoulder as he leads us down the stairs.

"She what?" I ask and then shrug. Why am I not surprised? "I guess I need to go and see them too, make the rounds and let everyone know I'm, ya know, alive and kicking."

"That's probably a good idea. But first, I want to hear

about Michael and Avalon!" He almost sounds like an excited little kid talking about going to a candy store for the first time. I sit at the table in the kitchen as he pours coffee and tell him everything about Avalon, leaving out the whole thing with Mom. He's lost enough, he doesn't need to know that I'm in some sort of crisis when it comes to her.

"Holy shit," he says, wide-eyed. "That all sounds… intense. So, you're like officially a Death Dealer again? That's so fucking cool. Want to hook me up when I get my wings? Pretty sure I'd make a banging Death Dealer." He waggles his eyebrows at me and I can't help but laugh at him.

"I'm pretty sure it's going to be a while till you give this life up," I say, when his face falls as I realize I put my foot in my goddamn mouth.

"If I have that choice." He shrugs, the laughter from seconds ago gone.

"I'm sorry, Colt. I will ask Michael to make finding this shit out a priority. You need to know, the burden I put on you by knowing… I'm sorry, it was so selfish of me. I just wanted you to be careful."

"Remy, it's fine. I get it. If anything, it's making small things seem more important than they ever have. Which is why I'm determined to fix this shit with Fallon once and for all. I just need her to forgive me for being such a dickhead."

"If I can help..." I say with a huge grin. The idea of the two of them finding happiness together makes me so freaking happy, but I know that there's a lot more to it than that.

"I'll let you know. You could always just keep that Demon asshole away from her? Or find a way for her to not go over to the Shadow Realm? I'm joking obviously, I'd never trap her like that, but still. Deacon's a prick."

"I know. But he was there for her at a really dark time."

"I'd have been there if I could!"

"I know that, and I'm sure she knows that too. New topic... Bauer. Have you made arrangements for him?" I ask, but when his face locks down, it hits me this probably isn't a better topic.

"He can fucking rot in hell," he says firmly. "No one is going to miss that asshole. We'll burn him and chuck out the ashes."

I don't entirely disagree with sentiment, but I also know he's going to need more closure than that.

"Colt," I sigh.

"No Remy. Dad's thing was bad enough, and that was before I suspected he had even more of a hand in the bullshit that's been going down. Bauer doesn't deserve shit from us, any of us. He doesn't deserve a Hunter's burial or a memorial. He can just burn." The pain and anger in his eyes keeps me quiet. This isn't the time, but then, I'm not sure it will ever be the time. Colt always seems like the carefree wonder child, and for the most part that's exactly who he is, but when he loves, he loves with everything he has. To betray that, the way our dad and Bauer have… he's more broken than he'll let even me see.

"We have a meeting tomorrow, the coven heads, the heirs and the elders. To try and finish sorting out this precarious treaty between everyone. If you and your guys want to come, it'd be more than welcome. Levi's presence tends to keep the Hunters in line, and we have a lot to catch people up on."

"You mean like me being an Angel, and Creek being part Demon?" I laugh as he nods and smiles. "Yeah, we'll be there. I could probably arrange for Caleb or Morgan to attend at some point too. Get them in on the treaty. It would be nice for the peace to spread further than just here."

"If you bring Caleb or Morgan, I'm bringing a camera, because the entire room are going to shit themselves," he says, barely containing his laughter. He's not wrong though.

"We'll see how tomorrow goes, but I'm sure they'd be down."

"You think Michael might come to the table too?" he asks.

"That might be more of a stretch. Especially with

Morgan at the table. Those two… they have history."

"Now that is a story I want to hear!"

"Maybe another time," I tell him, just happy some of the shadows in his eyes have retreated.

"I do have another surprise for you though," I tell him tentatively. "When I was in Avalon, we discovered a fun new power of mine."

"The sarcasm is strong in this one," he jokes and I swat his arm. "Oh come on, like being a conduit for Levi, and reading minds, oh wait and the healing thing. Like that's not enough. You need to share the love."

"Fine, I won't tell you." I stick my tongue out at him and he rolls his eyes. It feels like we've been thrown back ten years in that instant, but it brings me so much joy that I'm not even going to question it.

"Don't be an asshole," he says with a smirk.

"I have shadow fire," I tell him quietly.

"Ermmmm and for those of us who have no idea what that is?"

"It's pretty rare, and it's one of the only things other than Angel glass that can kill an Angel. Typically reserved for Demons, but a few Angels in history have had it," I say.

"Holy shit." He leans back, running a hand through his hair as his eyes go wide. "So you're like, a super badass!"

"Something like that. I've only had it appear once, and if I'm honest, I'm not exactly excited about using it again.

So, just keep that bit to yourself, yeah?"

"Your secrets are safe with me, little bit. You know that."

"I know." I smile at him and he claps his hands together.

"After all of those stark revelations, I'm fucking starved. Molly's?"

"Hell yes!" I say with a smile. "I'm driving!"

"That's fine, I get shotgun. Driving after decimating the amount of food I plan to isn't healthy anyway." His eyes sparkle with laughter and I follow him out of the house.

Maybe we'll survive this in one piece after all.

Creek pulls his truck up next to where I park Betty, in the spot where Colt and I parked last time we came to a Witches meeting, apparently Colt gave in and agreed to meet them all on their ground. Another reason, I think, that he asked us to be here. Roman looks like he's been chewing on wasps since we left. Unsurprisingly, he wasn't exactly thrilled about this meeting, especially since he has no answers if people start asking questions about the Lycans' loyalties. Though I doubt that's going to come up today. I almost feel bad for Kain sitting in the truck with him and what appears to be a pissed off Creek.

Levi sits beside me looking smug as fuck, since he called shotgun first. Which probably didn't help Roman's mood either. I get that they're all feeling a bit… let's call it protective rather than the straight up insanity that it is… about me after everything this last week, and I get it, I do. But I also really don't want dissent between the five of us, especially when things are finally getting to a point where they're good.

I climb from the Mustang, and walk around the back of it, waiting for the guys to join me. Colt said he'd meet us here when he texted me this morning, letting me know what time this was happening. I let Fallon know we'd be here too, when she rang me and cussed me out for not seeing her before now, which I totally deserved so I let her yell at me for a good five minutes before I told her I'd see her here.

It doesn't take long for Colt to show up, and we make our way up the rocky path to where we're meant to be meeting everyone.

"Remy!" Nasari waves as we reach the group, and I smile at him as Colt starts saying hello to everyone.

"Remy, you better not be hiding from me girl." Fallon's drawl hits me and I can't help but grin, even if she did chew me out earlier. I turn as she jumps on me with a hug. "Girl, I am so glad you're alive."

"Me too." I smile as I hug her back, glad that my friend seems more like her old self. Whatever it is she's been doing while I've been running around like a loon is obviously working. Guilt works its way up my throat about how little I've been around for her, especially considering everything that happened to her is basically my fault.

"Mama is looking for you, I think she has some stuff she wants to talk to you about," she says quietly. I open my mouth to ask her what it's about and she shakes her head. How cryptic.

"Okay, well we can hang out tomorrow, and if she's around we can talk? Or you guys can come to the house?"

"Sounds good to me. I miss you."

"I miss you, too."

"Okay, now let's get this show on the road, because your guys look ready to kill things, and well, I don't want to be here longer than I need to. I'll be back, got to go help Mama with the portals." She squeezes my hand before flitting back off to Marie, and I head over to where my guys are standing, their ears being talked off by the elders present. Colt looks almost disappointed as his gaze follows Fallon across the meadow. I guess they're still having issues, but I swore I wouldn't meddle. No matter how much I want to.

"Oh thank the fates," Creek mutters as I reach his side. He takes my hand and smiles down at me.

"Hey guys," I say to the elders speaking, taking their attention from the guys who look more than a little relieved. "I think Marie and Fallon are opening the portals, so we're about to get started."

They each nod and mumble as we move towards where Marie and Fallon are standing. Colt motions at us to stay back a few feet when the portals start opening. It doesn't matter how many times I see this stuff, it always amazes me. Theoretically, I can create portals, like the one I can create to the Shadow Realm, but I've never really tried to create one anywhere other than to or from the realm.

As each of the Witches and their heirs arrive, they take similar places in a circle as they did the last time we were here. Once they all arrive, Colt moves the Hunters to stand between the covens, merging the circles. My guys and I stay standing with Fallon and Marie. The Laveaus' are where my loyalties lie, always. The other Witches have done nothing to earn my distrust, but they've also not done a ton to earn my trust either.

I miss the mindset I had before I got my memories back. The ability to trust people until they taught me not to is gone. With everything that's happened, and getting my memories back, it's just not a part of who I am anymore. It might not be for the better, but it is what it is.

I tune out a little as the Witches and the elders start their treaty discussions. I only notice as Roman and Kain chime in, ensuring that their people aren't left to any detriment from the treaty. The agreement we made before pretty much turned to dust after Archer's latest awesomeness revealed betrayers in almost all of the factions.

"There is still no sigh of Lizzie, or her coven," one of the Witches says, snagging my attention.

"How is that even possible?" Colt asks, his frustration obvious from how he speaks through clench teeth.

"Lizzie is a very powerful Witch," the Witch huffs. "She has more than enough power and talent to shield herself and her coven."

"You sound like you look up to her," Nasari chimes in, eyeing the heir.

"This isn't going to get us anywhere," I say, loudly enough to be heard above the bickering. "Fighting amongst ourselves makes us weaker. If you can't give yourself to this new treaty and all it means fully, then leave. We'll be better off without you. A chain is only as strong as its weakest link." I am so sick of this constant bickering between the factions. "I know that centuries of resentment aren't going to be fixed overnight, but fucking hell. We're not children, it's not hard to be civil. So either buck up or fuck off."

I cross my arms, watching everyone in the circle. My brother smirks at me, and I restrain from rolling my eyes at him. I wait a full minute before nodding my head when no one leaves.

"Okay then, that's that. Can we not bicker like children, and just try to think of productive ways to pool our resources to find these people? We are four factions. Surely they can't hide from all of us." It's on the tip of my tongue to say I could bring in the Four Horsemen, but Colt is right, people would shit their pants on the spot. These people don't even know about my relationship with the Shadow Realm, let alone the rulers of it. There's going to be a whole lot of revelations today.

"In the spirit of being open and honest, there is also something you should all know," I say, with my head held high. I look to Fallon who nods, and I move to the center of the circle. I look back at my guys who all smile at me, except for Levi, who looks like he's ready to smite anyone who so much as looks at me wrong. I contain the laughter that threatens and roll my neck, stretching out. While I'm aware that these people lack the tools to kill me, they could still hurt me, so I cross my arms again and eye each of them seriously. "Do not freak out."

I take a deep breath and unfurl my wings. The gasps that usher across the meadow feel loud as thunder, but I know in reality they're not.

"How is this possible?" Nasari asks. The wonder in his voice is evident. "You did not die?"

"Actually, I did. In the Shadow Realm. This was the result," I tell him, giving them just enough information, but no details. They don't need to know the details.

Chatter starts up from almost everyone around us.

Questions are thrown at me, but everyone's talking over each other and it's essentially chaos, which I was prepared for, but fuck. I literally just said about not freaking out.

A whistle screeches through the air, and I look to Fallon who has her fingers in her mouth, making the noise. "People! Get a hold of yourselves. This is nothing but an advantage for us, against an unknown enemy."

Her words make me smile. I knew deep down that she had no issues with what I am now, but it makes me feel better to hear her say it out loud. I catch Colt watching her, a proud smile on his face before I look at my guys, each looking as fierce as the next, ready to throw down if it's needed, but Fallon's words cause a silence from the people around us. I can't even begin to imagine how they'll react when they find out about Creek. But that's a revelation for another day, and goes firmly in the, they don't need to know, column.

I walk back over to my guys, and Fallon and Marie both smile at me warmly.

Marie steps forward and clears her throat, taking the meeting back under control. "Now then, back to finding Lizzie."

Before the meeting finishes, we have a new plan of attack for Lizzie and her coven, some damaged relationships have been fixed, and thanks to me keeping my wings out, people seem to be coming to terms with the fact that I've changed. Again.

I have no doubt that when they get the chance, the Hunters will pepper me with questions about how it was possible, without taking the true death, but that is a story for another time. They don't get to know everything about me, regardless of the fact that we're all in this, seemingly because of me.

Once Marie draws the meeting to an end, the Witches start to portal out, back to their own corners of the Earth, and they take some of the elders with them, to start with the hunt for Lizzie. Once we're alone again, Marie pulls me to one side. I look at the others, Colt trying to talk to Fallon, my guys barely taking their eyes from me, as they continue talking, I assume about the parts they need to play in the coming weeks. I turn from them and give Marie my full attention.

"Remy, I won't keep you long," she says in hushed tones, which makes the butterflies in my stomach kick up.

"What's wrong?" I ask, trying not to worry.

"My vision, it's changed," she says, her eyes dart to the group behind me. "I haven't told anyone else, because I don't fully understand it, but it's changed. The war… the path has changed. There is no longer utter death and destruction on a battle field, but someone who can get close to you is not what they seem. Their face is hidden from my vision, which makes me think they're working with a Witch, to try and hide their intentions. It must be a very powerful Witch to block them from me. Be careful, Remy."

She squeezes my hand before walking back to Fallon. She told me alone for a reason. But it couldn't be one of them. It just couldn't.

Right?

TWELVE

"We haven't done this in forever." Fallon laughs as we drop into the chairs at the coffeeshop we used to spend more time at than at home.

"It's fun. Even if my poor plastic is feeling some pain." I drop the multiple bags from the morning of shopping we've done so far.

"This was way better than staying in with all those surly guys of yours. What was wrong with them? You not putting out enough?" I laugh at her words, if only she knew the pelvic sorcery I've been experiencing since I got back from Avalon.

"Hardly, I'd just already said something about going out with you, without a chaperone, and they all went into overprotective alpha mode," I say, rolling my eyes and picking up the menu.

"Girl, why are you picking up the menu, you and I both know you're going to order the same as always." She laughs at me and I join her. I feel like some semblance of myself for the first time since I got back home. She's not wrong, I've ordered the same thing from here for about four years. I drop the menu just as the server approaches with a smile.

"What can I get for you ladies?"

"I'll have a pumpkin spice latte, extra whip, extra shot, with a cheese and ham croissant." Fallon grins at me as she orders the same thing she orders every time at this time of year.

"I'll have a peppermint mocha with extra cream, with a chicken and bacon toastie." I smile at the girl who nods and turns on her heel back towards the counter.

"I can't believe it's almost Christmas," Fallon sighs. "I feel like it's come out of nowhere this year."

"Tell me about it. It's going to be weird as fuck this year. I don't know what we're even doing." I sigh, and put my head in my hands. "Do you think it would be weird if we just ordered Italian, and spent the day watching movies?"

"Girl, after the year you've had, you can do whatever the fuck you like, and no one can say shit. Though I'm pretty sure there's going to be more than a few people that want to be with you guys that day. Including Maddie and Nate, though Nirvana will be home, so that could be interesting, and Colt will want to be there too… We could just do a big movie day? Goddess knows you guys have enough space to have everyone. Everyone could bring their own dish, and we can just do presents, food, and movies?"

"That sounds like a perfect day. A day with nothing to worry about except how stretchy my pants need to be so I can eat all of the things." I sigh wistfully. Even just the idea of it makes me feel lighter.

"Then let's do it!" Fallon pulls her excitement in a bit as our coffee and food arrives, the girl just smiles at us as she drops it and practically skips away. Oh to be so oblivious and carefree.

We sit and talk about nothing but light and happy things before we head back to finish gift shopping. It doesn't take us long, before we head back to the manor. Fun as this day has been, the drive home feels a little tense. We've avoided speaking about anything that's been happening to either of us recently, and now we're heading back, I know I need to speak to her about it all.

It's not an uncomfortable silence, but when we pull up at the manor, I'm not sure who jumps from the car first.

"Oh my girls are back, let me feed you. Too skinny you girls!" Nonnie fusses over us as we haul all of our bags into the house.

"Let us get this stuff to my room, Nonnie, and then you can feed us all you like." I'm not telling her we ate, it makes her too happy to feed us, and well, I'm never one to turn down good food. Thank the fates for Angel metabolism.

We drop the bags off in my room, stuffing them in a back corner of my closet, ready for me to get my wrap on, and then head back to the kitchen.

"Where are the guys?" I ask Nonnie, dropping a kiss on her cheek as we take a seat at the island.

"They were fighting in the gymnasium, silly boys. They're fine, but look at you, you need to eat more." She fusses again and starts spooning what looks an awful lot like chicken Alfredo into two bowls, before placing them in front of us, and pulls garlic bread from the oven. "Eat, eat. Do you like?"

I take a bite and groan around my fork as my tastebuds burst to life. Fallon moans beside me too, her eyes closed as she tastes the dish. "Nonnie, I think you've outdone yourself."

She beams at my words and I smile. "I'm glad, yes, very much. I hid you a treat in the little fridge in the pantry for later." She winks at me, and leaves Fallon and I alone, heading towards the side of the manor where her room is. I have no idea what she does here, but she seems set on not returning to the castle in France. I wonder how many people there are cursing me for stealing her away.

"So…" Fallon starts before taking another mouthful.

"So… I nearly died, again," I say with a sigh. I tell her everything I remember about what happened with Bauer, and then waking up in Avalon. Everything that's happened until now, the memories that have come back to me. Not leaving out any details, except for what her mom told me. While I'm sure it's not her, Marie would have told her if she wanted her to know.

"I mean… holy shit, Remy. If this was anyone else, I'd call them a straight up liar, but all of this could only happen to you." She sits blinking at me, wide eyed. "I don't even know where to start. Michael, your mom, the Archangel council—Gabe sounds like fun, just a side note—but fucking hell. I have no idea how you even find the strength to get out of bed, I'd have quit on this shit long before now."

"Enough about me, what's been going on with you?" I ask, because it's been a while since we talked about everything going on with her.

"I'm okay. I've finally managed to get my power under control, well, ish. Bryce spoke to me a bit after the whole Michael thing, once Levi said you were safe. He gave me some tips for controlling the power inside of me, and they've been working. As for everything else in my life, well, that's a whole other story. But not one I have even close to figured out yet."

"So that's your way of telling me not to ask how things are between you and my brother?" I ask, laughing softly.

"Pretty much." She shrugs with a small smile. Shadows appear in her eyes, and I wish I could take them from her. The guilt of everything she suffered because of me is real, but I know that really, that was on Archer and whoever it is that was pulling his strings.

"You know I'm here if you need to talk right? I'm never too busy for you," I tell her softly. I hate how little time we get to spend together these days.

"I know, and ditto. Once this madness is over, and we get to the bottom of everything, I vote we go somewhere sunny, with white sands, and hot boys that can bring us margaritas."

"That, my friend, is a plan."

We spend the rest of the night avoiding heavy topics, and it's nice to just pretend we're normal people, with normal problems that aren't more complicated than eating too much ice cream and what tv show to binge next. The guys give us space, only dropping in to let me know where they are, and when they head to bed. I know the latter is because they're hoping I spend the night with one of them, but I convince Fallon to spend the night rather than me driving her back so late, and we move the contents of my bed to the sitting room, so we can binge movies all night.

It's everything I didn't realize I needed, wrapped up in

one day. Just one day of being a normal person, without the turmoil that's been haunting me taking over. I laugh at the cheesy romcom we decided to put on, and notice Fallon's dropped off, so I shut off the move and turn down the lights. Maybe everything will be all right after all, as long as I have people around me to remind me who I am and what's most important.

"You know he'll keep sending us out scouting together until you stop your bitching about wanting not to go out in the field anymore right?" I whisper-shout to Nevin as we creep towards what leads have told us is the camp for the higher Demons that are causing this stupid fucking war in the first place. We've tried to find them for years, but we've either been too late, or the intel was wrong. That or we have a mole, but Leviathan refuses to believe that possibility—that one of his Death Dealers is betraying him. The man I love is a stubborn one, loyal to a fault, it's part of why I fell in love with him, but it's also a total pain in the ass sometimes.

"Maybe he'll stop sending me out with you when you learn to think before diving into reckless situations," he grumbles. I mean, he could be right, but it's kind of a part of who I am. I protect the people I love. The ones I care about. Looking after myself always comes second. Or it

did, until about two weeks ago, when I learned that I'm no longer the only one depending on my survival.

It's made me more cautious, but, I'm still not going to sit on the sidelines and do nothing. It's not who I am. It never will be.

"How about we just focus on getting the information we need and getting back undetected and in one piece?" I say, and he rolls his eyes at me.

"I'm not the one who's likely to get us discovered," he huffs. Ever since Tobin died, Nevin has been a little gruffer. I get it. Tobin was always the lighter one of the two of them, he'd pull Nevin from any funk he was stuck in. And now Tobin is gone, he doesn't have that anymore. I can't help but feel guilty about it, even though there's no way we could have known that the Demon had shadow fire. It's so fucking rare, that even Nevin didn't have a clue what it was until he'd spent weeks researching.

It might have been nearly ten years ago, but that's nothing but a drop in the ocean to an Angel. His grief is still as raw as it was the day it happened, and no matter how many times he tells me it's not my fault, a little part of me will never really believe that.

We move our way into the Demon camp, sticking to the shadows that I manipulate to keep us hidden, without it being obvious. It steals some of my concentration, but it's necessary for us to get the information we need and to get it back to Leviathan, so we can try and end this war once and for all. Morgan has enough chaos going on in the Shadow Realm to deal with everything on Earth, so outside of her helping me eventually seal the realm, her and the Horsemen aren't going to be of much use. Plus, there's that whole, Hell on Earth thing that we'd all like to try and avoid. We've got enough chaos going down without adding them to the mix.

Nevin starts taking a note of what Leviathan asked for, while I keep us covered, but we keep having to move further into the camp, almost too far to be able to remain undetected. This was not the plan. I never wanted to get this far in, and I can tell Nevin isn't exactly happy about it either, but I know for a fact that he's as unwilling as I am to go back without the details we need.

"I think we've got it," Nevin whispers. "We need to start to try and get the fuck out of here."

I nod, and we try to move back to the edges of the camp, so we can get back, but there are a lot more Demons here than when we started, and we're so far in, that it's going to take us a minute to get the hell out. We move as swiftly as we can, and I focus so hard on keeping the shadows wrapped around us, that I don't see the dip in the ground. Nevin trips in front of me and falls into a weapons rack. The crash of axes and spears creates so much noise and garners so much attention, that we're truly fucked.

I freeze as Nevin scrambles back to his feet, but I pull my karambit knives from their sheathes on my thighs, and prepare myself to fight our way out of here. This was not the plan, but I have too much to live for right now, we are getting out of here, though this will put a huge stop on all of the plans we've been making.

Fuck.

This literally couldn't get any worse.

It's like the calm before a storm, like someone inhaled and held it. The silence. The stillness. Before all hell breaks loose. Nevin and I work as we've trained. Back to back, using every tool in our arsenal to get us the hell out of here. It's too tight to be able to unfurl our wings and fly the fuck away, we just need to thin the herd enough that we can do exactly that. I barely even pay attention to what I'm doing, beyond making sure I'm protecting myself a little bit more than usual. Mine isn't the only life I'm looking out for here.

We work our way through as much as we can, when the opportunity shows itself, I wait until Nevin is in the air, and then follow suit. Trying not to focus on the aches and potential breaks in my body, just on getting back to Leviathan.

"Fuck!" Nevin screeches even as a sizzle fills the air. I look over my shoulder and see balls of fire being thrown at us from below while they ready their archers. Fuck. We're

still in range of their arrows. Nevin slows, and the burnt flesh of his wounded wing hampering him.

Fuck, fuck, fuck!

The incoming spear will hit him and I move before thinking, throwing Nevin out of its path. I thought I'd moved high enough to avoid it, but instead of piercing my heart, it punctures my stomach.

No!

"Come on Amantara, we just need to get out of range, and then we can stop and get that thing out of you." His concern barely touches me as the realization hits me.

My baby.

Our baby.

The one I didn't get a chance to tell Leviathan about yet.

I keep my wings beating, keep the hope in my heart that my baby is okay. Angel children are so rare as it is, the thought of losing one is devastating. The thought that it's my own fault, I'm not sure it's something I'll survive.

I follow Nevin up and into the distance, barely paying attention to anything but the wound in my stomach, and the beat of his wings. We don't stop until we're back at our camp. I was flying without saying a word, so I guess he assumed I'd be okay to get back. I don't really remember the flight, it's all just a blur. A numb blur while I tried to tell myself I didn't just kill our baby.

Leviathan is waiting for us when we land, the concern on his face breaks my heart, because he doesn't know, and if the worst has happened, I can never tell him. He will never forgive me. The pain of it will be too much.

"I'm fine," I say to him as he reaches me, and I wince away from his touch. "I just need to take it out, and I'll be fine." He reaches around me and snaps the back of the spear away, before tugging the front so it leaves my body. Blood rushes down from the wound, but I can feel it already starting to heal. I just need to be alone for a minute. I need to find out if I hurt him. I don't know it's a him, but it's just a feeling I've had since I found out I was pregnant. That I was carrying our son.

"Amantara..." Leviathan starts, but I shake my head.

"I'll be okay, Nevin has all of the details, I just need a minute," I say, and walk away from him and his all-seeing stare. If I stay, I'll break, and then I'll have to tell him. I walk as quickly as I can manage back to the wooden house we've been calling our own, and head straight for the bathroom. By the time I strip out of my clothes, the wound is sealed, and there's not even a mark on my body to show that there was damage, just the dried blood.

I place my hand on my stomach, willing for the movement I had felt before, but there is nothing. A sob wracks my body as I climb under the waterfall Leviathan created for us in here, letting the water hide my tears, and wash away the blood staining my skin. I refuse to believe that he's gone, not until I have proof. I step from underneath the water and dry off, dressing in clean clothes, and go in search of Elysiel. She was the healer who confirmed the pregnancy. Until she tells me all is lost, I refuse to let go of that small spark of hope.

I move with purpose towards her tent. I swore her to secrecy with a blood vow when we found out the news. Pregnancy is a wonderful thing, but it's also a very dangerous time. It makes people of our kind do insane things, so it is safer to keep it as much a secret as possible.

I enter the tent silently, and find it empty. So I sit on the bed and I wait.

It feels like days until she returns, and when she sees me, she looks to my stomach instantly.

"Is he gone?" I ask when she looks back up to meet my eyes.

"Lie down," she says as she moves towards me, but I can feel it in my heart, the truth I'm unwilling to accept until she says the words. I lie back, and she lifts the hem of my top, placing her warm hands on the flatness of my stomach. She hums softly as light emanates from her hands. I want to close my eyes, but I can't. I need to know.

She pulls back and a tear slips down her face. "I am so sorry, Amantara."

I shake my head as I sit.

No.

This can't be happening.

Why did I do this?

"There will be some bleeding, so you will need to stay close for a day or so. The infant was too young to be able to survive such an injury. I am so sorry. Is there anything I can do?"

I shake my head again as I stand, unable to speak. Guilt floods every part of my system. Our baby is dead and it's all my fault.

The days pass, and I'm unable to function. The day after I saw Elysiel, I bled, and I sobbed the entire day, hidden away from everyone so that no one else would know the truth.

That I killed our baby.

I can't bring myself to tell Leviathan. It would break him. And to say the words, it would break me too. I'm still unsure as to how I'm going to survive this. I know that Leviathan knows something is wrong, but I pretend to be asleep when he returns at night, and I pretend to sleep when he awakens in the morning. I have never hidden from anything in my life, but this… this I hide from. I can barely function.

It's been a week since I killed our baby, and I nearly

got myself killed again yesterday. This guilt is eating me alive. I don't know how to cope, how to not get anyone else killed when so many rely on me being Leviathan's right hand. So this morning I made a decision, one that I can barely live with, but I can't see another way. It's why I left our camp hours ago in search of a Witch.

I heard of a powerful one living in a town not far from our camp, and I'm convinced she is the only one that can help me, before I ruin the lives of everyone around me.

It doesn't take me long to track her down, Witches are a rare commodity, but even humans need healers, especially now with this chaos in their world. They may not believe it is magic, but they sure as hell don't question the results.

I knock on the door to the wooden house, and wait a moment. The door opens and a young woman with long dark hair and dark skin opens the door. "I have been waiting for you, Shadow Walker. I am not sure I can do what you need."

"Will you at least try?" I plead. She hesitates but she nods, and steps back from the door, ushering me inside.

"You understand that it may be impossible to undo this once it is done?"

"I cannot live with this guilt. Please. I need to forget," I practically beg, as tears run down my face.

"The mind is a maze. I cannot guarantee it will work, but I will try to take the pain from you. I cannot erase the

memories, but I can lock them away, and the emotions you feel will go with them. I can replace the holes with something else, but are you sure you wish to forget the life that was lost?"

I shake my head, but I know that this is the only way.

"Please. Please make me forget. I cannot go on knowing what I did." She frowns at me, but nods her head.

"I will try. Lay down over there, and we shall begin."

I wake up in a cold sweat, panting, my hair stuck to my face. What on earth did I do? How could I have done that? My stomach rolls and I run from the sitting room to the closest bathroom and lose the contents of my stomach.

I was pregnant, and I lost the baby.

Levi's baby.

And he has no idea.

Guilt creeps up my extremities until it reaches every depth of me and sobs wrack my body.

What have I done?

I scramble from the bathroom, and throw on the first clothes I put my hands on. Anything, just something. I grab a pen and paper and scribble a note to the guys, begging them not to come looking for me. That I'm safe and I'll be back in a few days. I just need to get the hell away, and there's only one person I can think of that will understand. I know she will.

I grab the bottle of Morgan's blood, and the extra vials of mine, just in case they don't listen and head outside, I try not to wake Fallon as I rush out of the doors. The minute my bare feet touch the grass, I spill my blood with Morgan's, and say the words I need to open the portal.

It takes three tries to get the words out between the sobs I can't seem to control, but the minute it opens, I jump through the portal, leaving the shattered remnants of my heart behind me.

THIRTEEN

I can barely catch my breath as I stumble into the throne room.

"What the fuck?" Caleb's cursing reaches me seconds before I'm wrapped in his arms. "What did they do, Mara? I swear to god, I was just starting to like them, but I'll tear them apart. Every one of them."

I try to speak, but every emotion I've stuffed down for eternity is hammering me all at once. All I can do is cry. We sink to the floor, his arms still around me, and he holds me while I cry.

"Go find Morgan," Caleb hisses, but I can't see anyone else, with my head buried in his chest.

"What happened?" Bryce's voice filters through my sobs but I can't move from the hold Caleb has on me as I fall apart.

"I have no fucking clue, but you bet your ass I'm cracking skulls. Now go fucking get Morgan. I have a feeling that she's the reason Mara is here."

"I'm right there with you, brother. I won't be long." The air ripples after Bryce finishes speaking, but I barely feel the tingle on my skin while Caleb rocks me and strokes my hair. The tears won't stop. I have no idea how to make them stop. No idea how to stop just feeling *everything*.

The world outside of us disappears as I lose the battle against the war inside of me. I try to shut it all back up, but I can't do it. The guilt, the pain, everything I've tried to avoid. My stomach rolls as it just hits me, like wave after wave of the ocean. Just when I think I've caught my breath, another wave takes me down.

Caleb holds me the entire time without hesitation or movement beyond telling me it will be okay and stroking my hair. I didn't mean to break like this. Not on him. But the comfort he offers comes with no judgment, and no strings. It's exactly why I came here. It's why I'm breaking.

"I'm sorry," I hiccup as I catch a breath, and he shakes his head.

"You have nothing to be sorry for. What happened?" he asks softly. He looks down at me with such affection, it's like another stab to the gut.

"I… I killed him," I stutter, and the tears start to fall

again as Morgan sweeps into the room. Caleb stands, taking me with him, and passes me over to her.

"What on earth?" Morgan says, but I can't answer.

"I have no idea, but whoever it was, I'm going to kill them." Caleb growls. A chorus of 'me too' join him and I realize that all of the Horsemen are here. I try to catch my breath, pulling away from Morgan to compose myself, but it's a losing battle.

"Can you guys give us some space?" Morgan asks them softly, and despite the groans of protest, they leave the room, and shut the door.

"They're going to wait outside of that door until they know you're okay." She sighs with a soft smile. "Now how about we have a cup of tea, and you tell me what is going on?"

I nod, managing to finally get a hold of myself, but silent tears still run down my face. With a wave of her hand, the table appears, with a full tea spread, including the little sandwiches and cake. If I had it in me to laugh, I'd be laughing my ass off right now, but the most I can manage is a smile, and even that hurts.

She pulls me to the table and I sit beside her as she pours us both a cup of tea. "It's chamomile, it should help calm you."

I take a sip, wincing at the sharp taste, but I take another, hoping for anything to calm the storm inside of me. She sits in silence, watching me, waiting for me to start talking, but I have no idea where to even begin. And after such a dramatic entrance, I feel like a complete idiot, but I still can't stem the tears fully.

"Whatever happened, you know we're on your side, right?"

I nod, and take another sip of the tea. Anything to buy myself time from saying any of it out loud. I take a deep breath and try to steel myself against the words I know I need to say out loud. Otherwise I'll never even begin to start working through the mess inside of me.

"I remember…" I start, and have to take a deep breath again as the guilt and shame rises up, threatening to make me throw up again. "I remember everything. Including the thing I bound myself from remembering…" Her eyes go wide at my words.

"You bound your memories? Mara… that's… I wish you'd have come to me instead, it's so unhealthy to do that."

"I had no choice, there was no other way to survive it. To not bring him down with me. To not put other people in danger because I was a zombie. I couldn't function." My voice catches again as she takes my hand.

"Whatever it was, I'm sure that you did what you thought was best." She squeezes my hand and the tears start to trickle down my face again.

"I feel so lost, Mor… like I don't know who I am, who I'm meant to be. There are so many different versions of me inside my head, and I can't work out which one is the right one."

"You are all of them, and none of them. There is no right one, Mara," she whispers, her hand not leaving mine.

"I killed him," I say quietly, and her eyes flash again, but she remains unmoved.

"Who?"

"My son… Levi's son." Her gasp is audible at my words, and it's like another dagger to the heart. "I was reckless, careless, and he died, before he even had a chance to live. Levi didn't know… doesn't know."

"Oh Mara, being reckless doesn't mean you killed him," she says softly, squeezing my hand again as the tears spill down my cheeks steadily again.

"But I did. I should have been more careful. I should have done something different. I should have protected him!" I tell her almost hysterically. "It's all my fault."

I tell her what happened, about the guilt and shame that ate me alive after it happened, that threatens to swallow me whole now. She sits and listens as I pour my heart out to her, about everything, all of the things that threaten to swallow me whole, without interruption.

The door to the throne room creaks open as I finish speaking and the guys heads appear around it.

"Is everything okay?" Caleb asks.

"Told you." Morgan chuckles as the door opens wider. "We're fine. I'm sure you guys have plenty of things to be doing, right?" She raises an eyebrow at them, but they all just look at me with so much concern it makes me want to cry all over again. I give them a watery smile, shaking my head as Caleb takes a step towards us.

"I think…" Caleb starts, but Morgan interrupts him.

"No skulls need breaking. You're off the hook. We just need to talk it out some more." He stops at her words and Bryce tugs him backwards.

"We'll be back soon," Bryce says as he leads the rest of them back out of the room and closes the door.

"I'll be amazed if they're gone for an hour before they check back in. Other than me and Mireya, you're about the only person they actually care about. So seeing you like that, when they've never witnessed it before, they're going to want to make sure you're really okay," she says, and I sigh.

"I don't know what to do, Morgan. I've always known, I've had a plan, there's been a mission, or orders, but right now. I don't know which way is up."

"That is the guilt talking. But Mara, you have nothing to feel guilty for. You were grieving, but what happened is not your fault. While I think you should've told Leviathan rather than hiding, I understand why you did what you did.

But you can't hide anymore. As for everything else, you can stay here as long as you need, to work through your past, but I think the best way to do that, really is with your guys. They've been through a lot with you. They're going to understand this."

"Maybe." I take another sip of the tea, and slump in my chair. "But I feel like Levi isn't going to understand."

"He might get angry, and he has every right to, because as much as you keep telling them not to keep stuff from you, you've done the same to him. That all being said, he won't be angry at you about what happened. I know him well enough to know that he won't blame you, because it was *not* your fault."

"But…"

"No. Mara. Nothing about what happened is your fault. It was a bad situation, and a really terrible thing happened. But it happened to you. You did not cause it. You did not ask for it." she says firmly, and I look down at my hands in my lap. I really want her words to be true, they just don't feel it, not in my heart. "Now, let's get you some food, and then get you to bed. I imagine you're exhausted. Then we can talk some more in the morning."

"Thank you," I say, my voice small.

"Mara, I will help you however I can. Just know that none of us will think any differently of you for any of it, and we all love you. No matter what."

I wake up, my eyes feeling scratchy from all the crying, and my throat dry as the Sahara. It took a while to go to sleep after Morgan got me settled last night. The tears just wouldn't stop. I didn't know I could cry this much, that I had that many tears in me.

I know that my tears aren't over yet though. Now that I opened the dam, every single thing I've put off dealing with is pressing down on me. It's like an elephant is sitting on my chest and I can barely breathe. Which is why, despite feeling like I do, I don't move from the fetal position I woke in. I welcome the darkness of the room. Not even a slither of daylight makes its way in here, but that suits me.

The darkness around me matches the darkness I feel inside.

I've never been one to wallow. I've always just picked myself up and got the fuck on with things. But I guess that's part of the reason I'm here now. Every time I stuffed it down, and just carried on, that emotion didn't disappear. It festered.

And now I'm drowning in it all.

The pain of being betrayed and murdered by my family. The hurt of losing my children. The one with Levi, and the loss of my child from when I was human. The loss of Everly. The knowledge that my mother wasn't strong enough to fight for me against my father and grandfather. A few small but epically important moments from a millennia of memories that keep pushing me under the waves of my pain and grief. There are just lifetimes of love and loss churning around inside of me.

What makes it even harder, are the many different reflections of myself. I don't recognize myself anymore, I don't know which of them I'm meant to be. I've been so many things to so many different people. What if the guys don't love the me I'm becoming? Fate knows I'm not the girl they fell in love with. Any of them. They each loved different versions of me. Each with different fears, different drives, different loves.

And now, I feel like a shell of them all. Like I'm watching a movie about someone who looks and talks like me, but isn't me at all. There's just so much loss in my heart that I haven't dealt with, and it keeps pulling me under and threatening to carry me out with the tide. I've never felt so hopeless in my life.

I pull the covers up over my head. Even in the darkness, it's like an extra shield against the world outside. Even if the torture is coming from within.

At the click of the door opening, I stifle the groan that threatens.

"Mara?" Caleb's voice is quiet, but I stay still, because I'm not sure I'm ready to face him, or anyone yet. I've never broken like I broke yesterday. To have shown up here and just fallen apart like that, crying all over him, shame makes my blood heat. “I know you’re not asleep.”

The bed dips in front of me and I sigh.

“I’m not going to let you wallow Mara. That’s not who I am, and it sure as hell isn’t who you are. Talk to me. Let me help you. I couldn’t sleep last night worrying about you. Morgan wouldn’t tell us anything, and I’m hurting because you’re hurting. You know I’m here for you. No matter what. We will literally unleash Hell on Earth if that’s what you need.”

I crawl out from under the covers, and he gets in next to me, pulling me into his side.

“You might think differently when I tell you,” I say softly and he squeezes me tighter. It feels wrong almost, telling him before I tell Levi, but I know deep down, that Caleb’s being honest. Nothing I say or do will change things between us. We’ve been us for too long, that bond between us runs too deep. I know that my pain will be hurting him because of it. I wish I could make it stop, but I know I can’t.

I take a deep breath and tell him everything. Every little thing that has been haunting me. Every single pain that I stuffed down and never dealt with. All those things that happened when I didn’t know he existed, but I know if he had known what was happening, he’d have tried to keep me here and never let me out ever again. I know this by the way he gets stiffer beside me as I tell him everything. I can practically feel the rage coming from him, but it's almost comforting, because I know he's not directing it at me.

"Mara," he says, practically growling. "You are the person you've always been. Just because there are different forms of it, at the root of it all you're still you. The person who helped us overthrow a tyrant. The person who risked everything to save my life. Who gives so selflessly, and feels so deeply. All of this pain, it isn't who you are, but it has helped to shape you. You're like a phoenix and you'll rise from this, stronger than before. And I will be there every step of the way to help you get your strength back, so you can face the ones you love the most, and tell them the most important bits of what you told me. You, Mara, are a fighter. Your heart is bigger than any other I've ever known. What happened, all of it, was not your fault. Not one fucking bit of it."

Tears spill down my cheeks again at his words. Sitting here, being torn in two, all of my darkest parts on display. The chaos inside of me quiets a little at his words, even if the guilt of everything still threatens to choke me. He pulls me in closer to his side and leans the side of his head against the top of mine, and just lets me cry, and mourn the child that I lost.

FOURTEEN

I've been here three days, trying to heal enough to be able to go home and face my guys. To tell them not only what I'd done, but also why I ran. And the thought terrifies me. The thought that they might leave because of it makes me almost immovable.

But I've been working with Morgan and the guys on building my power, they've been giving me all the space I need, but also plenty of distraction as I try to work through my guilt and grief. Though the guilt of still being here, rather than going back home, knowing what the guys must be going through—even though it will have only been about a day back home—it still hurts me.

I hate that my first instinct was to run. That's not who I am. At least, I don't think so.

There are only so many times you can hurt like that without it changing you. While I might not have completely reconciled all of the pain inside of me, I have found a fraction of peace in being here. Just enough to get a handle on the measure of healing I still need to do, but I know I need the people in my life around me to do that. I accept that I love them all, despite the changes in me, I just have to hope that they can accept me, with all of my past on show. Morgan and the guys showed me that it's possible, but they've dealt with enough pain and change themselves that I know that's exactly why I came here.

That's the other thing being here has given me chance to work on. Who I am now that I know this. Now that I know everything. Caleb was right in one respect, fundamentally, I'm the same as I've always been, but the pain and scars I carry now have definitely changed me.

I find myself less willing to trust people I don't know. But I guess that's just a part of my trauma, and how it has shaped me.

I know the people I have around me are ones I can trust. They've shown that time and again. Despite Marie's vision, I refuse to believe anyone still in our circle would be the one to betray us. If whoever is behind this is working with a Witch—which does make me suspect Amelia more, after everything Michael has said—they could have manipulated Marie's vision more than she realized. Another war could still be coming, and I refuse not to be prepared.

Morgan agreed with my deduction when I spoke to her. So did Bryce, and considering he is literally War, it makes me trust my instincts just a little more. I decided once I get home, I'm going to look into it a little more on my own while the guys focus on the bits they've already been looking into. I'm not going to burden them with this in case I'm wrong.

"Mara, come on. Don't take it easy on me," Malik says as he bounces on the balls of his feet. Sparring with the guys has shown me one thing the last few days. I really do remember everything. It's one of the few things that has made me smile. A little like the maniacal smile I wear right now.

"You need me to take it easy on you." I wink at him, and he scoffs.

"Please. I can handle you," he says launching at me, no holds barred. I duck and parry, rolling out of the way of his attack, searching for a weakness to flip the tables. But they're not called the Four Horsemen for no reason. That being said, I wasn't a notorious Hunter for centuries for no reason either.

I find my opening and take it, using the parts of me I hadn't realized were lost, and pin Pestilence himself. I smile down at him, my blade at his throat and he grins back. "There's my Mara."

I laugh as I remove the blade and stand. I offer him my hand, and he takes it, while Caleb and Killian grumble and Bryce laughs, winning the bet they had. At least one of them had some faith in me I guess.

"Thank you, Mara, for showing me I need to spend more time working out, rather than resting on the stories of how badass I am." Malik laughs and takes a swig from a bottle of water Killian hands him.

"You are a badass," I tell him with a grin. "I'm just a bigger one." Caleb laughs and strips off his t-shirt.

"My turn now, right?" His cheeky grin makes me laugh just as Morgan enters the room.

"Caleb, that is hardly a fair fight. She'll beat you in a heartbeat," Morgan teases, but Caleb takes it in his stride.

"Maybe she will, maybe she won't. Won't know unless she tries," he taunts.

"Did you tell her yet?" Morgan asks the guys, who grin but shake their heads.

"Tell me what?" I ask.

"Tell you about the treasure we stumbled upon," Bryce chuckles.

"What treasure?"

"A certain soul might have found its way down here, and into my lap. He's been so much fun to play with," Bryce tells me, while the others just grin.

"I already knew you had Jack."

"Yes, but you didn't know that while Caleb gets to play with Jack. I get to play with Archer."

"You really think the Hunter's curse is broken? That they don't cycle anymore?" I sit on the bed cross legged, opposite Morgan, taking in everything she's been explaining to me.

"It seems that way, it's rare for us to get any souls from Hunters, but we've had more than a few recently. It could just be that they've been rejected from Avalon after choosing the true death, so I can't say for sure," she says with a shrug, that somehow still looks regal on her.

"How many others?" I ask.

"A good few. I know the boys are hunting them to see if there's anyone with information about everything that's going on is in the mix. Hence Caleb and Bryce locking up Jack and Archer."

I lean back on the mass of pillows behind me and try to take it all in. After the bomb they dropped earlier, Morgan demanded girl time, so we came back to my room, I showered and found her sitting on my bed, and that's where we've been since.

"You seem more settled," she observes as she watches me. "Are you feeling better?"

"I feel a little less lost. Remembering fundamental parts of myself has helped, rather than clinging to that darkness, and working out with the guys, proving to myself that I am still who I thought I was, even though I'm different now," I tell her quietly. "But I think I just put another plug in the pain and guilt. If I think about it, then it's still there, that darkness wanting to swallow me whole."

"Telling Levi might help with the guilt." Her voice stays steady, but her eyes practically pierce my soul.

"I know, I'm going to, as soon as I go home." I bite the inside of my lip, because I know her next question.

"When are you going home?"

"I don't know. I know I need to. I need to face them. Explain everything. But I'm also so fucking terrified. What if, I tell them and it changes how they see me? What if this version of me isn't the one that they loved? What if they can't get behind the new aspects of me, now that I'm more than I was?"

"Remy, I've been you, remember. You were with me in this exact same situation, worrying that the ones who loved me wouldn't love me once I became more than I was. Just like my guys still loved and cherished me, so will yours. We are lucky, you and I. Not everyone is so blessed to be loved so much."

She's right. I know she's right, but the fear is so fucking real. Which pisses me off too, because I've never had any doubt in the love from my guys before. I hate being this insecure, but that guilt keeps suffocating me and riddling me with doubt.

"Mara, you can take on the Four Horsemen and come out victorious. If you can do that, you can do anything," she says, leaning forward and taking my hand. "Including going home and facing your guys."

"Are you kicking me out?" I ask, laughing softly.

"I would never. But I do think that you've gotten everything you came here for. Now, you're just hiding. And as much as Caleb is going to pout when you leave, I think you need to. Facing your Demons is the only way to exorcise them." She smiles sadly at me but I nod. I know she's right. Just like in my life as Amantara, the Shadow Realm is my safe place. My home away from home. With the family who are the family I chose. That chose me. The best kind.

I just have to remember I have that on Earth now too. No matter how scared I am to face them.

"You're right. I know you are. It doesn't make it any easier though."

"I know. And if you need to come back, we will always be here for you. Hell, Caleb might follow you back at some point to make sure you're doing okay. The only time I've seen him as freaked out as he was that night, was when Mireya was born. If it didn't hurt so much, I'd have spent the entire time laughing at him."

"You know you guys can come to see me whenever,

right?"

"We know. And I'm sure we will, it's harder for us all to go with Mireya, but I'm sure you'll see one of all of us at random points. Just remember, you are loved. And what happened, none of it is your fault. We all carry guilt with us for something, but this, all of this, is not your fault. Levi will see that and understand. And if he doesn't, considering the power inside of you now, and the things you've worked out with the guys the last few days, you could probably kick his ass anyway." She laughs and I can't help but join her. I'm still terrified, but she's right, I have to go and face them. Face him. Tell him the truth.

"Probably. I know I need to go back. I will. Probably tonight, because I can only steal your clothes for so long before I miss my snarky t-shirts. Plus, I miss them."

"Exactly. You can do this. It's the middle of the day back there, so it's the perfect time. You've barely been gone as far as they're concerned. Also, Caleb wanted you to have the knives he got for you so long ago. I'll get them for you before we send you home."

I sigh, I know she's right.

"Okay, let's get this show on the road and send me home. To whatever fate may hold for me."

I step out of the portal to the Manor, and arrive to complete fucking chaos. I guess the Witch coven showed themselves. I duck as a fireball flies towards my head. My gaze sweeps the scene in front of me. My guys are scattered across the madness, Colt is here, so are Fallon and Marie. But that's about it for people on our side.

My rage blankets me. How fucking dare they attack my home! I pull my shadow fire to my hands, those few days training with the Horsemen, along with getting all of my memories back really did do me some good.

I unfurl my wings and shoot to the sky, since no one seems to have noticed my arrival yet. I use the shadows inside of me to create protective bubbles around my family, which draws people's attention to me, but I just smile and then unleash fucking hell down upon the people trying to hurt the ones I love.

The shadow fire releases from me, and the screams it causes make my blood sing. I unsheathe the blades from my thighs, silently thanking Caleb for regifting them to me, and cut through the Witches still trying to attack me. As I swoop down and draw blood, portals start popping open, but I call to that darkness inside of me, and block those portals.

No one will escape my wrath this time.

The screams get louder as I hold my family captive and wipe away the filth that dares to threaten what is mine. I have had enough of being targeted. I release one portal, to allow a message to get back to Lizzie and whoever she's working with. I will not be fucked with, and it's going to take one hell of a force to stop me now.

When I dispose of the last Witch, I release my family who all just stare at me like they've never seen me before. I feel the blood drying on my face and hands, and put my wings away so I can focus on the here and now.

"Holy. Fucking. Shit. Remy, you're kinda of terrifying, you know that?" Colt says, his eyes wide, and his voice full of awe. I shrug at him, and stand there, feeling awkward and exposed, waiting for someone else to say something.

"You're back," Creek says softly, his gaze running over me as if to check that I'm okay.

"Where did you go?" Kain asks, moving towards me.

"Why the fuck did you leave?" Roman growls.

"And, on this note, we're going to leave," Fallon says, moving towards my brother.

"But…" Colt starts, and Fallon glares at him as she reaches his side.

"Call me and we'll catch up later," Fallon says, tugging on Colt's sleeve to make him leave with her and Marie. He grumbles an objection as they start to walk away, but honestly, I think he'd go anywhere for her.

"I will," I respond to her, before turning back to my guys, the adrenaline starting to leave my system, replaced by those butterflies creating a tornado in my stomach. My guys are all standing there staring at me.

The anger and confusion, mixed with a little awe is bad enough, but the sadness, the disappointment, that's what guts me.

"I know I shouldn't have run, and when I tell you what happened, you'll understand why I had no choice. I'm sorry. I didn't mean to worry you, but I couldn't stay here," I say as I wring my hands out. "I promise I will explain, but can I shower first? And then we'll talk."

Creek smiles at me softly before moving towards me. "You can always speak to me, Remy. But I get it. Sometimes, the people closest to you are the last ones you want to see you at your worst. I'm not angry, I know you wouldn't have left if you didn't have to. Even if that note could have given a little more detail. I'm glad you're back and that you're okay. Talk to me when you're ready beautiful."

He kisses my cheek and then stuffs his hands in his pockets and moves towards the Manor.

"What he said," Kain says, tipping the corners of his mouth upward. "Though, I'm going to start on clean up out here. Come find me when you're ready."

I look to the other two. The two I knew would be the most pissed off, though Levi has no idea how much more pissed off he's going to be, and it guts me just thinking about it.

Levi softens first as I feel my eyes start to well up. “Go and shower, angel.”

He moves behind me to help Kain dispose of the massacre in the back yard, while Roman just stands there watching me with his arms crossed.

“You can’t run like that. Not again. Do you have any idea what it was like to wake up and find you gone? With no idea where you were, even if we suspected?”

“It was selfish, I know. I’m sorry.”

“Don’t be sorry, Remy. Just don’t do it again. No matter what it is. We are the ones you run to. Not the ones you run from.” He finishes speaking and stalks over to where Levi and Kain are, to help them.

I bow my head and go inside to my room to shower and try to work out the right words to explain.

FIFTEEN

I stand under the scalding water, which has finally stopped running pink and brown, wishing for the right words to pop into my head, but I know this conversation isn't going to be that easy. There isn't a magic thing I can say that will make this easy. That will make it not hurt.

I climb from the shower and wrap the towels around myself, dragging out every movement, trying to delay the inevitable. But when I open the door and find Levi sitting on my bed, I know my time is up. I open my mouth to speak, but close it and head to the closet. I'm going to at least need clothes for this conversation. I'd prefer a suit of armor and a shot or six of whiskey, but at the very least I need pants.

I dress reasonably quickly, because I know he's not

going to give me much more time, all things considered. Except, he doesn't know anything yet, and I almost want to delay that so I don't have to tell him everything.

I pull on some thick, fuzzy socks, because they make me feel so comforted, and pull on a big knit cardigan, wrapping it around myself before heading back out to my room to face him.

"Levi…" I start as I walk back into the room, but my mouth dries up. He's in jeans and a black t-shirt, freshly showered himself. I didn't pay much attention when I ran into my closet. How the fuck am I meant to even start this conversation?

"Let's start with where you went. I'm assuming from your entrance, and your… show, that you went to Morgan?" I nod as I sit in the almost never used chair in the corner of the room.

"I couldn't face you guys," I say quietly as I stare into my lap.

"What happened?" he asks patiently. There's shuffling as he comes to stand before me. His feet appear in my line of sight first, until he squats down and lifts my chin with his finger.

"I remembered… the thing that I had blocked. And..." My voice catches as the memory washes over me again, and guilt consumes me.

Fuck.

I have no idea how to tell him.

He stands and leans forward, scooping me up into his arms, and then moves us to the bed, so I'm cradled against him. I don't deserve this comfort, but I stay where I am, too selfish to move.

A tear spills down my cheek as I open my mouth to speak. "I was pregnant. So, very, very long ago. There was a night, when we were here, during the war, and Nevin and I went to scout out the higher Demon's camp. I was stupid and careless. I lost him. Our baby. It's all my fault."

He holds me tight, even as I rush the words out between sobs, and I feel his shoulders shake as he buries his face in my neck.

"We were going to have a son?" he asks, his voice hoarse, and I nod. His grief is painted all over his face. I'm not sure he even knows that he's crying as he holds me against him.

"We were discovered, and we were trying to escape."

"I remember," he says with a shudder. "You took a spear to the stomach. Nevin said you saved his life. It was laced with venom, that he wouldn't have survived, but he's not a Shadow Walker."

"I didn't know that, but yes. The spear took our son's life instead. I was foolish. Reckless. I should never have even gone." The words are like ash on my tongue, and my stomach rolls as guilt threatens to overwhelm me once again.

"It wasn't your fault Remy. I wish you would have told me. We could have mourned him together. I remember you were a mess for weeks, but we put it down to the effects of the poison. I am so sorry you went through that, through all of this, alone."

"You're not mad?" I ask, shocked.

"Of course I'm not mad. I'm fucking devastated, but I'm not mad. At least, not at what you think. I'm mad you didn't tell me, and that you ran, but it's not your fault it happened, Remy." I cry even harder at his words, I didn't realize how much I needed to hear them from him. He holds me and we cry together, mourning the loss neither of us got the chance to know about before now.

I don't know how long we sit there, but he holds me until the tears stop and lays us down with him holding me from behind. I feel a small semblance of peace having told him, but despite his words, the guilt still lays heavily on me.

He strokes my hair as we lay in silence, and I slowly let the world slip away.

I wake up in the same position I fell asleep in. Fully clothed and wrapped in Levi's arms. I feel at peace for a second before I remember everything. The guilt washes over me again until Levi's arms tighten around me, his silent comfort and support mean more than I can put into words.

"Morning, angel," he says, his voice thick with sleep. I turn in his arms, and put my hand on his cheek as I look into his eyes, searching for any hidden resentment. Nothing but love shines out of those stormy eyes as he meets my gaze.

"Hi," I say quietly, as I stroke his cheek with my thumb.

"We should probably get up. Roman is never going to let you out of his sight again," he chuckles, but his eyes still hold a haunting of sadness. Which is to be expected considering what I told him.

"I suppose." I sigh.

"They won't think any differently of you either you know," he says before kissing me softly.

"Maybe," I utter, and he rests his forehead against mine. He might be right, but he could definitely be wrong too. I'm still not completely convinced he's not just holding it together because I ran, and he doesn't want me to do that again.

"Stop it. I can see your mind whirring," he says with a small smile which I match. He always did know me, better than I know myself sometimes.

"I suppose we should get moving then."

"Indeed. At least now Nonnie can stop attacking us with that wooden spoon of hers. She's lethal with that thing." He chuckles softly, the shaking of his shoulders moving me with him. He kisses me again, this time I feel every piece of him with it. His sadness, his hunger, but mostly, his unconditional love. He steals my breath away, and a little piece of my heart heals with his kiss.

He pulls back and rolls us off of the bed to standing before letting me go. I sway for a second at the loss of his touch, but catch myself. "I'm going to go change. I'll see you in a few?"

"I'll be there. Time to face the others."

"I can tell them, if you'd like?" he offers, but I shake my head.

"Thank you, but I think it needs to come from me. They need to know where my head was at. That I'm sorry. Plus, you were right, there's no way Roman is going to let me off the hook even if the others would accept the story from you. His wolf won't believe I'm really okay and here unless I tell him myself." I sigh at the thought of saying it all out loud again, but the hurt doesn't cut me so deep now that I've told Levi. I guess I really did need to do that.

"Okay, well I'll see you in a few minutes." He smirks at me before swatting my ass as he leaves the room.

Bloody Angels.

I strip out of my clothes and jump in a super quick shower, before arming myself with a nice pair of jeans and another snarky top, courtesy of Everly. This one says *more issues than vogue* and it feels fitting for today. I grab another pair of fluffy socks, because they feel like another layer of armor against the crushing waves of guilt I know are coming, and head down to the kitchen.

Creek is leaving his room as I pass, and he walks with me in only a slightly awkward silence - despite his smile and the fact that he takes my hand - to the kitchen where we find the others already sat at the table. Levi and Roman with a mug of coffee each, Nonnie and Kain with a mug of blood, while she cooks whatever it is she's making today.

"Remy girl! There you are! You sit down, I'll get you coffee and sort you food. These broody boys have been driving me round the bend! You sit, I'll look after you!" Nonnie fusses and ushers me into a chair while Creek chuckles as he heads to the coffee pot.

"Thank you, Nonnie. You really don't have to though. You should sit and enjoy your own breakfast."

"Oh hush. Let me, it makes me happy to do it." She waves me off and heads to the stove, and Creek sits beside me, handing me a giant mug of coffee. I take a sip and sigh. It still isn't Angel coffee, but man I love it.

I feel them watching me. I look up to Levi first, because he already knows and he just smiles at me, supporting me, but not rushing me. I already know Kain and Creek will wait if I asked, but Roman is bull headed, and I also don't want to drag this out any more than I have to. I don't want to have to keep reliving it.

"So… I suppose I should start talking," I say quietly. No one else says a thing, but Nonnie drops a plate in front of me, grabs her mug of blood and leaves the room. Fates bless that woman for being so kind to me.

"You don't have to if you're not ready," Kain offers, and Creek nods agreeing, while Roman remains a statue. I know he won't push if I tell him I really need the space, but I also know that he's pissed that I ran. I get it, I'd be pissed if I was him. Taking a deep breath, I clutch my mug in front of me, almost as an extra shield between me and them, and start to tell them everything I told Levi last night.

It hurts to say it all again, but I know this will be the last time I *have* to speak of it. Fallon and Colt won't push. They know me well enough. I cry again as I relive it, speaking the words aloud. Creek and Kain take one of my hands each in theirs and just hold me as I tell them how I remembered, and why I ran.

When I finish speaking, the room is silent. Roman stands up and walks away without a word, and my heart breaks all over again. I knew someone wouldn't understand. That someone would blame me. I try to speak past the lump in my throat but it chokes me and steals all of my words.

"He will calm. He's likely just upset on your behalf, mon amour. Give him time and he will come to you." Kain tries to soothe me, but all I can see is Levi practically shaking with anger.

"Levi…" I start, but he shakes his head and storms from the table following Roman.

"Well, that's going to end well." Creek sighs before looking back to me. "Remy, they are not your problem. How they or we feel about things is no reflection on what happened to you. That being said, I'm more just sad that you couldn't talk to us about what happened without leaving, but I also totally understand it. It took me a good while before I was able to face my parents after we came home from the Shadow Realm. It's wildly different, but fundamentally a similar thing. What happened to you was not your fault. You were not reckless, you were not careless, and you didn't kill your child. What happened was the fault of whoever threw that spear. Even then, if it had hit you anywhere else, it would likely have been a different outcome, but if it had been, well, maybe you wouldn't be here today, living with us as you are. Everything happens for a reason."

"I second that," Kain agrees. "I wish you had come to me, to us, but I understand the trauma and the toll it must have taken on you. There are few losses like the loss of a child. Add that onto everything else you had going on inside your mind, and all of the things we're still fighting for. It is understandable that you wanted to escape, but you can tell me anything, precious. Anything. I will never judge you for any of it."

"Thank you," I croak, trying to stop myself from crying again. Morgan was right, of course they'd understand, but the guilt still coats my stomach and makes me want to throw up. Though I don't expect that to leave anytime soon, I know that with my guys at my side, I can deal with pretty much anything.

"I should go find Roman," I say as I stand.

"I'd maybe give him and Levi time to work out their differences first," Kain says with a small chuckle.

"No, they shouldn't be fighting over this," I sigh.

"Remy, sometimes guys just need to fight to get it out of their system. It's good for us to take a hit every now and then, keeps us in line and on our toes," Creek jokes. "But in all seriousness, they obviously have their own shit to deal with, you don't need to carry that too. Roman will come to you when he's calmed down. He's probably more pissed off at what happened to you than at you, he just doesn't know where to point that anger."

I sit back down and rest my chin on my hands with a sigh. Creek's theory is definitely plausible, Roman and his wolf hate it when anything happens to me, and he probably deals with me crying the worst out of all of them.

I take a breath take a bite of the food Nonnie made for me. It's cold, but I know I need to eat, so I swallow down the omelet and wait, hoping that the guys are right, and that Roman isn't about to up and leave on me.

After breakfast I decided to try and forget everything by running. Which is how I find myself bent in half, panting, after pushing myself until I felt like I was going to throw up after running laps of the property.

Roman and Levi still haven't emerged from the house, and I have no intention of getting in their way. Kain and Creek are right. Guys just need to fight it out sometimes. I wish girls were that simple.

I dropped Fallon a text earlier to let her know that I'm alive, and sent one to Colt of a similar fashion. I gave them both a much briefer explanation, and it was much easier to do via text. I pull my phone from my arm cuff and see that I've been out here nearly two hours. I respond to both Fallon and my brother, and head inside where I find Roman, sitting on his own in the lounge room, seemingly waiting for me.

I pause after I close the doors and wait to see if he's going to say anything. The tension in the air is so thick, you could cut it with a knife. "Roman…"

He doesn't even look up at me, so I head to my room to shower because I'm not going to argue with him. If he's still angry, I'm going to give him space until he's ready. I'm at the door to my room when the sound of heavy footsteps coming down the hall reach me, so I sit on my bed and wait.

"You shouldn't have run from us," he growls as he slams the door closed behind him. I stave off the flinch that threatens at the crash of the door closing, and wait in silence as he paces the floor in front of us. "You said you wouldn't leave again, and then you left."

"I'm sorry," I offer, but I'm not sure he even hears it.

"You should have come to me. To any of us. Running is never the answer. Running can get you fucking killed. Do you have any idea the stress, and the worry that you put us through… The not knowing where you were and if you were okay. There were tears on the fucking note Remy. We knew you weren't okay." He continues to rant as he paces, and a fresh wave of guilt hits me for leaving.

"I never meant for you guys to hurt, I just needed to escape. Escape myself, and the pain. The overwhelming guilt. And so much shame. Do you have any idea how much it hurt to fall asleep and that was what I remembered? To be hit with all of it as if it was happening to me right fucking then? I get that you don't like that I left, and you are entitled to feel how you feel. But goddammit, Roman. Do you get that I couldn't come to you? To any of you! Because my pain was so extreme, the guilt, the shame, that all I could think of was the child I lost, and how I wouldn't survive losing any of you too," I pant as I shout at him. Anger over-riding everything. He just stares at me, still as a statue, wide eyed.

"I fucking hurt. Every inch of me. And I didn't want you to see that," I say. "I needed to escape who I am as much as anything. You obviously stopped listening during my explanation earlier, otherwise you'd know that. The very many different versions of myself in my head, all of the crazy that came with it, and I was just about coping. But this, this pushed me over the edge, and I knew I had to get away and speak to someone who doesn't care who I am, or what I've done. Doesn't care who I've become."

He stalks towards me, grabbing me by the throat and waist, and kisses me until I'm breathless. I melt at his touch as he overwhelms every one of my senses, until there's nothing left in my head but him. He fists my hair and walks me backwards until we fall onto the bed and he cages me with himself.

"You won't run again. You've worked your shit out, but, Remy, you need to talk to us when shit is going on in your head rather than stuffing it down and breaking like this. All of this doesn't work if you don't let us in. I know you're not the girl I met so very long ago, but I still love you. Who you were then, and the bad ass bitch you've grown into. Your heart is the same as it was then, and that is what fucking matters. You do not run." His growl sends tingles straight to my core as his hand tightens in my hair, keeping my eyes on his.

"I have no intention of running again," I tell him as I squirm beneath him.

"Good."

SIXTEEN

It's been a week since I got back from the Shadow Realm, and we seem to have found a relative peace. Even if it still feels like Roman watches me like prey. We've finally settled into a new sort of normal. One where people don't walk on eggshells around me. Where we know that someone, somewhere, still pretty much wants me dead, but we don't want it to take over our lives.

We now have such a big network of people, that its almost easy to feel safe. We know we've fucked with whoever it is that's coming against us, or at least, their numbers. So the threat, in theory, should be reduced, I'm looking forward to a new normal where whoever it is that hates me this much, isn't fucking with us.

I'm still pretty sure this isn't all about me. I'm still

convinced this has more to do with the factions and hierarchy. With someone wanting a bigger piece of the pie than they have and that I just threaten that somehow, but everyone else seems convinced someone is out to get me. Considering the attempts on my life in the last year, I shouldn't be so remiss to throw their suspicions out, but I also don't want someone else's crazy to rule my life.

So in between Roman jetting off to the compound for two days, and calling me pretty consistently, and Kain still looking into leads for Amelia, things have been reasonably relaxed. Creek and Colt have been training with me since I levelled up with all of my memories, kicking their asses has been beyond fun. Fallon came and reset the wards around the manor, we did facials and pedicures after.

So all in all, pretty mundane. Which is why I'm so excited that today is Christmas Eve. I've spent the entire morning wrapping the presents I bought. I left the guys putting up the ridiculous tree I bought first thing, under the strict instructions to put the lights on before the baubles. Hearing them bicker about what goes where has been brilliant, and I totally snapped some ninja photos for the scrap book I got the other week too. Our first Christmas.

Nonnie has been in the kitchen prepping all day, I haven't dared even go to that side of the house, and I'm not alone in that either. After Creek got chased out earlier by Nonnie with her wooden spoon, everyone has just steered clear. Though, I'm not going to lie, watching a grown ass, half-Demon, man run from an old Dracul is definitely going to be a Christmas highlight that I'll never forget.

I stash away the last of the wrapped presents and head back to the sitting room to see how badly they've massacred my tree.

"Wow," I gasp as I enter the room. "You guys did this? Alone?"

I blink, fixed on the spot, taking in the fight before me. It's freaking beautiful. The warm twinkle lights on the tree, with the white decorations. The garland across the fireplace also has twinkle lights and is sprayed with fake snow.

"Do you like it?" Kain asks, smiling brightly at me.

"It's amazing." I notice the gifts already under the tree, and my grin widens. Creek walks towards me and envelopes me in a hug.

"I knew you would." His voice is so low as he embraces me, I'm sure the others don't hear it, but it gives me goosebumps. The thought of spending our first Christmas together makes me giddy, especially after the shit show that was thanksgiving. The smells coming from the kitchen alone make my mouth water. I get the feeling that Nonnie isn't letting me have my vision of pizza, instead, it's a European Christmas for us. Which considering Kain, I'm not too bothered about. I've spent Christmas' all over the world, the Europeans definitely eat like they're my people.

I tug on Creek's hand and get him to help me bring the gifts from my closet to put them under the tree. I might have gone a little overboard, but it turns out I like shopping when it's not for me. We all curl up on the sofa, and I put on the best Christmas movie ever.

Die Hard. Because it's not Christmas until Hans Gruber falls from Nakatomi Tower.

Despite the moans from Levi, he lets me snuggle into his side, and with my feet in Creek's lap we relax properly for the first time in forever, only occasionally laughing at Nonnie's cursing in the kitchen.

The doorbell rings halfway through the film, and Kain excuses himself to answer it, despite my offer, which admittedly was only halfhearted because I am most definitely snug right now. The extra voice makes me sit up properly and Creek pauses the film as Kain returns with my brother in tow.

"Hey guys," he says with a wave to the room.

"Hey," I say as I get up and give him a hug. He's been awesome this last week, he's just treated me the same as ever, not bringing up what I told him about why I left last week. He's just been my big brother. "You're early."

"Yeah, sorry. They're forecasting snow though, so I thought it was probably best to head over a bit earlier than planned. I did text."

"I left my phone in my closet," I laugh, and he joins

me.

"Of course you did." He drops the sack in his hand to the floor and pulls out a gift, handing it to me.

"You remembered!" I gasp, and rush to the tree to get the similar box for him I had waiting.

"What did we miss?" Kain asks, confused while Creek shakes his head chuckling.

"I forgot you guys do this."

"Christmas Eve presents!" I exclaim, and hand Colt his gift. I rummage under the tree and get the guys their matching boxes and hand them out. This is one tradition I never want to lose. I open my gift from Colt and bark out a laugh when I see the contents.

"These are perfect!" I say pulling out the purple pajamas with dancing takeout coffee cups on them. I pull them out and find a packet of hot chocolate, some marshmallows, and a pack of Cheetos in there along with a book. Same as every year. It really is perfect.

I watch in glee as the guys open theirs and find their matching reindeer onesies that absolutely slayed me when I found them and knew I had to buy them. Colt has a Christmas elf one, because I knew he'd be here and it was too perfect not to. The only difference with their boxes are they each got a naughty coupon book I found in the lingerie store too. I wasn't going to get them, but Fallon threw them in my cart and it didn't bug me enough to take them out. C'est la vie and all that.

"We have to wear these?" Roman asks, just kind of blinking at me, even though the others all look almost as amused as I do.

"That's the tradition," Creek confirms for him, his eyes practically sparkling with laughter.

"I love it, thank you," Kain says, coming to kiss my cheek, still chuckling as he does. "I'll go and change now." Just the thought of my well put together, always in a suit guy in the reindeer onesie about does me in, I'm so childishly excited about the Christmas photo I'm going to make them take with me.

Colt heads out of the room with Creek to go and change, and I just change where I am once he's out of sight.

"You really want us to wear these?" Roman asks, and I smile.

"I really, really do," I grin.

He sighs, but Levi leads him from the room with a smile.

I head into the kitchen, and find Nonnie singing away as she preps more food than I think I've ever seen.

"Woah, Nonnie. You feeding the four thousand?" I joke, and she scoffs.

"Silly girl. You think this will be enough? I think not. This is nothing."

"How about you come and relax with us for the rest of

the night?"

"No, I enjoy doing all of this. It might seem silly, but seeing the joy in your eyes, in everyone's eyes, at the sight of all the food brings me the greatest happiness, my beautiful girl. I have as much fun doing this as you do torturing those boys." Her eyes light up. I guess she caught part of the unboxing.

"Okay, well if you want to come and rest with us, you are more than welcome. I'm looking forward to helping you tomorrow."

"There is no way on this planet I'm letting you in my kitchen, Remy girl. I want Christmas dinner on the table, not in the bin." She winks at me and I can't help but laugh.

"Fine, fine. My culinary skills are not the best. Can I at least make some hot chocolate for everyone?"

"You go on, I'll make it and bring it through."

"You, Nonnie, are a freaking treasure. And if anyone tries to say any different, I'll take their heads." I walk over to her and kiss her cheek softly. She waves me off, blushing a little, but I can see her smile as I leave and it warms my heart. She will never replace Everly, but her presence here makes this place feel more like home.

I wake up in a puppy pile, excited as a kid for Christmas and practically bound out of bed. I'm very aware that

Santa didn't drop the extra presents sat under the tree this morning, but that doesn't stop my eyes widening when I take in the sheer amount of gifts under the tree. I think my guys *might* have gone a tad overboard. It's like freaking winter wonderland in here.

I squeal as I bounce towards the kitchen, and find Nonnie already cooking.

"Nonnie! Merry Christmas!" I exclaim as I wrap her up in a hug.

"Joyeux Noël, Remy girl," she says as she squeezes me back. "You want breakfast before or after gifts?"

"Breakfast? You think I've got space for breakfast with this amazingness you've been preparing for the last day? Not a chance! I'm not taking up the space with breakfast! Pfft." I grin at her as I pour myself a mug of coffee, because even with my extra giddiness, coffee is still necessary. It's always necessary. As shown by my Christmas pj's from Colt, obviously.

I finish my coffee, watching Nonnie fuss around the kitchen, humming Christmas songs as she goes, trying to be patient for everyone to wake up. A knock on the door makes me jump and I rush to the door, because it's freezing outside and who the hell is here this early today?

Opening the door, I come face to face with Fallon, Marie, and Rebel. "Merry Christmas!"

I grin as she shouts their greetings and usher them

inside so I can shut the door against the chill. Behind Marie floats a bag of gifts and I chuckle to myself as she floats them into the lounge without even looking. "I didn't know you guys would be here this early!"

"Well, we weren't going to, but then we figured what is Christmas about if it's not about family. You're family, so here we are!" Fallon tells me as she hugs me.

"What she said," Marie says with a smile. "And I have a feeling more people are on the way. I hope you have enough space under the tree."

"Holy shit," Fallon exclaims from the sitting room. "Mama, there is definitely not enough space under the tree."

We join her and Rebel who are just gawking at the tree. "Yeah, the guys went a little overboard, I think."

"We certainly did not," Kain says sleepily as he appears in his reindeer onesie. I grin so hard as Fallon and her family try not to laugh. I can't wait for them to see the others.

"You got them to wear them?" Fallon snickers.

"Of course."

"There's coffee in the kitchen, but beware, it's mania in there," I tell them all, and take my spot in the corner on the sofa, as I wait, oh so very impatiently for the others to wake. Though after the Laveaus' loud arrival, I daresay it won't be long till everyone stumbles out here. Fallon reappears and brings with her two mugs of steaming goodness and hands me one. She sits beside me, snuggling against my shoulder and we just sit in silence, enjoying the sounds of laughter around the house.

Colt is the next to appear, he stayed in my room last night, and as promised, he's in his elf onesie, looking proud as hell as he struts into the room. "Merry Christmas, little bit."

He ruffles my hair before turning to Fallon. "Merry Christmas, Fal."

She looks over at me and takes another sip of her coffee, before smiling softly at him. Trying not to watch them too closely, I peer down at my coffee until he heads towards the kitchen, where by the sounds of it, the other three guys are now too. I sit and wait for them, because there's no way I'm giving up my primo spot, but it's not long before everyone files into the sitting room sipping coffee, or hot chocolate in Rebel's case, waking up properly before the unwrapping begins. I'm so excited to see their faces when they see what I got them, though they all made it very clear last night that they were happy about their coupons. Not that we've done much of anything since I got back, I'm back to being treated like a china doll. Before the end of the holidays I will make sure to see an end to it, but for now, I'll leave it and enjoy the day I have.

Levi takes charge and starts handing out gifts. I'm

glad I put my ones for Fallon and her family under the tree too, though they bought enough of their own that no one appears left out. Even Colt has a decent pile in front of him.

I, however, feel almost embarrassed at the amount of boxes left under the tree there are for me. Having four boyfriends is awesome, but it means a lot of unwrapping. Especially since it seems they thought gift buying was something of a competition. I don't even really know where to begin.

It takes a while, but we get through a decent amount, and I decide to finish opening the rest of mine tomorrow, when it's just the five of us, because it's obscene the amount of gifts I have. Not that I don't love every single thing I open. From the new set of throwing knives, to the coloring books. Each and every single thing is amazing, and I love them. It just really is a bit much.

Fallon helps me stash my opened gifts in my room, and I go to get dressed, ready for the day, when Fallon hands me another black gift bag. "What is this?"

"This, is something I knew you'd love and I had to get it for you, but I didn't want you to cry if you did in front of everyone on Christmas morning." I eye her warily, half worried, but mostly anxious about what's in the bag. "That makes it sound way bigger than it was, just open it and you'll see."

She rolls her eyes as I tentatively open the bag, and pull out a colorful sweater that reads *this is my ugly Christmas sweater* and I laugh so hard.

"I know this was like a you and Everly thing, but I saw it and I knew you'd love it." She shrugs and I hug her.

"I do love it, it's perfect, thank you." I pull the hideous green sweater over my head and she huffs.

"How is it you still look good even in that thing?"

"It's a gift." I wink at her, before linking my arm with hers and heading back to the others for what is shaping up to be one of the best Christmases ever.

SEVENTEEN

Christmas was a beautiful escape from the real world, but today, everyone's back at their own places, we still have enough leftovers to see us through a month and I'm so bloated still, that yoga pants are the only type of pants I'm going to be wearing.

It's also my second small Christmas today. Astrid and Olivia are coming over for a while, and I'm both terrified and excited. It's been a while since we saw them. I meant it when I said I wanted Astrid to get a real childhood, and around our madness, that just isn't going to happen. I never meant to not see them for so long, but yet again, life got in the way.

Nonnie offered to make us a much smaller dinner for today, and considering my severe lack of culinary skills, I accepted with thanks. I set up the small tree in the kitchen and popped their gifts under there, since we still haven't cleared the madness in the sitting room and I still have to go through and finish opening all my gifts. The guys seem okay with me spreading them out, as long as I open the same amount from each of them at the same time.

"You doing okay in here?" Creek asks when he finds me in the library, pouring over my old journals.

"I'm good, I just wanted to do something productive this morning that would distract me from the bloated feeling."

"Not hiding from your anxiety of seeing Astrid and Olivia?" he asks, eyebrows raised. He knows me too damn well.

"Something like that," I sigh, and open another journal.

"What are you looking for?" He settles in beside me.

"Something about Amelia. We still don't know enough about her, and I've been wracking my brains about issues between us, but even though I have all of my memories, I'm not all knowing. There's stuff I've naturally forgotten. So, I was hoping there might be something in here to help jog my memory."

"Any luck yet?"

"Nothing. I haven't even found her name mentioned. It's as if she didn't exist to me, but I know we had interaction. It's so fucking strange." I groan and drop my head onto the table.

"You think someone could have messed with your journals?" he asks, examining one of them.

"I doubt it. These were hidden in Avalon. Levi had my place pretty locked up, but nothing is impossible. Still, I don't see why anyone would do that. Amantara… I mean, I was dead. No one could've known I'd get my memories of that life back."

"It's still weird that you talk about that life as if it's a different person," he chuckles. "But, if whoever it is has a seer like people have speculated, it's entirely possible they'd know."

"Amantara feels like a different person. It's hard to explain." I shake my head. "But yeah, I guess you're right about the seer thing. Just seems like a lot of trouble to go to."

"You don't think Amelia is the one behind everything, do you?" He looks at me closely and I shake my head, confirming his suspicion.

"I don't. It seems too neat. Too tidy. Too… easy. Plus, as hard as I think back, I can't think of one thing that I could've done to inspire such hate from her. She wasn't quiet, but she wasn't exactly in your face either. I get why people would suspect her, but my gut tells me we're looking in the wrong direction."

"Any ideas who it might be in that gut of yours?" He

smirks as he speaks and I roll my eyes. He puts his hands up in surrender and chuckles. "Hey, your gut has saved our lives more than once, I trust you, and you trust it."

"Hmmmm." I narrow my eyes as I look at him, but he's only teasing me a little. "I honestly don't have a clue. I can't think of anything I've ever done that would cause someone to do something of this scale."

"Maybe it really isn't about you," Creek offers. "It could just be that you stand in the way of something. I mean, with Archer, his shit was definitely about you. It was about a power play. Maybe that's what this is on a greater scale. God knows he was getting instructions from somewhere."

"Maybe…" I muse.

"You realize that Olivia and Astrid are meant to arrive in the next thirty minutes, right?"

"What?" I screech. Time has not bent me over like that. I glance at the clock and curse again.

"Fuck, shit." I scramble to my feet, trying to close the journals as quickly as I can.

"You go get ready, I'll put these away and put the locked chest back for you," he offers. I clasp his cheeks in my hands and kiss him.

"You are the best. I love you. Thank you!" I rush from the library to my room to get myself ready. Thirty fucking minutes. Shit.

At least my distraction worked I guess.

I take the quickest shower known to man, and dress quickly, but try to look as presentable as I can. Why the fuck do I feel so nervous? I take off the blouse I put on, because I feel awkward and sweaty in it, and go with one of my last t-shirts from Everly which says *I'm only sarcastic when I speak.*

I wipe my sweaty palms on my pants before opening the door and paint a wide smile, that I hope doesn't look as nervous as I feel, on my face. "Hey you guys! Merry Christmas!"

"Merry Christmas!" they shout back at me. Astrid darts in and hugs me tightly.

"She's feeling extra huggy today," Olivia says with an apologetic smile, but I wave her off.

"Hey, that's what Christmas is all about, right?"

"Right." She smiles and I wave her in as Astrid stays attached to my side.

"I'm glad to see you're both all healed up and doing well. I'm sorry I haven't seen you much since you were in the hospital," I apologize, and lead them towards the kitchen as they strip out of their coats. Astrid runs over to the Christmas tree I set up and coos over it while I pop their coats away.

When I get back to the kitchen, I find both of them with Nonnie, a mug of hot chocolate each, while Astrid talks a million miles a minute explaining what Santa brought her already. Oh the joy of kids at Christmas.

My heart pangs, a brief memory of Christmas with a child of my own hits me and disappears almost as quick. I shake it off and bring myself back to the here and now, to celebrate with the family I have now.

"I see you found the tree," I say as I reach them.

"We did! Santa must have come here for us too, because I saw my name!" Astrid exclaims excitedly.

"You did, huh? Wow, you must be really grown up to know your name!" I say, crouching down to her level.

"I turned five."

"Five? Wow, that's really grown up. I guess if you're really grown up, that means you can wait until after dinner for your presents," I tease.

"No, silly!" she says, pushing me with her tiny hands. "Presents are for before dinner!"

My heart clenches at the giant smile on her tiny little face. She's so freaking adorable it almost hurts.

"Okay, well if you say so. You better check with your mom that it's okay."

"Mom! Please! Is it okay for presents before dinner? Even though I'm a grown up? Please."

"Well, since you said please, I don't see why not,"

Olivia says, laughing softly, before looking up at me. "Are the others joining us?"

"They thought we might want to do presents alone, but they'll be by for dinner."

"Oh, no, don't hide them away on our account. Astrid has been looking forward to seeing the big wolf and the Angel." She winks at me and I can't help but laugh.

"If you're sure."

"Yes please! I want to play with the wolf!" Astrid squeals as she spins on the spot, so I pull my phone from my pocket and text them all, because I genuinely have no idea where they've all disappeared to.

"Okay, well I'm sure they'll be here soon. How about you finish telling Nonnie and I what Santa already brought you?" I say as I sit at the table, and Nonnie hands me my own hot chocolate before sitting down with us to listen to the sweet girl's tales.

It doesn't take long for the guys to find us, and to finish our hot chocolate. While they keep Astrid and Olivia busy, as Astrid regales them with her stories too, I grab a box from the tree and head over to Nonnie who is back cooking away.

"Nonnie," I whisper. She looks up from her pan and smiles at me, until she sees the box in my outstretched hand. "Merry Christmas!"

"Oh, Remy. I told you no gifts!"

"I know you did, so I didn't give it to you yesterday, but there was no way I wasn't getting you something." I smile at her, and she almost looks like she's going to cry.

"Silly girl. I will open it later," she says, dabbing at her eyes.

"Okay, Nonnie. I just want to say thank you, for everything." I give her a quick hug before she waves me off and I head back to the others, where Astrid somehow has my guys in Santa hats and they're handing out presents. I sit back down in my chair and watch as they melt around that little girl, and almost get wistful. It's not like we can have children, at least, most of us, and it doesn't seem fair to just have a child with one of them. Plus, other than the exception as a human, I never really saw myself as a mother. But watching them with her warms a part of my heart I didn't think would ever see light again.

"Remy! Here's one for you from me." Astrid skips over to me and hands me a gift bag.

"Wow, thank you, honey!" I smile down at her while she stands there, beaming up at me. I open the box, and my smile grows. "I freaking love it! Thank you so much!"

I pull the black cat plush toy from the bag and hug it tight.

"Since Sushi lives with us now, I wanted to make sure you didn't get lonely. Mom said we couldn't get you a different cat, but this one would be okay. I call him Sushi

Two."

"I love him, he's perfect. Just like you." I pull her in for a hug and she wraps her little arms around my neck and squeezes.

"More presents anyone?" Creek asks, and Astrid squirms in my arms.

"Me please!" She jumps down out of my hold and rushes back to the guys, and I sit back and watch as the afternoon unfolds, while Astrid wraps those four big strapping immortals around her little finger.

It isn't long before Nonnie announces it's time to wash up, and the guys lead Astrid and Olivia to a bathroom, while I help her set the table.

"You have a beautiful family, Remy," Nonnie says softly.

"Thank you, we're glad you're a part of it."

A knock on the back glass door sounds, startling me, and I look questioningly at Nonnie.

"Are we expecting anyone?" she asks, and I shake my head. The blinds are down, because we wanted the twinkle lights on, so I can't even see anything.

I open the door and gasp, tears springing to my eyes.

"Merry Christmas, sweetheart." Everly's voice wraps around me seconds before she pulls me into a hug.

"What? How is this possible?" I ask, holding her tightly.

"Keeping guests out in the cold, little bird. I thought you had better manners," Michael jokes.

"Don't you start, you leave her alone," Everly scolds him, and I can't help but laugh.

"Merry Christmas, Remy," Michael says softly. "I couldn't think of a better gift, though she sure does speak her mind."

"That's what makes her the best," I sigh. "Oh my fates! Astrid and Olivia. Come in!" I usher them in and close the door, while Everly eyes Nonnie in the kitchen.

"You, you are the one from the photos. The one who looked after my Remy girl, yes?" Nonnie asks, and Everly nods.

"Thank you. Thank you for keeping her safe and loving her," Nonnie says with a warm smile before turning back to me. "You see, it's a good thing I cook too much."

"Everly?" Levi looks stunned as he reenters the room. She rushes to him and hugs him tight.

"It is so good to see you!" she says before hugging him again.

"I guess this gift just keeps giving, huh?" Michael says quietly beside me.

"Oh you have no idea. Really, thank you," I tell him.

"Anything for you."

Tears fill my eyes as Olivia and Astrid enter the room and see her. A lump chokes me and Michael slips an arm around my shoulders as the emotions become overwhelming. Levi glares at him momentarily before seeing my tears and then softens.

The others join us again, the reunion taking every second until dinner is served. We eat too much, laugh, cry, and joke as we catch Everly up on everything, all while I try to ignore the looks my guys shoot at Michael. I know they won't ruin this day. Not this day. Not with Everly here. Bickering can wait. I want this day to stay as perfect as it's been so far.

I've never been more glad for my yoga pants than when Nonnie presents me with a giant cheesecake all to myself for dessert, and Everly laughs when I say about not being able to eat it all.

After the food is all done, and I feel like I'm going to have to be rolled from the table, Olivia takes Astrid to my room so she can have a nap, and I've never been more jealous of a five-year-old. The thought of a nap is so freaking appealing, but also, I don't know how long Everly gets to stay, so I don't want to miss a thing.

"Fancy a walk, Mom?" Olivia says when she returns, and Everly stands.

"I'd love to."

Olivia grabs her coat and they head out the back doors while I watch them wistfully.

"How long does she get to stay?" I ask Michael quietly,

and all other conversation seems to halt.

"Just for the day. She is not an Angel, just a soul in Avalon. I granted her the pass for the day, but I can't do more than that. You know the rules."

"Fuck the rules," Levi growls.

"The rules are there for a reason, and you know it Leviathan."

"Doesn't mean I agree with them," Levi counters, and crosses his arms.

"Please don't argue. Not today. At least not here. Let us have this one perfect day. That way, I got two, right next to each other, that I'll never forget," I sigh.

"Sorry," Levi apologizes, and Michael joins him.

"Thank you."

"Should we clear up and then move to the sitting room?" Kain suggests, standing and gathering plates. Michael grins and clicks his fingers. In a blink, the table is cleared, the mess is gone and I sit looking at him in wonder.

"I really need to learn that trick."

"Stick with me, kid," he winks, and Roman growls but I just roll my eyes and work out a way to pry that nifty little trick from him.

We head to the sitting room and Creek turns on the lamps and the twinkle lights, while Kain pours everyone a glass of wine. It seems so grown up, being here with all of them like this.

"This old woman is going to take a nap too, since there's no cleaning to do," Nonnie says as she refuses the drink from Kain. "I'll see you all later."

She wanders from the room, a chorus of goodbyes follow her, and then I'm left in the room with just my guys and Michael. To say the tension level rises when Michael sits beside me on the sofa is an understatement, but other than the odd glare from Roman and Levi, everyone keeps their promises of a good day.

We settle in on the couch, and Creek puts a Home Alone on the TV.

"What is this?" Roman asks, and Creek and I look at him wide eyed.

"You've never seen Home Alone?" Creek asks, almost horrified. Roman shakes his head, and when the others all admit they've never seen it either, we hunker down in silence and watch the film that Creek and I could probably recite by heart at this point, while we wait for Everly and Olivia to return.

The guys head outside with Michael after making some stupid bet that I wasn't really listening to, so I leave them to it and make a pot of coffee.

"I thought I'd find you in here," Everly says with a

smile. "Olivia is outside playing referee with those silly boys."

"Well, I'm glad someone can wrangle them. They only lasted a movie until they started with their bickering. I don't even know what it was about, I tuned them out." I laugh and pour us both a mug of coffee before we sit down.

"It is so good to see you, sweetheart," Everly says, squeezing my hand.

"You too," I say, my voice hoarse. "I am so sorry…"

"Remy, you have absolutely nothing to be sorry about, you hear me? My time was up, and I got to have a few months with you that I never thought I would get. Sometimes I wish I had more time, but I got today, which I never expected, and it is more than I could have dreamed for. What happened to me was not your fault," she tells me firmly. I open my mouth to respond but she shakes her head. "No, Remy. Absolutely not. I will not have you carrying this guilt on top of everything else you're carrying. Michael filled me in on a few things so I didn't put my foot in my mouth, and my heart aches for you my dear girl. You carry far more than you should, and this burden is not yours to carry."

She squeezes my hand again, and then wipes a tear from her eye.

"I wish I could be here to help you through all of this."

"Me too," I tell her, laughing a little through my tears.

"God knows those lot listened to you better than they ever do me."

"Well, they are very stubborn boys," she laughs.

We sit and talk, and I fill her in on the bits that Michael left out, and somehow telling her everything is like a weight being lifted from me, in a way it wasn't in saying it before. Maybe I'm accepting it more, or maybe it's because she became almost like a mother to me, which is crazily ironic, but still.

"Oh sweetheart. I am so sorry you've been going through all of this. But know, that if you ever need me, I will always have time for you in Avalon. Always, you hear?"

"Thank you," I tell her softly.

The back doors open and the guys swoop in with Olivia, bringing the cold in with them.

"We, should probably be heading back," Olivia announces. "I'm going to go and wake Astrid so she can say goodbye." She leaves the room, and Everly smiles sadly.

"It's probably time for us to go too," Michael says, and I hurt all over again. Everly starts saying goodbye to the guys while Michael pulls me to one side. "I have a lead on the Hunter's curse. I should get some answers in the next few days, so as soon as I know, I'll be back, okay?"

"Thank you for looking into this for me. I know you

have so much more going on."

"Anything for you, little bird."

"And thank you for bringing Everly today. It was exactly what I needed." I hug him tightly, because while he might suspect, he'll never truly know just how much I needed to see her today. I watch on quietly while Olivia and Astrid say goodbye to Everly one last time, trying not to lose the very thin hold I have on any sense of calm. Levi walks them out and Everly comes and hugs me one last time.

"I am always here for you, sweetheart. Always," she whispers before letting me go, and as her and Michael leave the manor, I don't try to stop the tears that fall down my face.

EIGHTEEN

It's officially the new year. We didn't do anything special, though you better believe I made them all stay up to watch the ball drop. Usually, I'd make resolutions around now, but this year, I'm not going to. We still have so much unresolved around us that it doesn't seem right to set even more expectations of the year. Fuck knows we've got enough to juggle for now.

It's been nearly a week since Michael and Everly left, and despite his promise for answers, I've not heard a thing from him. I'm very aware that I technically could go to Avalon, but I'm also aware that that isn't really a viable option considering what happened last time I was there. I'd really rather not get into an argument with the Archangel council and spark up with shadow fire.

Nope.

Not in any lifetime.

I've been feared and hated enough as it is, thank you very much.

That doesn't stop me sitting out here on the dewy ground, staring up the sky, like something out of a cliché movie, waiting not so patiently for Michael to make a fucking appearance. Really, I'm doing yoga, because even an Angel needs to stay supple and bendy, but still.

"How are you not frozen?" Creek's voice startles me, but I finish my stretch before sitting up properly to smile at him.

"I don't really feel it anymore," I tell him with a shrug. "Angel wins." He eyes me sitting on the ground in the yoga pants, sports bra, and thin jacket.

"Maybe you don't feel it, but it can't be great for you. Come inside and get some breakfast, I just made a fresh pot of coffee."

"Yay coffee." I jump to my feet and hug him. "Good morning."

His eyes smolder at me before he presses his lips against mine and steals my breath away. I feel every inch of him pressed against me and run my hands under the hem of his t-shirt, against the hard lines of him. He pulls back and leans his forehead against mine.

"Your fingers are fucking freezing," he says with a soft

laugh.

"I guess you had better warm me up then, hadn't you?" I tease, curling my fingers around the top of his jeans. He groans as he pulls my hands from the band of his boxers and holds them inside of his.

"Remy, you've been going through a lot, are you sure you're ready?" he asks, watching me closely. He's always been considerate, a gentleman to fault until I get under his skin enough.

"I'm not made of glass," I tell him, pulling back a little.

"I know that, Remy, but you also nearly died, found out one of the most traumatic things of your entire lifetime, and I don't want to rush you into anything." I take a deep breath at his words. He's not wrong, but I miss him. Damn him and his moral compass.

"Fine," I huff. "Let's just get some coffee." I follow him inside the house, trying not to feel rejected, even though his rebuttal stings a little, I know he means well. Doesn't stop my frustration being very real though.

We get inside and Nonnie is fluttering around the kitchen, humming as she moves. She waves her wooden spoon at Creek as he goes for the coffee pot, so he retreats, his hands in the air in surrender. He pulls a chair out and sits me in it, kissing the top of my head before sitting next to me.

The glass doors we just entered from opens and

Michael enters the room.

"What are you doing here?" Creek asks, his arms folding as he stands to face Michael.

"I came to speak to Remy," Michael answers him, practically dismissing him. I roll my eyes at the testosterone showdown going on in my kitchen, while Nonnie clicks her tongue behind us. I guess the whole, me staring at the sky cliché thing actually worked.

"Do you want to join us for breakfast?" I ask him as Creek lets out a sigh, but remains in the same position he was in.

"Thank you, I'd love to," Michael answers with a smile, and sits in the chair on my other side. Hopefully, Levi is asleep, because that move alone is going to be enough to piss him off. I can feel it. Nonnie clicks her tongue again but says nothing as she heads back to the stove, before bringing over three steaming cups of coffee.

I can't help but laugh as Michael winces when he takes a sip. I guess when you spend all your time drinking Angel coffee, you get a bit spoiled. "Thank you."

Nonnie blinks at him before giving a nod and heads back to where she's cooking. I guess even she isn't immune to the charms of Michael. I sip at my own, trying to enjoy the moment of peace, despite the awkward silence around me, because I know when the others get here, it's only going to get worse. They might have got on, just barely, the day after Christmas, but I have very little hope that that peace will be extended any further.

I already know Levi only held his tongue for me and because Everly was here.

I just hope we don't kill whatever allegiance we have with Avalon, because I'm pretty positive that whatever feelings Michael may have had for me once upon a time… isn't going to be enough if we need their help.

Nonnie brings over a plate for me, stacked with eggs, steak, and hash browns. I grin at her and she returns it. "Thank you, Nonnie!" I dig in, my hunger overriding any manners that might be expected of me. She returns with three more plates, and hands one each to the guys, and then sits at the opposite end of the table to me, as if not taking sides and staying away from the chaos. I don't blame her.

We eat in more awkward silence, but the food is so good that I can't find myself to care. That is until I hear footsteps padding towards us. Roman and Kain arrive together, talking quietly until Roman stills at the entryway, his eyes zeroing in on Michael at my side. A low growl escapes him and Kain sighs.

"Breakfast boys?" Nonnie asks, standing to clear her empty plate.

"Thank you, that would be amazing," Kain says softly before dragging Roman to the table. Roman drops into the seat beside Creek, still scowling at Michael, while Kain comes over and kisses me good morning before sitting down beside Michael.

Thank God one of them can at least put aside the macho dominance bullshit. Even if it is just for breakfast. I groan a little, because I can almost foretell how this day is going to go, and I don't want to deal with it.

It's not long before Nonnie drops a plate of steak and eggs in front of the two of them, then Levi rounds the doorway and stops just inside the room.

"Why are you here?" Levi asks, his voice cold and clipped.

"I came to speak to Remy," Michael answers, barely looking over to Levi. He looks relaxed, like he's just enjoying the food in front of him. If I thought he was that guy, I'd presume he was doing it to fuck with Levi.

"Then speak," Levi barks, crossing his arms in front of him. The room crackles with electricity, and Nonnie places another plate on the table for Levi before catching my eyes. I nod slightly, and she leaves the room. Bless her heart for making sure I was okay before she left. I don't blame her for leaving though. The tension in here sucks all of the air from the room.

"You asked me to look into something for you," Michael says turning to me. "Well, I finally got some answers."

"You got answers?" I ask after the wave of panic releases me.

"I did, I found out a few days ago, but I wanted to make sure the information I had was one hundred percent so that I wasn't giving you… I don't know… false hope I guess. I don't even know if what I found out is good news or not."

My heart rate picks up at his words, and I try to take a few deep breaths.

I jump when the front door slams open and one of Roman's Lycans crashes into the room. Everyone jumps to their feet, ready to go to battle.

"Emmett, what's going on?" Roman barks as his eyes glow.

"We found them," Emmett pants, as if he's ran for miles.

"Found who?" Roman asks.

"The traitors. We found the traitors."

I called Colt and told him to gather the elders. I didn't tell him why. I don't even know how I'm going to say the words out loud. There's so much going on, so much that we still need to work out, but this…

My stomach rolls just thinking about the consequences of the things I set in motion. I was so focused on making everyone equal, evening the playing field, that I didn't consider anything like this could happen.

I take a deep breath as I pace in the council chambers. It's been a long while since I was down here, and I don't know if it's a past life where I suffered claustrophobia, or if it's just my anxiety, but it doesn't feel like there's enough air down here.

No one else is here yet. After Michael gave me the news and Roman's visitor came crashing in like that, to say the manor was chaos is an understatement. Roman disappeared, and Kain went with him to try and keep a lid on his anger. Stopping world war three seemed like a good idea. Levi is back at the manor with Michael, with Creek playing referee there for me, that meant that this was something I had to face alone.

It feels right to do it this way anyway, considering that this all started with me. Now I know how the histories got things a little mixed up, it's going to take a lot of explaining to make everything make sense. Which will be fun, since it doesn't seem entirely real to me yet.

Colt comes through the door, and brings the others with him. He waited outside for everyone to arrive while I, essentially, hid. I made myself busy, dragging tables and chairs from the other rooms into the center of the chamber to make like a board table, but still. I was definitely hiding.

I work my way through a round of hellos before everyone takes their seats while I remain standing, more because the thought of sitting still at the minute makes me want to crawl out of my skin.

The room goes quiet and everyone turns to look at me, stopping me in my tracks.

"Okay…" I start, letting out a deep breath. "Thank you all for rushing here to meet with me, I know that it was, quite literally, the middle of the night where you were, but this is something we need to discuss face to face."

I pause, wracking my brain for how to even to start to explain this, but really, I just need to tell them and then explain. I run my hand down my face and face the elders again.

"The Hunter's curse is broken." The room is silent, people looking at me confused, but I realize, that on its own doesn't mean much because they don't know the whole story. Though Colt's face devastates me. I hate that I took this from them.

"Okay, let me start at the beginning," I say with a sigh, and then tell them the real history of the Hunters. How humans were only meant to be granted temporary Angelic gifts, to assist in the War of the Fallen. I tell them about the war from my own memory, and how without this, we would have lost.

"And then, I was dying, and so Leviathan, in his grief, transferred my essence into a human form, essentially, making me a Hunter. Except, what he didn't know at the time, that in doing so it would upset the balance of power.

Of nature itself. And so, the Hunters, any families who had been gifted previously, became cursed, to reincarnate each life. To be stuck in the cycles they were in, and for the curse to pass down generations. It is why there are different time periods between lives, because the loop has to almost reset. But someone's great-great-grandmother, is also their great-great-granddaughter… I swear that made more sense in my head. But essentially, the curse is why the Angels gave us the option of the true death, because they found a loophole, should anyone want it." I shake out my hands and take another deep breath, not wanting to stop, because I'm not ready for questions.

"The curse is the reason for the cycles we've all been living, and the link was cursed to my life. Except… I died, and I became immortal again. We were not sure whether or not the curse would be broken, because I was essentially still alive. We have looked into it extensively, with Michael, and confirmed that the curse is broken. So, the Hunter cycles will no longer continue. We do believe however, that as children have been born with the gifted Angelic powers, that the Hunter lines will continue in this manner."

It's as if the whole room has held its breath, and then, in the blink of an eye, chaos erupts. There are questions being shouted, some people are up and moving towards me. Others are still seated, dazed by the information I have given them.

I get it. All of it. The anger, the confusion, the sadness.

Their lives have just been irrevocably changed, and its completely my fault.

“Everyone shut the fuck up!” Colt yells across the room, and it’s like a switch is flipped. Suddenly there’s silence. “I get that this is a lot to process, but if you have questions, you’re not going to get answers by shouting over each other, so sit the fuck down, and let’s talk this out like civilized fucking people.”

I sit down once everyone else has pulled themselves back together. I knew this would cause pandemonium, but I completely understand. This doesn’t just affect them. They still need to pass this on to the people that they represent. That isn’t something I’d wish on anyone. Just telling the elders is enough to make me want to vomit.

I sit and wait while they talk amongst themselves, but it’s Nasari who turns to me first. “Is there any way to reverse it? Can the curse be reinstated?”

“Honestly, I have no idea, but it is definitely something we can find out before you tell anyone outside of the council. I understand that sitting on information like this is awful, but I think it would be better for me to get answers to any and all questions from you guys before we tell anyone else.”

There is a murmuring of agreement around the table

and I feel a little calmer. At least panic isn't going to spread across the entire faction just yet, but I make a note to ask Michael just as soon as I get a chance.

"Who else has questions?" I ask and a dozen hands rise into the air. I run my hand through my hair and let out a deep breath.

This is going to be a long meeting.

NINETEEN

It's been a week since that awful day facing the elders. I still have no extra information for them, we're waiting on Michael finding out the information from the people he has looking into all of this. Meanwhile, he's still hanging around the manor, which has made the last few days both tense as fuck, as well as slightly comforting.

There's a big part of me, now that I have my memories from my life as Amantara, that is very much used to having him around all the time. I mean, except for the war, I saw him almost daily from the time I came into my powers and my parents essentially abandoned me. In fact, if it wasn't for him, I probably never would have met Levi, and my life wouldn't be what it is.

There's just a very strange feeling around the whole

house.

However, Roman and Creek have been preparing the basement, because Tobias is due to arrive today with Theron and the traitor, Laurent. Aryna's second. I have very little idea how they discovered it was him, or how they confirmed it, but the information I got was that he was sedated and being brought here.

After that, the house was a flurry of activity. Roman's Lycans have been here with him, helping him reinforce whatever it is that Levi already had set up downstairs. No one is taking any chances it would seem.

I'm happy to have absolutely no part in it, so I've been hiding away in the library for the most part, still poring over my journals trying to find something that explains anything over my past lives that could have sparked all of this insanity. While I have all of my memories, that doesn't mean I just know everything. It's been good to help jog my memory, but beyond that, I've found nothing.

I sigh and drop my head onto the open journal in front of me and try not to despair. While I'm glad we found the Lycan traitor, I'm still not a fan of torture. Even if it is to get us information to stop whatever the fuck it is that's coming.

I take a deep breath and sit back up, closing the journals as I do.

This isn't getting me anywhere. I have too much

nervous energy to keep focusing like I am right now. I need to burn some of it off. I put the journals away and head to the pool. Fuck knows where the others are, but swimming off this restlessness sounds like a good fucking idea.

I duck into my room and change into a slightly revealing bandage one piece, that I'm almost positive someone other than Everly picked out, but it covers me enough, and I can't be fucked to keep searching for another suit. I have no fucking clue where the others are, but after checking the hall and seeing no one I strut to the pool in nothing but my one piece and close the door to the fitness suite behind me.

Pulling my hair up and into a braid using the hairbands around my wrist, I stretch out and then dive into the pool. The icy water washes over me, stealing my breath momentarily, but it doesn't take long for me to adjust as I slice through the water.

I have no idea how much time passes when a pair of hands grasp my waist and pull me from the water.

"So, this is where you've been hiding," Levi says, his voice so low it makes me shiver.

"I wasn't hiding, just burning off some energy. I got restless," I say as I wrap my arms around his neck. He lifts me up slightly, and my legs automatically close around his waist as his mouth comes down to mine and he bruises me with his kiss.

"I can think of better ways to deal with that." I feel the

rumble of his words on every inch of my body. He nips my chin, and I give him access to my neck, which he kisses, licks, and bites down to my collarbone, my core tightening with each touch.

"Hmm, I have no idea what you mean." I give him the sass he loves to hate all the while offering my exposed flesh to his undivided attention.

"You're lucky I tolerate you, angel, or else you'd be flying back into that pool."

As he speaks, his arms tighten around my waist and his mouth devours me a little more as though his body instinctively rejected his words.

"So back to burning off energy the old-fashioned way?" I squeeze my legs tighter around his waist, my feet crossing at the top of his ass, searching out more of his hardness against my needy core.

"The old-fashioned way, huh?"

He plunges us beneath the surface, and I squeal a little as we go under, the surprise of it all catches me completely off guard.

As soon as I can breathe again once we resurface, I'm sputtering and coughing through my nervous laughter, my eyes catching on a rare moment of Levi's lightheartedness. He's smiling, I love his smile, rare as it is, especially this smile. This smile is just for me. He's unbelievably handsome. All hard lines and soft words, when they are addressed to me at least. Levi is the responsible one. The planner, the thinker, the strategist. But when he smiles at me like this, it takes ten years off his tired eyes making him even sexier than ever.

Wrapping my arms as tight as possible around his neck, I brush my lips to his and whisper, "Are we going to keep talking semantics or are you going to fuck this restlessness from me?"

I see his eyes dart to the right then the left, as though trying to figure out which side of the pool is the closest for him to push me against.

"Your wish, angel, is about to become real and in high definition."

With my back against the tiled wall of the pool, I close my eyes as his mouth slams onto mine, his tongue possessing every inch of space beyond my lips, his grunts echoing off the walls. I'm about to wrap my legs around his waist again when I feel myself flying out of the water and set down on the cold concrete. The fabric covering my pussy is suddenly gone, split in two, never to be used again, pieces. I'm too shocked to protest, staring down at myself as though the idea of Levi going completely caveman on me is new.

It's not. This isn't my first rodeo when it comes to Levi's jealous and possessive side, the part of him that will never admit to any type of insecurity. Michael being here will be bringing out that side of him.

I know him, I know exactly what he needs to feel reassured.

Spreading my legs further apart, I make sure the message I want to send him is loud and clear.

I'm yours. All yours. My heart, my mind, my pussy. All yours.

When he looks away from my bare skin to focus on my eyes, we share an entire conversation in just a few, silent moments.

With a quick, mischievous grin, he plants both of his hands on my thighs and spreads me even wider.

The view of him licking his lips as he stares at my core sends a rush of heat through me, as his teeth bite onto his lower lip and his fingers dig into my flesh.

When the warmth of his tongue travels from one end of my slit to the other, I cry out. I actually sound like an animal in heat. It's raw and natural, just like his desire for me.

Our gazes meet and his eyes burn with want. Something so primal and unguarded that it takes my breath away. I'm already shaking with my need to come as the tip of his tongue circles my clit right before he sucks it into his mouth and flicks it again.

My cry catches in my throat and my arms give out from the intensity of his attention.

"Levi, oh, I…"

"Shhh, angel," is all he says, the vibrations from his words running over my sensitive skin, before he resumes his own form of perfect torture.

My hips seek him out, my legs trembling with the effort to stay open. My toes are curling so tightly I'm afraid I'll lose feeling in them.

And then it happens.

As he stands there, waist deep in the beautiful cerulean waters of the pool, the blue lighting intensifying the feeling of intimacy, he sinks his teeth into the swollen flesh of my clit and I fly far from any earthly location.

I can't hear anything, I can't see anything.

I can only feel.

I feel his warmth, his need, his desire and mostly his love for me.

I feel it all and I don't ever want to return back to Earth.

Blinking away the haze of my orgasm, I can only see blurry lines, a moving figure that is slowly coming into focus.

It's Levi. A beautiful, smirking, oh so very proud of himself, Levi.

"Welcome back, angel. How's your energy level going?" The cocky tone to his voice is enough to bring my sass back.

"Is that all you've got? Because I could still swim a

few laps."

I barely have time to finish my phrase when I'm hoisted back into the water, and slammed down, right onto his hard, awaiting cock.

I gasp at the feel of him, the thickness that is all him, that is invading and controlling me from within.

Fates, he feels so fucking good.

"Hold on, Remy, I'm about to show you how to burn off excess energy."

I'm not an idiot so I do the only thing I know I should do. I wrap my arms around his neck and let him take complete control of me as he fucks me against the side of the pool like a crazed animal. He's got one hand clutching my ass cheek and the other on my nape of my neck holding me in place as he pistons into me.

"Whose cock is fucking you, angel?" he grunts the words as though I could possibly forget.

"Yours," I answer anyway, because he needs to hear it.

"Who owns this fucking pussy, angel?"

"You," I moan.

I can feel the wet tiles sliding up and down my back with every powerful thrust inside me.

"Who do you belong to, angel?" he grunts, and I practically see stars from his voice alone.

"You." The word comes out raspy, because I can barely breathe, let alone speak.

I don't know how he can still talk. Every one of his tendons is tense from the effort. He's fucking me with every muscle and every possessive intention. He's making sure I know that no other man, human or otherwise, can mistake what is happening between us.

I give him this moment. I don't make fun, I don't sass.

I give him exactly what he needs.

Me.

"Harder, Levi. Harder. Please."

That's exactly what he does. He retreats almost all the way before slamming back inside me and making me shudder with how good he feels.

My mouth is at his neck, my teeth aching to bite him, to brand him as mine. Like a possessive lover, I want to suck his skin into my mouth and make sure everyone can see him wearing my mark.

With another grunt, Levi slides out and then thrusts back inside me so hard that I do bite him.

He grunts his approval, a feral sound that is part animal part ethereal creature from some unnamed world.

He's lost to his desire for me. He's completely absorbed by his need to fuck the world out of my mind.

"Come all over my cock, Remy. Fucking do it. Now."

His tone is the reason my juices coat his dick as though I can turn it on and off. He demands and my body reacts instantly.

With a finger from his hand on my ass, he pushes inside my hole just as he slams back inside my pussy.

We both cry out into the silent room, the echo bouncing around us.

We don't dare move. His cock is deeply seated inside me as is his finger. My teeth are practically drawing blood as I shake and tremble from this second, more intense orgasm.

I feel like it will never end. Like my body is going to be in a continuous state of orgasm.

Once my breaths are less erratic and I can finally feel my nerve endings, I remove my teeth and lick up the few drops of blood that I've stolen from his collarbone as he pulls his finger from inside of me.

"I think I got your message," I say breathlessly.

"What message is that?" he whispers, kissing up and down my neck, in no hurry to remove himself from the warmth of my wet pussy.

"When I'm feeling restless, I just need to come and find you." I grin at him lazily as he holds me.

I don't know how long we stand there in the blue hues of the pool, united by our love and our lust, but we make no effort to separate and go back to the real world until it's absolutely necessary.

I was asleep when they brought Laurent in, so I didn't hear a thing, and I'm kind of glad that the basement is sound proofed. Though I am very intrigued, because Michael and Roman went down there together this morning after Creek headed over to see Colt after everything that happened at the meeting, he's spent quite a bit of time over there.

To say that was a bromance I never saw coming is the understatement of the fucking millennia. They've been down there all morning, while I've been in the kitchen with Nonnie, as she tries, and fails, to teach me how to cook.

"Remy, how on earth did you manage to burn this? I told you, you need to constantly stir," Nonnie clucks as she waves me away from the very ruined hollandaise sauce that's burnt to the bottom of the pan.

"I did, I swear," I tell her, trying not to laugh. The smoke alarm starts to blare and Levi and Kain rush into the kitchen on high alert. "I tried to cook, I failed, false alarm," I say, facepalming.

Levi just smirks while Kain barks out a laugh.

"I've never known anyone so hopeless at a stove," Nonnie sighs, throwing her hands in the air.

"She's been this way in every single life she's lived," Levi tells her and she shakes her head.

"I just don't understand it."

"What can I say, I'm obviously just designed to never have you leave me, Nonnie," I joke, but her face falls.

"What? What did I say?"

"I must go home," she tells me, frowning. "My granddaughter is expecting. I must go home and make sure they are okay. They will need me when the baby comes."

"Oh, Nonnie. I promise I will be fine, I was only playing with you. I survived before I met these guys, plus, Levi and Roman can both cook. It will all work out. I am so excited for you!" I clap my hands together, but she still looks distraught.

"How about you try and teach me something simpler? Like Chicken Alfredo? That doesn't turn quite so quickly, right?" My gaze bounces between the three off them, almost panicked. I don't want to be the reason she doesn't go home to her family when they need her.

"Nonnie, I already told you, Remy will be fine. We all will. Luc will be glad to have you make. Apparently Taura has taken over the kitchen since you've been gone." Kain winces with the words and Nonnie clicks her tongue.

"That girl over seasons everything. She cannot run my kitchen!" She paces in front of the stove before stopping and turning to watch me. "You promise me you will eat properly until I return. A girl needs to keep her energy up. If you don't eat, I will know." She waves her wooden spoon at me, and I move towards her and wrap her in a hug. She freezes for a moment before returning it.

"I promise, Nonnie. You don't need to worry about me.

I love to eat. The guys won't let me go hungry. They're as good as you are at making sure I look after myself." I wink at her and she scoffs.

"These boys, they don't know what they're doing. I cannot go."

"Nonnie, you must go. It would make me so very sad to know I was the reason you were not with your family. Please, trust me. I will make sure to take care of myself until you can come back to us, okay?"

"As long as you are sure, I would hate to see something happen to you, Remy girl." She hugs me tight and then looks over to Kain. "I am already packed, if everything is okay here, I would like to go home very soon."

"I will sort out arrangements for you now," Kain tells her with a small smile, before she bustles out of the kitchen.

I let out a deep sigh and slump into one of the stools at the island counter, then Roman's and Michael's voices filter into the kitchen, and they both arrive not long after. Their t-shirts both have evidence of their morning's work, but I guess they mostly cleaned up before they came up here.

"I see you've both had a good morning," Levi says, an eyebrow quirked.

"Fun, yes. Productive, not so much," Roman says as he and Michael sit at the table. It's very strange seeing him here in our space with my guys. Especially Roman.

I thought they'd be the least likely of friends, considering Roman's tendency to be an asshole first, and think about the consequences of it later.

"So he didn't say anything?" Levi asks almost smugly as he looks to Michael.

"Not yet," Michael tells us. "But I have plenty of other ways to make someone talk. And if all that fails, then I have my ultimate trick."

"You'll look inside his mind?" I ask

"I will," Michael confirms.

"Why not just do that first?" Kain asks.

"Because if people have too many defenses, and you have to break through them, it can break the person's mind. Which means what you see isn't always reliable," Michael explains. "Angels and humans are the easiest for me to read, followed by Hunters as a hybrid. Witches and Lycans are harder, they're from a different kind of magic to mine. Dracul and Demons are the hardest. Nothing is impossible, I'd just rather not use it if we don't have to."

Kain looks a little comforted by Michael's explanation, I guess the thought of having him inside of his head isn't all that comforting, not that he has anything to hide, but still I get it. It's why I never really resented the other Angels' fear of me. I mean, they didn't know me, they had no way to know there was no way I would pry inside their minds. Fear is a powerful thing.

"That makes sense." Kain nods. "Well, if you guys have things handled here, I'm going to take Nonnie to the Laveaus and portal her home." He strides across to me and kisses me softly. "I'll be home later tonight, okay?"

"Okay," I say with a smile and kiss him again. He adjusts his tie once he steps back from me, not that it needed doing, even with running in here, he was perfectly put together, not a hair out of place. I watch him as he goes, and I feel my cheeks heat when I realize everyone is watching me stare as his extremely biteable ass as he walks away from me.

"Well, we should eat, grab a bottle of water for Laurent, and head back downstairs," Roman says, clapping his hands together once.

"Nonnie made lasagna. It's in the oven," I tell him, and he grants me a huge smile.

"I do love some lasagna," Roman says, rubbing his stomach.

"I don't think I've ever had it," Michal comments, and we all just look at him in shock.

"You've never had lasagna?" I ask.

"No, I don't think so." He shakes his head.

"Oh my fates. You are about to experience heaven in your mouth." I grin as Roman plates up two portions, grabs two forks, and brings them over.

"If you don't need anything, Remy, I'm going to go and

check in with Nevin and Serafina," Levi says, grabbing my attention.

"Okay," I say smiling at him. I know he's struggling having Michael in our space, but as I told him last night, he won't be here for much longer. I think he's just having fun ruffling Levi's feathers more than anything, but he does seem genuinely invested in finding out who is causing all of these issues. Though how he can be away from Avalon for this long is beyond me. He wouldn't even leave for the war. I walk over to Levi and let him lead me from the room with his arm around my waist.

"Call me if you need anything while I'm out," Levi says softly as he moves me so my chest is against his.

"I will." I smile up at him.

TWENTY

I spent the rest of the day feeling more than a little useless. Everyone else has something they're working on, and for the first time in a long time, I'm not really needed. I get the feeling they've been taking on more themselves because of everything recently, but it's kind of left me at a loose end. It feels weird. I've wanted time to relax for so long, and now that I have a minute to catch my breath, I have no idea what to do with myself.

So, I've been, very carefully, trying to make dinner. Mac and cheese, so not something I haven't done before, except this isn't mac and cheese out of a box. Who would have thought making it from scratch was this hard?

I stir the sauce into the macaroni and then move it to the ceramic dish, putting extra cheese on top, because there's no such thing as too much cheese, and pop it in the oven. I manage to set the timer, and then load the dishwasher before turning my attention to the garlic bread. I pull Nonnie's homemade garlic butter from the refrigerator and slather it generously over the bloomer that I sliced in half, just like the recipe I found online said, then I wrap it in foil before popping it in the oven too.

I take a swig of the whiskey I poured out earlier and feel pretty proud of myself. I didn't burn anything to the ground, or set off the fire alarm. My biggest worry, is that there's too much salt, but I mean, the cheese will totally mask that right?

At the very least, I tried.

I drop a text to all of my guys to let them know that dinner will be ready in about twenty minutes. Whether they decide to show is another matter. Their health could be at risk either way. I smirk to myself, because it's going to be so funny watching how trepidatious they all are eating something I cooked. Personally, I think it will be amazing. I can't be that terrible.

I take another sip of whiskey when Michael and Roman appear in the kitchen with smiles on their faces. "You look pleased with yourselves."

"We are," Michael says, moving to the sink to wash up. Roman moves towards me, I scan him, but he's already clean. He wraps his arms around me and kisses me with so much heat it leaves me breathless and wanting more.

"Wow, you really are pleased. What happened?" I ask.

"We got him to talk." Roman grins as his words hit me.

"You did? What the fuck did he say?"

"The others are on their way back, I'll tell once everyone is here." Roman squeezes me tighter.

"I, however, have to get back to Avalon. I'm going to be more use to you there, and I've already been gone too long," Michael says as he watches us. I catch a glimpse of sadness in his eyes, but it's gone so quickly, I almost question if I saw it. I pull slightly further away from Roman, not because I don't want to be there, but I realize I've not even thought about Michael maybe still having any kind of feelings for me the last few days that he's been here, which is terrible.

"Are you sure you can't stay for dinner, at least?" I ask, trying not to sound as apologetic as I feel, because I know he'd hate that more than seeing me with the guys.

"You cooked?" Roman asks, shocked.

"I did, without burning anything down. It shouldn't be long." I smile, because I really feel like I accomplished something.

"I can't stay, little bird. But if you need me, you know how to get in touch. I'll be keeping an eye out too. Be safe." I remove myself from Roman's grasp and move across the kitchen to hug Michael.

"Thank you for everything," I tell him softly, as he hugs me back even tighter.

"It was nothing. You know you don't need to thank me," Michael says lowly, watching me closely. "I'll always be here for you, Remy. Always. No matter what." His eyes flick up to Roman across the room with his final words, before he releases me and takes a step back. He nods over to Roman, and then heads out of the back door. There's a brief flash of light, and then he's gone.

I sit at the counter, and Roman pours me another drink while getting himself one, when Kain and Creek appear together. "Fallon portal you guys home?"

"She did," Creek says with a smile, kissing me before he goes to get himself a beer from the fridge, and Kain comes to sit beside me.

"Nonnie get back alright?" I ask him as I lean into him and rest my head on his shoulder.

"She did, though she felt very guilty for leaving you." He kisses the top of my head. I sigh contentedly and stay tucked up against him while the guys talk, but Roman doesn't really explain much, because we know that Levi will be back soon.

It takes about twenty minutes, and the timer on the oven dings just as Levi walks into the room, so we serve dinner, and no one dies, even if there is the odd comment about too much cheese. Straight up blasphemy if you ask me. Once we get cleared away, Levi clears his throat and pins Roman with his stare. "So, you have news?"

"I do. It took some pretty persuasion, but that's always been my favorite kind. Laurent told us that he wasn't the only Lycan working against us. I've already sent word to Theron but I have a feeling that Aryna and the other Lycans he told us about will have already scattered and gone to ground."

"That's great. One less thing to worry about," Creek says, clapping Roman on the shoulder.

"That's not all he told us. He mentioned a name that I think you'll all be very interested in…" Roman says, pausing to the point where I want to throw my glass at his head.

"Who?" I ask, unable to wait any longer.

"Amelia."

Three fucking days.

That's how long this bombardment from the Demons has been going on, I'm not sure how much longer we can sustain it. Even with all of the power we have over here with the Death Dealers, they have numbers on their side, and there's only so many times that Leviathan can unleash that monstrous power inside of him before he's wiped out. I see him after he uses it, and it hurts my heart to see him so tired, so drained, but so unrelenting. He is the first one out there, and the last to return. He doesn't ask of others what he isn't willing to give himself.

It's what makes us all willing to follow him to the ends of existence. I finish cleaning the blood from my hands, I've been helping in the medical bay because Leviathan thought I could try and use some of my healing powers here. He knows how much I struggle to bring that particular power to life, and this time has been no different. There is just something in me that doesn't seem to connect with that particular ability, even if every Shadow Walker in existence has had it. I've not been that much use here.

"I thought I'd find you back here." Serafina's voice is harsh as she pushes into the medical tent and storms over to me.

"Well, this is where I've been relegated to." I shrug, I'm not going to hide my unhappiness about it. I'd much rather be out there with the rest of them. "What's up?"

"We need you out there. You have got to speak to Leviathan about this insanity. You're our best archer. We're losing more ground and he's just being fucking stubborn about it." She huffs as she folds her arms and I roll my eyes at her.

"You think I haven't tried talking to him? You said it yourself. He's a stubborn ass."

"It's so stupid. And Nevin has been fretting about you

the entire time. It's weird not having you with us. Our team just doesn't function the same. The three of us plus Leviathan, that's how is been since I joined the team. He's being ridiculous."

"Trust me, I'm very aware of it."

"Well don't just be aware of it, fucking fix it." She turns on her heel and storms from the tent, her dirty blonde hair flying out behind her.

Shit.

I knew it was bad, I mean, I've been jittery as fuck being behind the lines, not being able to help them, but if Serafina is shook, then something is really wrong. She's a fucking ice queen, and we rarely see eye to eye, so for her to come to me directly… Yeah it's bad.

I take a deep breath and leave the tent in search of Leviathan, and walk smack into a hard chest. I look up and see Nevin, his hands on my shoulder, keeping me steady. The bombardment is still going on, but if Nevin and Serafina are back here, that means Leviathan must be too.

"I was coming to find you," Nevin says with a sad smile.

"Everything okay?" I ask.

"No, we need you, Amantara. It's a fucking shit show. Serafina and Leviathan are going to kill each other if you're not there to even them out. He can't even seem to focus on the strategy, because he's worried about you. It's insane.

Come back to us." He takes my hands and squeezes.

"I'm trying." I give him a small smile and kiss his cheek. "Where is he?"

"He wouldn't leave the lines, you know how he is."

I sigh at his words and shake my head. "That I do. Come on then, take me to where you left him. Let's get this shit resolved."

My shoulders tighten with anxiety. Facing off against the Archangel of War isn't fun for anyone. Even me. Even if he does love me. Sometimes that makes it harder, because he is so fierce about protecting me, that he's literally impossible.

It's impossible to ignore the screams from both sides as we move through the chaos. I'm still surprised that Gabe didn't want to come and join the fight. He loves creating a little extra chaos, and we could really use his soul destroyer tricks.

Hell, at this point, I'd take any extra help, but I know it's not coming. Michael didn't want us interfering as it was, and Leviathan only got him to agree by limiting the amount of interference in the human world. We've already gone way beyond the realms of our agreement. Granting humans some partial Angelic power to help our numbers was genius but it's also definitely going to piss some people off. But that's a problem for the future, and also, totally not my problem. It's not like they'll live forever, the problem will resolve itself eventually.

I bring my mind back to the here and now as Nevin runs beside me, protecting me by using himself as a shield as we get closer to Leviathan's position. I can see him from here, giving out orders, but everyone looks frazzled. We might not need as much sleep as humans, but three days is still a long time, especially with everything going on around us.

"Leviathan!" I call out but he's already watching me, as if he sensed me coming, even amongst the anarchy. It doesn't take more than a minute till I'm in front of him and wrapped in his arms.

"What are you doing here?" he asks, his eyes wild. "Is everything okay?" He pulls back and looks me over, and I raise my hands to his chest.

"I'm fine. Everything's fine," I say and take a deep breath. "Well, almost fine. You need to let me come back to the front lines. Look at you, you're a mess. You're not taking care of yourself, and it's driving me nuts back there, I cannot access that healing power, no matter how hard I focus."

He looks me over again, his narrowed eyes shoot over my shoulder to where a silent Nevin stands. "Did he put you up to this?" He almost sounds jealous, which is fucking insane. Nevin is like a brother to me.

"No, Leviathan." I reach up and grasp his chin, pulling

his face down and his gaze back to me. "I want this. Please don't push me away. I need to be here with you. With the team."

"Fine." He lets out a sigh and softens against me momentarily.

"Now, you need to go and rest, and fucking eat something," I tell him with my hand still clasping his chin. "I've got this covered."

He looks like he might argue, but then he smirks at me. "Okay, hellion. I'll go and grab a quick bite and a nap, but you bet your ass I'll be back soon."

"I had no doubt." I smile and release his chin as he cups my nape before kissing me, his tongue tangling with mine. A moan slips from me, and he pulls back, smirk firmly in place.

Roman's revelation last night turned Levi into the war machine that he is. There has been no sleep, and a flurry of activity, barked orders, and general mayhem since the words registered with him. Nevin and Serafina have been with him in the kitchen since the early hours of this morning, and despite Michael reinstating me as a Death Dealer, the whole strategy thing was never really my bag.

I peer into the kitchen to see if it's safe to get coffee, and they're all still standing around the table, with the biggest map I've ever seen.

"Clara, the Witch, can we track her? She'll be easier to find than Amelia if she's in hiding. She was always the best ghost we had, she knew exactly how to disappear, but a Witch's power is an easy trace," Serafina asks them.

"Erm…" I say as I round the doorway. "If she's a Witch won't she be dead by now?" Serafina rolls her eyes at me like I just said the most stupid thing in the world.

"Some Witches have access to power that can extend their lifespan. It's not practiced so much any longer, and it takes a severe amount of magic, and has an equally severe cost, but it's possible. And someone of Clara's level… it's definitely possible that she could still be as alive as you or I," Levi explains, and my eyes go wide, as the fragments of a memory come to me. He's not lying, not that I would've thought he was, but I already knew this, I just didn't remember.

"Right, of course," I say as my cheeks heat. "So, can you track her?"

"We likely can," Nevin answers as I move farther into the room. "We'd need a Witch though."

"Well, we have plenty of Witches, but Fallon would help in a heartbeat," I tell them.

"Then she'll do," he says, barely even looking at me as he speaks.

"What is the plan when we find her?" I ask, because as

we know, killing an Angel, not that easy, and I daresay if she's evaded capture for this long, she's not as helpless as she once seemed.

"We kill her," Levi says, with no hesitation, and no remorse. "She has come after us and ours too many times, we've lost too much. There is no mercy for her once we find her."

"Levi…" Serafina starts, but he cuts her off with the shake of his head.

"No. Michael will back me on this one. We find her, and she dies, before she has chance to kill anyone else."

"And how, do you propose we do that?" Nevin asks. "It's not like we have an abundance of ways to kill her."

Levi looks over to me, and a shiver runs down my spine. He wants to use my shadow fire, I know it. Though I'm shocked he'd even think about letting me that close to her, considering how protective he's been of late.

"Morgan," Levi says, still looking at me, telling me silently that he's lying. "Her and the Horsemen have walls and walls of Angel glass on level six. I have no doubt they'll lend a hand when they find out we know who is behind everything."

"Of course, the Shadow Queen… of course she'll help." Serafina rolls her eyes as the sarcasm rolls from her. "You guys really do make some fucked up friends."

"Hcy!" I start, but Levi stops me.

"Enough, you two. We don't have time for this, we need to get Fallon, and then we head out to scout." His voice is low and demanding and does all sorts of scandalous things to me.

"What about the rest of us?" I ask.

"Nothing, nothing else happens until we know for sure. The last thing we want is word of what we know getting out," he tells us all, and without saying a word, he storms from the room.

"I guess I'll text Fallon," I mutter, and head in the direction Levi left, because there is no way I'm staying behind with those two. I don't have the patience required to stick around for their bickering. They're like brother and sister, they wind each other up beyond compare and it drives me fucking nuts. I don't care how well we all work together as a team, or how many times they've saved my ass.

Just nope.

I text Fallon and tell her that we need her help ASAP, and she lets me know she'll be over in a few. I head to find Levi and find him standing by the door to the basement with the others. Small whimpers come from the open door, but any semblance of guilt I might have once had are now buried. While I might not want to help extract the information, I'm not against it. These people made their decisions, they picked their sides. It's their own fault for picking the losing team.

"I texted Fallon," I say as I reach them. "She'll be here soon."

"Thank you. I was just updating everyone," Levi says.

"What's the plan for the rest of us?" I ask Roman.

"He let slip the hiding place of the Witches, so Kain and Luc are going to take his generals and have an old school Witch hunt." Roman's grin is purely animalistic. Apparently, Levi isn't the only one feeling bloodthirsty at this point.

"We have Witches who will be coming with us," Kain tells me as his fingers brush against mine. I hadn't realized I'd stiffened, but I relax a little with his words.

"Okay, good. But what about him?" I ask, tilting my head down towards the basement.

"Him… Creek and I are going to see if he has any other pretty words, see if he knows where the other Lycans are being held up. And from there, I haven't decided yet. But I'm leaning towards he dies." The whimpers from the basement get a little louder and I flinch a little, despite my resolve.

Who am I to question an alpha's ruling?

TWENTY ONE

It's strange being the one left behind.

Creek and Roman are in the basement with Laurent. Levi, Serafina, and Nevin are scouting the location Fallon found for them. Kain took a portal back to the castle, and he and Luc are out hunting Witches, which leaves me, home alone with nothing to do.

Which on the one hand, I understand. The guys don't want me in the thick of things, they're trying to protect me. But, on the other, it pisses me off. I don't need to be protected. Still, I'm trying not to be an asshole about the whole thing, and so I'm trying not to get too bent out of shape.

However, that does mean that I'm still here basically twiddling my thumbs. I've trained, and exercised and meditated every other time they've left me alone. Colt is still dealing with the elders freaking out, so he's beyond busy right now, and Fallon… well, she's seemed a little distant lately, but I get it. She's got a ton going on, helping with the hunt, trying to master her new power, attempting to rebuild her life after Archer and Azriel stole so much from her. She's not really been the same since we got back, but again, I get it. She's not really talked about everything she's been through, but I can imagine, and that alone is enough to make my blood run cold. She seemed like she was back to herself at Christmas, but I'm also very aware of how easy it is to slip into the mask of who people want and expect you to be.

I sigh and drop down onto the sofa, picking up the remote and channel hopping. I have no idea why, I didn't even watch cable before my life got turned upside down. I don't want to put the Chicagos on, because well, we still have shit to do, and I don't want to get sucked in right now.

Turning off the TV I stand and head outside. Ever since I got my wings back, there's just something calming about being outdoors. Now I know the truth about myself, my entire lifespan, I realize that some parts of my life when I was Amantara filtered through, even without the memories. I've always enjoyed being outside, felt calm in the outdoors. It's one of the things Roman and I always had in common.

I tip my head back, and let myself soak up the limited sun rays. The power inside of me makes itself known as I worship the little sun we have. Of course it likes the sun, there are no shadows without the light. I push the power to my hands and my shadow flame ignites, climbing up my arms. I feel the cold burn of it, but there is no pain.

I pull it back inside of me, and hold it, like holding my breath, until my skin burns with the need for it to be released. I push the power out of me, and it's like I'm the epicenter of a bomb site. The power explodes out of me in a 360. I redirect the blast from the manor meaning the tree line gets an extra hit. The sizzle and pop of the flame as the trees turn to ash before my eyes are so loud.

Another pop sounds and I stagger backwards before I feel the burn in my shoulder. Blood runs out of the hole in my shoulder, and I feel a little lightheaded. The wound isn't healing, and it occurs to me I'm still here out in the open. I have no idea which direction the shot came from. Another pop rings out and I fall to my knees as I struggle to breathe as blood pours from another hole, this time, in the chest. A lung hit.

I try to breathe in, but its barely more than a wheeze.

Why the fuck am I not healing?

"Remy!" Roman's cry reaches me, and I turn, seeing him start to run towards me, but the ground at his feet is ripped apart as bullets continue to fly. I shake my head to stop him from coming to me. I try to speak, but blood splutters from my mouth as I attempt it.

My vision goes blurry, but I don't understand. It can't be Angel glass, it doesn't burn like Angel glass did. But I'm not healing. At least, not as quickly as I should.

A body falls to the ground a few feet from me, and then I see boots before I fall back, my ass hiding the ground with a thud.

"Why isn't she healing?" Roman roars as he drops behind me and pulls me into his lap.

"It must be because she was reborn in the Shadow Realm. She has different strengths and different weaknesses," Serafina tells him as I struggle to hold onto consciousness.

"I've got Fallon, she'll be here in less than thirty seconds." Creek's voice reaches me, seconds before I see his face in front of mine. "Just hold on, Remy. What the fuck did he shoot her with?"

"Smells like salted iron. It's almost lethal to Demons, definitely fatal if you get them with enough of it. It must be because of the Shadow Realm. There's no other explanation."

"None of this makes any fucking sense," Roman curses violently behind me.

"Out of the way," Fallon says calmly, as she glows softly before us.

"Can you heal her?" Creek asks, his panic hurts my heart.

"I'm going to try, but I need you all to get out of the way." Her calm makes me smile. She might have been distant, but she is always there when I need her.

"Fal..." I croak.

"Oh Remy," she sighs as she drops to her knees beside me. "Look at the mess you got yourself into now."

"This is what I get for trying to exercise," I laugh, blood sputtering from me again.

"No more talking," she says, as I try to breath, and I just nod as she places her hands on me. The heat from her hands stings, like a hundred needles pricking my skin, but I seal my lips against the cry that rises and hope like fuck she can heal me.

I'm not ready to die.

I creep up the stairs and into the nursery. He's so very little, but just the sight of him fills my heart with so much joy that I think I might burst. I never imagined that I'd be here. It took so long for us to be able to have a child that I'd almost given up hope, but Luca always had faith. Faith that the gods wouldn't forsake us like that.

And he was right.

Two weeks ago, the light of my life was placed into

my arms, and my world righted itself. It didn't matter that I'd lost my parents and brother to a fire. It didn't matter that I'd spent most of my childhood homeless, living on the streets, protecting myself from the dangers that plague this land.

Luca saved me. He was my salvation when I thought all was lost.

I went to the arches, prepared to beg the gods for a sign. A sign that things would get better. A sign not to give up and just let myself wash out with the tide. To give me a reason to keep going.

That's where I met Luca.

His eyes were the kindest I had ever seen. His dark hair was short and tidy, he looked very important. I had learned in my short life, that usually the men who looked important, were the cruelest of their kind. But something about him was different.

He took me back to his small but well-kept home. He gave me a chance to bathe, and offered me fresh clothes. No one had offered me such kindness in such a long time that I cried as I redressed, feeling safe for the first time since my family were taken from me.

I learned over the coming months, that he was a carpenter. His strong hands shaped wood, to build things for the town. He was very well respected and liked here, and more than a few of the women in the town would glare at me being on his arm, though I couldn't have told you why at the time.

He was my friend for a while before he kissed me. He was so shy and gentle that I gave myself over to his kiss, and realized just how much I loved him. Realized that I hadn't let myself love him for fear of losing someone else.

We were wed not long after that at the arches where he found me. The priestess joined us with ribbons, and declared our love to the gods. Blessed us and our union before the gods, and asking for us to be granted all the things we wanted from life.

It took us years to get to this place. Where I would volunteer at the children's home in the town, looking after the children who were like me, while Luca worked during the day. To be blessed with a son of our own.

"Is he sleeping?" Luca asks as his arms circle my waist from behind. He looks over my shoulder, down at our son in the crib he made with his own hands. I feel his smile as he leans his chin down on my shoulder. "He looks so peaceful."

"He does. I don't want him to ever know the pain and loss I felt. I want to protect him from everything bad in the world," I say quietly. Luca pulls me from the room and back to the main room downstairs. I move to the kitchen and fix him a plate for dinner. He's gone such long hours, even now that our son is born. Sometimes I wish he was here more, but I know that he only works so hard for us.

"I met an interesting fellow today. He wants me to work with the blacksmith to make him a special kind of chest," Luca tells me as he sits at our table, which he also crafted. He crafted the entire house.

"Oh really?" I enquire.

"Yes, strange fellow. Very serious. You know the type, the ones who look like a smile might break them." I laugh softly at his description, because yes, I know the type. Our town governor is exactly the same type. Dreadful man.

"Are you going to do the work?"

"I think so, he offered a very handsome fee for it. It would be enough to buy us a bigger house. A much finer house," he tells me, and my eyes go wide.

"It must be some chest!"

"That it is, he wants a set of them, built of oak and salted iron."

"Well, isn't that so very peculiar."

"It is, but the blacksmith seemed to think it wouldn't be a problem. Apparently salted iron is good to ward off evil," Luca says with a smile. "I'm thinking of adding some to the windows of the house, unless of course we buy another."

"I'm happy if you're happy," I tell him with a smile, before placing his dinner in front of him.

"Well, then maybe I'll do it. But first, I must make

these chests for this Leviathan fellow. Odd name to match the man."

"Very odd indeed."

Roman lays me down gently on the corner couch, and then stands above me, arms crossed, like a sentinel on duty. Fallon might have healed me but I still feel like I've been hit by a Mack truck. I try to sit up, but Creek puts his hand on my shoulder as he perches on the sofa in front of me.

"You should rest, it will help you finish healing." A tick in his clenched jaw gives away the anger he feels despite the softness of his voice.

"I'll be fine," I say, my voice hoarse.

"You should listen to him," Fallon adds as she sits on the floor. I look around but there's no sight of Serafina.

"She went to find Levi," Creek says, noticing me searching for her. I wince, thinking about how well he's going to take the news of my new found weakness. I mean, I'm not exactly dancing on the ceiling about it, but these guys were already overly protective when I was near invincible.

I try not to groan out loud at the thought of it. This time, I do push myself up so that I'm sitting, because it's too weird to be lying here with everyone watching over me like this.

“Do you need something?” Roman asks, but I shake my head.

“Have we heard anything from Kain about the Witches?” I ask.

“Nothing yet, but I’ve let him know what happened,” Creek confirms, and I groan.

“But I’m fine, and now he’s probably going to come back here when he doesn’t need to,” I sigh, and as I finish speaking, a portal opens up in the living room, and out walks my Dracul king, looking furious enough to decimate worlds.

“Is he dead?” are the first words he utters.

“Serafina dropped him before we even knew she was here. Apparently, Levi left her behind to watch the house. He was a Hunter. Not one any of us recognize, so he could be new, but we have no idea who he is,” Roman tells him, his words clipped.

Kain strides towards me and Creek moves aside so that he can see me properly. He crouches in front of the couch, looking me over from head to toe before standing and leaving the room without another word. The sound of glass smashing has Creek following him and I sigh. He’s pissed. Not that I blame him, but I hate how much the smallest thing can anger them all so much.

Okay, I realize this wasn’t that small, and yeah, I could have died, *but* I didn’t. Fallon got here in time, and I was healing. Just much slower than usual. I have no doubt that Morgan and her guys will beat themselves up about this too if they find out, because that's what they do. While all of this makes me feel loved and cherished, I can't help but hate how upset they are right now. That's before Levi even gets back.

Fallon disappears into the kitchen, while Roman just watches me, and comes back with a soda and a bar of chocolate for me. "The sugar will make you feel better, plus, ya know, chocolate."

I smile as she plonks down next to me and puts the TV on. She flicks to a TV series about a mom and her daughter that we've watched a million times and snuggles up next to me. Roman pulls a blanket from the chair and puts it over us before sitting down too.

I sip on the soda and nibble on the chocolate, because I still feel a little nauseous, and just sink into the sofa enjoying the mindless reprieve. It's not long before Kain and Creek join us, and find their own spots on the sofa. I smile at having everyone around me, even if it's because I got shot. I got so used to be alone so often in previous lives, I never thought I'd want or need this many people. But I wouldn't give this up for anything.

A crash sounds outside and Kain heads out followed by Roman, Creek stays on alert beside me, but I can feel the static from here. Why they think I'd need protecting from the storm bearer is beyond me.

"You need to calm the fuck down," Kain says, Roman's growl accompanies it.

"You two need to get the fuck out of my way. Where is she?" Levi's voice booms, the power rolls from him and I can feel it, even in here. It takes a minute or so, but Kain and Roman must move because Levi is in front of me and lifting me out of my seat and into his arms.

"You're okay?" he asks softly, looking down at me, but I'm not sure he's even really asking, more just reassuring himself, but I nod regardless and cup his chin in my hand. He might still have that static rolling from him, but he'd never hurt me. I'd risk my life on that time and again.

"I'm okay. I was healing, just slowly. But Fallon got here quickly and helped me heal faster so I didn't bleed out," I tell him, my voice barely more than a whisper while everyone else in the room is essentially frozen. I get it. Each person in here is a big bad all of their own, but they've never seen him truly unleash the power inside of him. They can feel it as much as I can, but even that is restrained. He truly could wipe us from the Earth with barely a thought. I've seen it for myself. I hate that they still fear him a little deep down, because he would never hurt me, which means he'd never harm them, so I kiss him softly until he relaxes beneath my touch. "I'm really okay."

He rests his forehead on mine, when Serafina clears

her throat.

"Sorry to break this love fest up, but Amelia escaped with the Witch."

"She escaped? But you and Nevin were on her when I left." Levi's voice is low, but he holds me tighter. He's beyond pissed, but he's controlling himself.

"She had a few tricks up her sleeve, but I'm fine, thanks for asking. Nevin wasn't so lucky, but he's healing. He shouldn't be far behind me," she says, rolling her eyes.

"I'm glad you're okay," I tell her, because my brute sure as hell isn't going to. I can practically feel him shaking with anger that their target escaped. While I'm disappointed, everyone I care about is alive, so I'm not upset. "And thank you for everything."

The guys all grumble their thanks, but Serafina waves it off. "I was just doing my job." I've never really understood her whole ice queen thing, sometimes she looks so sad and lonely, it's heartbreaking, but then she's a dick, and no one really pays attention to the fact that she's kinda broken, but I see her and she hates it.

She moves to the corner of the room, standing like she's on guard, while my guys shift around the room and get comfortable. Levi keeps me in his arms and sits in the spot he lifted me from. I let out a deep breath as I snuggle against him, and we all sit, watching the TV, just enjoying our time together.

TWENTY TWO

"We nearly lost you again, precious." Kain sighs as he lays me down on the bed. Usually I wouldn't allow them to treat me like glass, but I can see the fear in every single one of them, and I don't want them to be afraid. If that means conceding a little, and letting them look after me, even when I don't need it, then I can do that for them.

Creek enters the room, shutting the door behind him, and drops into the chair in the corner, watching me, looking like he's aged ten years in the last day or so. So, I got shot. Yes, I nearly died, but we also learned something new.

I'm not completely immune to all things.

Better that we know now, when there was a chance for someone to heal me, than me being so careless, and me ending up dead because I thought I was invincible. I prop myself up on the pillows, they're both watching me, and it hits me.

The best way for them to get that I'm okay, is to show them I'm okay. I look at Creek and pat the bed beside me, motioning for him to sit with me, while Kain watches me from the end of the bed. He smiles, and I'm sure he can see my intentions written all over my face, but I don't care. I want this. I want them. Now. Both of them.

Creek seems too tense to smile, too raw, but he stands and slowly makes his way to the bed. His steps are heavy, like he's just run cross-country with a ton of weight on his shoulders. I know I'm their priority. More than that, I'm their reason for being, the heartbeat in their existence. I know this. It's not pretentious and it's not conceited, it's simply a fact. I know this because each one of them is my lifeline. Five hearts beat inside of me, linking us on a cellular level and we wouldn't want it any other way.

At first, Creek sits beside me. His shoulders are rigid, his jaw is tight, and his eyes are shadowed with storm clouds but when I place my hand on his heart and smile, the tension ebbs just a tad. He's being strong for me or maybe for himself as well. Beneath my palm, the pounding of his heart is like a steady heavy metal rhythm, pounding incessantly. Any other time, this would be a clear sign that he's ready to fuck me, no holds barred. Tonight, though,

I'm sure it's a mixture of fear and stress mixed with desire. With his back propped up against the headboard, he's watching my every move like a predator sizes up its prey.

I kneel on the bed at Creek's hip, and before throwing a leg over to straddle him, I give my attention to Kain who has been watching us the whole time.

He knows what I want, he always does, and with a quick jerk of his chin, he tells me everything I need to know.

Yes, we need this.

Get on top of him.

I'll be right behind you.

That's exactly what I do. In one quick move, I've lifted my shirt over my head and just as I'm about to stand to take my bottoms off, Creek stops me. His fingers are curled around mine, our eyes meet, and I can sense his next move before he acts.

With strength borne from the beast inside of him, Creek tears the clothes right off my body. Literally ripping the fabric in two in a heartbeat and discarding them as though they were mere pieces of paper.

I frown, staring at the tattered remnants of my wardrobe. I love that my men are so feral but goddammit, why do my clothes need to be the ones to be sacrificed every time we fuck?

"I'll replace them," Creek looks at me, a faint smile

breaking over his face like a new Spring day.

"You better."

Then it comes to me.

I could do the same. Why shouldn't their clothes suffer from our constant need to fuck too?

Of course, when I reach for his jeans, I don't even have to try to know that I'd never be able to rip them off. While I could physically, the alpha asshole thing just isn't how I play.

"Let me," Creek full out grins this time and it settles something inside of me that has been restless since the last attack.

He lifts his hips, keeping me on top of him, I push up slightly so he can push his jeans down and I feel Kain behind me pulling the legs off and throws them in to the corner. When I look back at my beautiful vampire, my smile grows at the sight of his beautiful naked body.

My fates, he's perfection through and through.

How did I get so lucky?

I feel sexy and wanted as Creek moves us further up the bed before reaching up and running the backs of his fingers down my cheek. Behind me, Kain is getting comfortable, the heat from his chest is warming my back as his hand clasps my hair and sweeps it to the side, leaving my neck vulnerable to his kisses.

Like a kitten, I purr at the feel of his lips on my heated

skin. That singular sound acts as a direct line to their libido making both their cocks jolt. One beneath my hungry pussy and the other at the small of my back. Emboldened, I adjust myself, pushing Creek so he's lying down, and I brace myself on my hands, positioning myself on all fours, teasing Kain with the sway of my ass. But my gaze is focused on the intense need in Creek's eyes. His hand is cupping the side of my face and his tongue is gliding across his own lips, wetting them, as though he can practically taste me.

"Kiss me, beautiful," he whispers, pulling me down to him.

Kain's fingers dance across the skin of my back from my neck to the apex of my ass, leaving goosebumps in their wake as I shudder.

I lift myself so I'm straddling Creek, when his impatience surfaces, he uses his abs to pull himself up and slams his lips to mine, slipping his hand behind my hair and clutching the back of my neck in a possessive hold. A hold that says more than any words could. He's telling me how much he needs me, how precious I am to him, how my life is linked to his own. In that kiss, he begs me to keep living and to never leave him.

I promise to try as my tongue follows his lead, dancing to the rhythm of his kiss.

I feel Kain at the small of my back, his lips are soft as

he trails a blaze up my spine, his cock nestling between my ass cheeks.

My pussy contracts, yearning for more. Begging to fill the void.

I mewl at the feel of them, prompting Creek to release my mouth and pull me closer so he can trap my nipple between his teeth.

I'm panting, the sensations from both of my men is like a shot of nectar that runs hot through my veins, making me drunk on lust.

"That's it, precious, let us take the reins. Let us make you feel good." Kain's words are sweet, just like the man himself, warming my heart as Creek sucks on my nipple a little harder than usual, but it feels so fucking good I don't even think about objecting.

Eager to feel them inside of me, I balance my weight on one hand and reach beneath me with the other, wrapping Creek's hard cock in my grasp and gliding it up and down the slit of my pussy. It all feels so good. So, fucking good.

Kain follows my lead, holding my hair with one fist and teasing the puckered hole of my ass with the head of his dick. Creek reaches for the lube and tosses it to Kain and seconds later I hear the top pop open and the cool, thick substance coats me, spreading around and around. I've got two cocks teasing my holes, preparing me for their invasion. Trapping my bottom lip between my teeth, I let my head fall back and beg, “Fuck me, please. Now.”

Releasing my hair, Kain is the first to push through. The head of his cock slowly breaching my ass and making me groan with the heady feel of him.

“So, fucking gorgeous,” Kain murmurs, pushing through, holding me steady with one hand on my hip.

“Fuck,” Creek curses. Looking down at him, I watch him watching Kain as he thrusts inside me. He looks like he’s mesmerized by the movement, the fact that another man is fucking my ass isn’t a problem for him, not anymore. Instead, I can feel his cock getting impossibly harder as he circles it around my clit, waiting for his turn to fuck me.

His eyes rise to what I assume is Kain’s gaze and then I feel it, his dick thrusts inside me just as Kain pulls almost all the way out. He seats himself for a few seconds, groaning, his fingers digging into my hips. He’s face is contorted in pleasure with a touch of pain. Creek is an open book, his every emotion is mapped out on his face when he’s this vulnerable. When he’s making love to me.

For a few minutes, they alternate their rhythm. One pulls out as the other pushes in. It’s a tandem of lust, a sharing of me.

But I want more. I want them both. I want the bite of pain as they both thrust in. I want to be full with them. I want to feel them inside me, together.

“More,” is all I can say as they accelerate their

movements, the need to fuck getting more and more fervent. “More,” I repeat, hoping they understand what I’m saying.

The thrusts take on a quick acceleration, like a Ferrari going from zero to sixty in no time. But that’s not what I need.

“No,” and they both stop, immediately.

I panic, not understanding why no one is filling me, fucking, making me scream with their dicks.

“Are you okay, beautiful?” Creek asks, panicked.

“Did we hurt you?” Kain inquires, turning my head to look into my eyes.

I almost laugh at their expressions but I realize that this is not the time to play with their emotions.

“No, I’m fine. I’m… great. I just, I need you both.”

Again, confusion swims in their eyes.

“At the same time. Both inside me, at the same time.”

The grin that splits across Kain’s face is nothing short of blinding.

“Ah, so, it’s not a ‘stop’ kind of ‘no’,” Kain starts.

“It’s a ‘fuck me deep’ kind of ‘no’,” Creek finishes.

I grin and nod my head.

They both pull out and as though they’ve been practicing this move their entire lives, they both push inside me at the same time, same pace, same depth. It’s fucking heaven. It’s everything I’ve ever wanted.

It all feels dirty but at the same time, the love they emanate from each with their moves is overwhelming.

"Oh God." Creek's finger is at my clit, circling as he slowly owns my pussy and Kain's hands are at my tits, playing with my nipples as he masterfully possesses my ass.

It's almost too much. My body is trembling from the sensations.

"Fuck, I'm gonna…" I don't finish my phrase as Kain's teeth sink into the flesh of my shoulder, his mouth sucking out the vital essence of my body while Creek pushes in one last time and pulls my mouth to his for a hard, possessive kiss. In that moment, we are all linked as one.

We all come as one.

Kain's orgasm coating the walls of my ass as Creek fills me with his seed. All the while their mouths are taking my blood and my breath, respectively.

Kain releases me, first from his mouth, his tongue lapping up any blood that escapes before pulling from me completely. He disappears into the bathroom, and I hear the sound of running water as I climb off of Creek, wincing just a little as I do, with the best kind of pain.

I lie on the bed, spent, hoping the bones in my legs reform from the jelly they are currently, when Kain reappears with a washcloth and gently cleans me while Creek disappears into the bathroom.

"That was…" I say, still breathless.

"It was," he chuckles, before throwing the washcloth into the basket and climbing into the bed behind me, pulling me against him so his chest is on my back with his arm tucked around me.

Creek reappears and shuts off the light before climbing into bed with us, facing me, his hand resting on my hip.

"Sleep. We can play more tomorrow," he says softly, and I feel Kain's smile in my hair.

"That we can."

Kain and Creek kept me as a willing hostage in that room for two days, feeding me and loving me, while Roman and Levi were off doing their whole war thing, and occasionally ducking into my room to join in the fun. I'm not one to complain, but today I'm more than a little sore, even if it is in the most fun of ways.

I glide through the water, doing laps to help stretch my body out. Something about being in the water settles me. Maybe it's because it's nature, and my love for the outdoors, or maybe it's just because I'm weightless, either way, I'm not going to dismiss the things that make me happy. Not anymore.

I lift my head from the water to take a breath and spot black boots at the edge of the pool. Stopping myself mid lap, I see Levi standing there, watching me with his arms crossed and a smirk on his face. "I do love it when you swim naked."

I grin at him as I tread water, because I really fucking love swimming naked too. "Fancy a dip?"

"Oh I sure as fuck do." He grins. "But you have visitors." The smile drops from his face and butterflies kick up in my stomach.

"Who is it?" I ask as I swim to the edge and pull myself from the water. He hands me a towel, his eyes darken as I pat myself dry before wrapping it around myself.

"Uriel and Ashera." His words make my blood run cold.

"Why the fuck are they here?"

"I don't know, they wouldn't speak to me." He refolds his arms and I start to pace.

"Well, they've not spoken to me since I fucking manifested my power. Why would they want to speak to me? My so-called fucking parents don't do anything unless it's a power play." I wrack my brains as to why they could be here. To say I lost the parent lottery both times I was given them is a fucking understatement. Though Uriel and Ashera make my Hunter parents look like a fucking dream. I stalk out of the suite and head to my room. I slam the door closed behind me, and dry my hair as quickly as I can, throwing my towels into the hamper. I grab the pile of laundry from my bed and find the snarkiest t-shirt I have and pull it over my head, leaving it around my neck while I rush on my bra, then finish dressing with a pair of jeans, and my boots because fuck if I'm going out there vulnerable in any fucking way.

I hide one of my throwing blades from Caleb in the back of my jeans, because it's always better to be prepared, and head out of my room where I find Levi leaning against the wall waiting for me. He looks so at ease, but the tightness around his eyes tells me he's almost as freaked out about my parents being here as I am.

I let out a deep breath, appearing to relax on the outside and nod at him. He stands up and takes my hand, and we walk to the sitting room to face my parents together. We find Uriel inspecting the artwork, while Ashera perches on the edge of the sofa, while my other guys stand watching them, looking ready to pounce should either of them so much as look at me wrong.

"Amantara, there you are." My mother clicks her tongue as she stands. A low growl comes from Roman, and I smile at him.

"My name is Remy," I tell her, staying standing where I am with Levi.

"Your name is Amantara," Uriel utters, moving to stand beside her. "We heard about this foolishness down here, disgracing our family name even more than we ever thought possible. If it's not bad enough that you're a… a Shadow Walker, you have to make a spectacle of yourself too."

"Who the fuck do you think you are coming into my house, speaking to me like this?" My words are as icy as they are full of rage. I release Levi's hand and take a step forward, letting my shadow fire come to my hand. I know they'd never breathe a word of it, for fear it would reflect badly on them, but watching the fear dance on their faces as they see who I am, what I'm capable of, gives me a bigger jolt of happiness than it probably should. "Why are you here?"

Neither of them speak, Ashera clings to Uriel like her life depends on it, but my father is far too selfish to sacrifice himself to save her. Apparently, she hasn't worked that bit out yet.

"We came to tell you to stop making a spectacle and return to Avalon, but you are too far gone," Uriel says, his voice on wavering a little, and I have to say, that almost impresses me.

"Avalon was never my home. Not really. This is my home. These people are my family. You mean nothing to me. As far as I am concerned, you are not my parents, you have no need to feel any sort of disappointment about who and what I am. You have not bothered with me for so very long, do not think that your words have any place in my life now."

"Amantara…" Ashara starts, but Kain cuts her off.

"Her name is Remy, and if you disrespect her once more, you will not have to worry about her fire, because I will bleed you out myself." His fangs extend with his words, and her eyes go wide.

"I think, if that's all you have to say, it's time for you to leave," Creek says, stepping forward to Kain's side, his eyes turning black. Roman joins them, his eyes flashing silver, as Levi's static fills the air.

"I told you, this is my family now. You're not wanted or needed here." I dampen my shadow fire, and move to open the door. Levi stays where he is, but I feel his eyes on me, while the others watch the parents, whose approval I once desperately craved. That girl is long gone, she died so very long ago.

Uriel and Ashera scurry from the room, and I finally see them for the cowards they are. Their standing and appearances are far more important to them than I could ever have been. Having a child for them was something they did because it was expected and made them look good. They should never have been parents in the first place.

As that knowledge falls into place, it's like a weight is lifted from me. I really don't need them, or my other parents. There's still a lot unresolved with my Hunter parents, but I don't truly need them. I have my family here,

I have Fallon and Colt, Morgan and her guys.

The thought makes me smile as Uriel and Ashera disappear from sight, until my guys circle around me.

"That was not what it seemed," Roman says ominously.

Levi tenses behind me and nods. "I fear you might be right."

TWENTY THREE

"Are you sure you're okay with this? We don't have to go?" Creek asks me for the umpteenth time as I finish sorting my hair.

"Of course it's okay, they're your family. I didn't see them over Christmas with you, and Nirvana goes back to school at the weekend." I pull the straighteners through my hair one last time, before putting another light coat of mascara on my lashes. I take in my reflection, the little black dress, the stiletto heels, I don't really look like me. Maybe the me I thought I'd be once I was a doctor or a professional dancer, living the high life. Not that I'd change the last year or so of my life for a minute, it's just strange, thinking about what might have been if I'd made the wrong decision.

“It just seems silly when there’s so much going on.” He sighs as he lounges on the edge of the bed.

“The guys have all of the crazy covered right now. If anything, there are officially too many cooks in this kitchen. Plus, after everything we’ve dealt with lately, I think we deserve a night of normal,” I say as I come to stand in front of him. His hands settle on my hips as his eyes rake over me.

“I don’t know, I can think of better things for us to be doing if we’re not helping out tonight.” He licks his lips but I shake my head.

“You’re not getting out of this dinner. I know you’ve not seen Nirvana since we got back from the Shadow Realm, and I know it’s dangerous, but she’s not going to notice anything. She’s a teenage girl. She’s got far more important things to think about than the possibility that the supernatural is real, and that she’s eating dinner with an Angel and demi-Demon… is that the right word?” He laughs at me and stands before me. kissing my forehead.

“Come on, let’s go, before I change my mind and you lose your dress.” He takes my hand and pulls me from the room. I grab my clutch from the dresser as we pass it and close the door behind us, yelling goodbye to the others as we pass through the sitting room. Creek doesn’t let us stop, and seeing the look in my guys eyes, I understand why. Maybe I should make more of an effort more often. Who knows, maybe I will when people stop trying to kill me.

Creek drives Betty, music playing softly in the background as we head to his parents' house. I haven't seen Maddie and Nate since Thanksgiving, and I haven't seen Nirvana since before my birthday. The fear of putting her at risk with us being there is real, despite what I said to Creek, but he needs to see his sister before she starts to worry about him. My fear is more from everyone being attacked because we're there than anything else, but Levi assured me that Serafina would keep a watchful eye over the house and the surrounding areas should any threats pop up.

Considering her track record of saving my ass, despite her ice queen front, makes me feel better that she'll be out there having my back. We've fought back to back more than a few times, so I trust her skills almost as much as my own.

I let out a deep breath quietly trying to expel my anxiety as we pass the sign telling us we've reached Salem's Bay. I wring my hands out in my lap, while Creek focuses on the road. It's dark out considering the hour, but the moon shines down so brightly that it doesn't seem so bad until we reach the streetlights that light up all of Salem's Bay. It doesn't take us long to reach his parents' place since the area isn't exactly huge, and his leg bounces as we pull up out the front of their house.

"It's going to be fine," I tell him, squeezing his hand, before we climb from the car.

"Creek!" Nirvana squeals as she flies from the house and Creek catches her. She might be getting older, but he still dwarfs her. "Holy crap, how did you get even bigger?"

Her laughter makes me smile, and I look up from them to see Maddie and Nate in the doorway watching them.

"So big brother, you finally got the girl I see." She winks over at me and I laugh again. "This is a story I need to hear, just without the gross stuff. I do not need to hear about your junk."

Creek's laugh booms from him and my heart warms. He was so scared about her seeing him and knowing he's different, but she's so blissfully ignorant. It's enough to make me sad that she's going to age up soon enough to awaken.

"I'm not sure I'm the best story teller," Creek chuckles as he moves her back towards the house, and I follow them up the porch steps. He hugs his mom and dad as we enter, and then they move to hug me.

"Thank you," Maddie whispers in my ear, squeezing me a little tighter. I guess Creek's resistance about coming here with Nirvana wasn't as unknown as I thought. I squeeze her back, not saying a thing, aware that Nirvana is only a few feet from us.

"So, the story is coming from you then right, Remy?"

Nirvana grins once her mom lets me go.

"Nirvana, go wash up. Dinner will be on the table in a moment."

Nirvana rolls her eyes at her mom's words but runs upstairs to wash up.

"Thank you," Creek says to her as we move into the dining room.

"Have you two decided on a story?" Nate asks as he sits at the head of the table.

"As close to the truth as I can," I tell him with a smile. Creek sits beside his dad, and I leave the seat next to him for Nirvana, taking the seat that will put me between her and Maddie. Maddie brings the roast over to the table and my mouth waters. It smells just like home.

Nirvana bounces into the room and takes the seat between me and her brother. She fidgets in her seat until her mom sits down and everyone starts plating up their food. The minute we start to eat the questions begin, and I tell her as much as I can about how Creek and I ended up together, without giving tons away, and also, without mentioning the three other guys I ended up with. We'll tell her eventually, just not yet. It's too hard to explain it all, and she's so young, I think if I gave her ideas, Nate would have a conniption.

"So, when do I get a niece or nephew? I've always thought I'd make a kick ass aunt!" She squeals with pure excitement, and Creek just about chokes on his food.

"Nirvana!" Maddie admonishes her. "You never ask those questions. A person's choice to bring another life into this world is none of your business."

"Sorry Mom," Nirvana says, her head dropping. "I was just excited."

"It's fine, Nirvana," I say, patting her arm while Nate and Creek sit a little shell shocked across from us. "Babies aren't on the horizon for us just yet, we're just enjoying the fact that we've finally found each other."

"What she said," Creek grumbles, before shoving more food in his mouth so he doesn't have to speak about kids. Fate knows that's not a conversation I'm ready for, all things considered. Though with Maddie's outburst, I wonder if Creek told her about the baby I lost. I assume she already knew about the human child I had, and the lives I was kept in the dark, considering how close she was to my mom. I shrug off that thought trail, because I don't want to go down the rabbit hole of pity party for one.

"Tell us more about school!" I say to Nirvana. "What's new with you?"

"School's okay, same old really. Though, a new girl did start last month, and she seems super nice." She grins at me, but I can't help the spike of panic that comes with it. I look over to Creek and I see the same fear reflected back at me. "Also, I have a boyfriend now, so that's new."

It's Nate's turn to choke on his food, while Maddie giggles. "You have a boyfriend? How come this is the first time I'm hearing about it?"

"Because if I'd told you when it was just the three of us, you and Dad would have ganged up on me, but Remy's here and I know she's got my back." Nirvana grins and I can't help but chuckle, while Creek goes all big brother on her.

"Who, exactly, is this boyfriend?" Creek asks, folding his arms across his chest, while Nirvana rolls her eyes at him.

"You see?" she says to me, exasperated. "He's just a guy in my year, he's super nice. His brother raised him, but he works a lot hence the boarding school. Their parents died a while back."

My stomach sinks as she keeps talking. It has to be a coincidence, there's no fucking way.

"What's his name?" Nate asks and Nirvana huffs at him.

"I don't know why that matters, you guys aren't going to know him." She folds her arms, much like her brother and I hold my breath. "His name is Dylan Dotoro."

This last week or so has been fucking insane. Between Levi going off the rails about losing Amelia, the new threat against me, Roman trying to get information from the almost dead Lycan in the basement, and me trying to get them all to realize I'm not broken… well, it's just been a week.

Serafina disappeared before I got chance to thank her again, though, after the visit from my so-called parents, I really wish I had her disappearing skills.

That's on top of Nirvana's little bomb about her boyfriend causing all sorts of fucking issues. It's not like I can tell her anything yet, she's too far from being awoken. But that, that is a problem for future Remy.

I pace in the sitting room, trying to make a decision about if my plan is really a good idea or not. I mean, I know it is, but still. It could blow up in my face. It's time to end this.

Taking a deep breath, I steady my nerves and open the door to the basement. The copper smell hits me first, and I realize why Kain has stayed away from this. It's a lot.

I make my way down the stairs to the basement, where I find Roman, chest heaving as he swings another metal spike covered fist at the Lycan chained to the wall. The sweat and blood mixes together with dirt on his bare chest. His hair is wild and free, almost matted from all of the spatter caught up in it.

"Roman." My voice comes out as barely more than breath. His fist stops moments before he hits the Lycan, who is already barely standing, being held up by the chains holding his wrists.

"You don't need to be down here, princess," Roman growls, his voice low, as he keeps his eyes on the Lycan.

"Then neither do you," I say softly taking a step towards him. His eyes flash silver, his wolf is so close to the surface, I swear if I touched him, I'd almost feel fur. He scoffs at my words, glancing at me over his shoulder.

"I'm going to get every last morsel from this traitorous asshole," he growls, and I can't help but smile.

"Roman, I don't think he's got any more to give."

The Lycan starts to laugh, and I raise an eyebrow. Maybe I was wrong. Roman grabs the guy's jaw, and the Lycan whimpers again.

"You got something to share with the class?" Roman demands.

"You'll never win. She's too weak. And she makes you weak, all of you. They'll win. They always win. Chaos will reign."

Roman roars and his clawed hand rips through the Lycan's throat, almost decapitating him. His chest heaves with each ragged breath. I move towards him, reaching out a hand to him when he spins and faces me, looking more lethal than I've ever seen him. Even covered in blood the way he is, there is something brutal and animalistic about him that calls to me.

His hand darts forward and clasps my throat. Not so firm that I can't breathe, but definitely enough that I'm not going anywhere. He closes the gap between us and bruises my lips with his kiss.

His tongue takes a tour of my mouth, searching out every corner and making sure he owns every inch. It's so feral, the hand to throat and the possessive kiss, that I feel it straight to my pussy.

Roman stops, releases my lips and closes his eyes as he takes in a deep breath, scenting like the wolf he is.

When he opens them again, the silver in his eyes is like a beacon, bright and inviting, but it's the ruthless grin adorning his mouth that has me biting my bottom lip.

"I can smell your arousal, princess. Fuck." He takes a step forward, closer to me, his blood-covered clothes pressing against my chest and stomach as he walks me backward and pushes me against the stone wall. "Your pussy is calling for me. Your scent is my siren, an irresistible calling."

When his hands slide up my face, I'm mesmerized by his stare, his eyes hypnotizing me. He's just gazing at me as though calculating his next move. As if he's visualizing me in his mind's eye.

Then he slams his mouth on mine once again and I find myself hauled in the air by my hips. Instinctively, I wrap my legs around his waist and let him take completely and utter control of this entire situation.

I know he needs it. The context of our lives is getting to him and since my safety is his number one priority any threat to that stability makes him unsteady, ungrounded. That's where I come in. I'm his reality check although, when I think about it, I'm also the reason he loses control half the time.

My back is to the Lycan who was left hanging and very much dead just minutes ago, so I can't see what Roman is doing. I'm too busy devouring his mouth, his chin, and his neck to care too much about the rest of the room, when I feel one of his hands leaving my ass. The sound of chains falling and then I'm standing again. Our lips never separate, his tongue never wavers, kissing me, owning me. Showing me with his mouth every emotion that is coursing through his veins.

It's only when I feel the cold bite of the steel closing around my wrists that I freak out just a little.

"Roman?"

"Shh, do you trust me?"

"Of course, I do." For a brief second, I have the slightest of doubts and it must be clear in my eyes because Roman starts to unshackle me, but I stop him again.

"Yes. I trust you, Roman. Always."

The relief is palpable. From the gleam in his eyes to the steeling of his spine, I sense immediately the importance of my words.

Trust is everything to Roman. His code in human and wolf forms. Without trust, his existence is meaningless.

"I trust you with my life and my heart," I continue, wanting him to truly know.

"Good. Close your eyes."

I do as I'm told and wait for new instructions, anticipation flooding me.

The tearing sound, I'm guessing is from his t-shirt, immediately has me imagining his perfect abs and chiseled chest. Licking my lips, I can't help the smile that breaks out on my lips at the mental picture I've created in my mind.

"Dirty thoughts again, princess?"

"So, so many."

That's when the damp fabric is placed across my eyes blacking out every spec of light and plunging me into total darkness.

"Use your upper body strength and make sure you hold on to that chain."

What in the world? Why on earth would he need me to…

The chain starts to rise through an electric mechanism, and I feel my body being pulled upward by my arms. When I'm on the very tips of my toes, the mechanism stops abruptly and Roman's hands are back on me, making me feel warm again.

The anticipation is killing me, the not knowing, the guessing and mystery of this little scenario of his.

As quickly as his hands touch me, they're gone again, along with my shirt and bra that he's ripped right off.

"You boys need to stop destroying my clothes or else I'll start walking naked everywhere we go."

That little quip earns me quick flick across my now naked breasts. I don't have to see to know my nipples are now hard as rocks.

"You can always stay naked for us, princess. But if anyone but the four of us sees you like that, I can't be held accountable for their chance of survival."

"Fair point." I can't help the smirk that crosses my face. He really is a jealous, possessive asshole sometimes, but right now, that makes me happy as can be.

Roman's fingers nimbly unbutton my pants then slide down my zipper before meticulously pushing the fabric down my legs, leaving me in only my panties.

"This color suits you, princess." His words are accompanied by the light tracing of his finger across the top of my pink panties followed by the expected snap of the strings on either side. "Too bad they have to go."

It's all worth it when his finger grazes my already drenched lips right between my legs.

"Hmm," he murmurs right next to my ear, darting

out the tip of his tongue and biting on my lobe, "I think someone needs a little more attention."

I whimper, my way of agreeing with him when the mechanism whirrs back into motion and I'm quick to latch onto the chains with my hands to alleviate the strain on my wrists.

I'm now completely off the ground, my toes no longer touching when Roman's large hands clutch my thighs and set me down on what I'm guessing are his shoulders.

At the first contact of his tongue on my aching pussy, I know I'm right.

"Oh my fates, Roman." He's not just eating me out, he's truly devouring me. Kissing and licking, biting and sucking every inch of my flesh while his large palms cup my ass cheeks, fingers digging in the supple flesh.

Using my upper body strength, I pull myself up and cross my legs at the ankle behind his head, pushing my core closer to his mouth. Without a single word I'm begging him for more. I'm telling him that what he's doing is perfection but that I need more. I need to be filled.

My head falls back as his teeth circle my clit and he bites down just hard enough to make me scream with pleasure and pain all rolled up with one excruciatingly talented mouth.

"Roman, oh fuck." I don't finish my thought as one finger, then a second breaches the tight rim of my ass and pushes inside me. The sensation is overwhelming. Between the workout with my abs, suspended by fucking chains and blindfolded, and his mouth showing me just how hungry my wolf is with the added bonus of his fingers fucking my ass, I'm not going to last very long.

And I am more than fucking okay with that.

Extending my arms so that I'm perpendicular to the floor, my head thrown back like a sexy, dirty dancer, I'm only tethered by the fact that Roman is holding me, cradling my ass as he brings me to the point of no return.

The tell-tale signs of ecstasy start at my toes, travelling up the length of my legs, then thighs as they squeeze the side of Roman's neck.

He knows what's happening, his nails scratching the surface of my skin as my juices fill his mouth like an offering.

The torture room is once again filled with screams but this time they are mine and they are all pleasure and the most exquisite kind of pain. My fingers are sore from holding myself up but I don't give a shit.

We both need this release, this invigorating push into bliss. It's our way of getting a little slice of normalcy back.

My breath catches in my throat as he sucks my lips into his mouth like he's trying to squeeze every drop of my juices from me for his own pleasure.

With no more strength left in my limbs from the force

of my orgasm, I let go completely. My ankles uncross, my fingers release the chains, my wrists taking the brunt of my weight but not for long.

Roman releases my pussy with one long, lingering lick before the mechanism turns back on and my body is slowly coming back down to earth. Both physically and mentally.

By the time my toes touch down and Roman unhooks the metal cuffs from my wrists, I'm lucid enough to hear the zipper of his pants and I know…

This is where I get him. All of him.

It won't be sweet, and it won't be tender.

I'm about to get fucked within an inch of my life and I can't wait.

"That was one," he declares, taking my blindfold off before reaching over to the wooden chair I'm guessing he'd used earlier.

The back of the chair is presented to me, and with a wicked grin on his lips he taps the wood telling me without a word that I need to hold on.

My hands and fingers are sore, but I don't care. I position myself like I'm dancing in a cabaret and the chair is my prop.

Roman gently kicks my feet apart and before I can even grasp the extent of his need, he slams into me with one long, powerful thrust.

I scream from the force of it, holding onto the chair

like my life depends on it.

"Your pussy is my salvation, princess. Without you, I'm nothing but anger and instinct."

His hand snakes around to my neck, covering the expanse right under my chin, his thumb and middle finger on either side. Turning my head, he bites on my ear lobe at the exact moment he thrusts back inside me with savage force. He's showing me his love, fucking his need right into me. With his second thrust, he bites my cheek hard enough to make my juices flow but not so much that it'll leave a mark.

He pulls back out and with his next slam into my pussy, he bites my bottom lip and I can feel the break of my skin.

Saliva and blood mix together as he glides his tongue along the flesh and continues fucking me like an animal who has lost all control.

His other hand slides over to my front and pinches my clit and I'm a fucking goner.

Again.

"That's two," he says, the gravelly tenor of his voice in my ear.

This time, I'm not even trying to keep any semblance of decorum. I'm shaking and trembling, bucking and screaming. The wood beneath my fingers splinters and the chair's back is a thing of the past. I'm still coming on his cock when he slides out and slams me against the nearest wall so we are facing each other.

In one swift move, he's back inside me, fucking me with fury, his movement erratic and without a predictable rhythm.

"Thank you, princess, for always knowing, for being what I need."

With those words, he takes my mouth once and fucks it just as he's fucking my pussy. Hard, fast, and furious.

"Three," he announces between harsh bites and lingering licks.

I'm about to argue that I don't have another orgasm left in me when his groin gives me the perfect friction against my clit just as his cock hits the promise land deep inside me and I jolt in his arms. I'm coming again, juices coating his dick all over again but this time, he joins me.

We're sharing each other's breaths, crying into each other's mouths as our orgasms slam into us at the same damn time.

Roman coming is a form of art. The veins at the side of his throat pulse with his pleasure. The almost liquid silver glowing from his eyes, the feral curl of his lip would make Da Vinci jealous with the beauty of it.

Fuck Da Vinci. Roman is mine.

My own personal, hungry wolf.

TWENTY-FOUR

Levi gathers us all in the library, he's officially rallying the troops. I don't know exactly what he's been doing with the guys the last few days, they've kept me as far from it as they could without outrightly banishing me from the library, which has become something of a war room.

The whole gang is here. Colt, Fallon, Marie, Serafina, Nevin, my guys, some extra Lycans and Dracul, even Caleb. How they managed to get him here is beyond me, but well, everyone has a simultaneous goal. Fallon is making everyone coffee, while Levi has a map out on the table in front of us all.

"So, we have scouted the area and confirmed Amelia and Clara are here. They have people with them, stationed in the forest surrounding the cabin so this isn't going to be an easy infiltration, but with enough teams of two, we should be able to neutralize those threats quickly and quietly enough that Amelia doesn't notice. The only unknown is if there are any magical wards, which we can assume there are," Levi tells us as he paces at the top of the table.

Fallon slips back into the room, handing mugs out to everyone. Ahhhh sweet nectar of bean. I sip the coffee and sigh. The bitterness will always be my favorite taste. After cheesecake. Maybe tied first.

"We'll be splitting into teams, so we can cover the perimeter easily enough. Roman, Theron, and Emmett. Kain, Luc, and Lysandra. Fallon, Nevin, and Serafina. Caleb, Colt, and Creek. Remy will be with me. Marie is going to stay here and track Amelia, staying in contact with us all to make sure we're updated. The rest of you will fan out between us to make sure there's no room for escape."

"There is no fucking way you're sticking me with the nerd," Serafina huffs. "Unless you want him dead too, I cannot cope with his incessant worrying and blathering."

"I'll go with Nevin and Fallon," I volunteer. It keeps me with Fallon, and I don't have to worry. The relief on Colt's face is profound, which means I now don't have to worry about him being distracted either. Plus, I know Levi only put me with him so that I didn't actually get to see any action. Not this time buddy.

Levi looks at me while Caleb smirks at me. I raise an eyebrow, daring Levi to object with me right now, and I see the moment he gives in.

"Fine," he says sharply with a nod, before glaring at Serafina who doesn't seem even a little bothered. "Everyone gear up, we leave in thirty."

The gold glowing dot on the map moves a little, and I realize that must be Marie's tracker on Amelia. I can't believe we're here. That we're this close. That all of this insanity could be over by the time I go to bed tonight.

I feel a little giddy at the prospect, but I push the feeling down. I've never been the kind of person to count my chickens and all that. I leave the others in the library and head to my room. While most of our accumulated weapons are in the library, my stash is in my room. There was no way I was keeping it too far from reach.

I pull my old trusty hooded cape from my wardrobe, and change into the buckled leather pants, corseted waistcoat combo that I wore on my very first hunting trip in this life. This outfit is just stunning, and why not look good while capturing the person who's been trying to ruin my life for well, centuries it would seem.

Once I've changed, I braid my hair before strapping my swords to my back, loading my guns into my thigh holsters, and tucking my throwing knives into spare spaces that are easy to reach. Lastly, I open the box and pull out my karambit knives. They're still as beautiful as they were when Levi gifted them to me so very, very long ago. I strap one to my hip and the other to my bicep before heading back out to the library.

Creek whistles as I leave my room and close the door. "Well damn. I fully understand why Levi wanted you plastered to his side today, but looking at you, I think you made the right call. Any of us would be far too distracted by you and probably get ourselves killed."

His gaze rakes over me hungrily and I smirk at him. "Well, if everyone gets themselves back here in one piece, maybe we can have one big play time as a reward."

"Yes, ma'am. That definitely sounds like the right sort of incentive." He grins as he takes my hand and walks me back to the library. Everyone else is already here, but I know the thirty minutes isn't up yet, I set a timer on my phone because there was no way I was going to be the reason the plan got off track. Not after the amount they've tried to keep me out of this as it was. I wouldn't put it past them to try to leave me behind.

"Remy," Levi says as we cross into the library. His hand clutches my hip as Creek leaves me with him. "Are you sure you're okay going with them? You're a conduit for my power, we'd be much better paired."

"You mean, you'd get to kick ass and I'd get to watch because you'd want me protected?"

"Maybe," he sighs. "I'd just feel better if I could see you."

"I will be fine. Amelia is the target, we have eyes on her, magical ones anyway. Marie will let us all know if anything changes, and I've got Fallon and Nevin with me. Nevin's saved my life more than a few times, and Fallon can heal me up if anything does happen."

He lets out a deep sigh before bruising my lips with his kiss. "You stick to them like fucking glue. If anything happens…"

"I will protect myself. I know the drill," I tell him as I rest my hands on his chest. "You look after yourself too. If anything happens to you, to any of you, I won't survive it."

We took off into the air not long ago, Nevin is carrying Fallon, since she has the map on her phone. Marie and Caleb are helping some of the others get there, but we needed air visuals, so anyone that could fly, ended up in the air.

Levi and Serafina are so competitive, that they disappeared into the horizon a little while ago, but then, they're covering the far side of the cabin, so they have a bigger distance to travel. Levi looked back at me once, silently telling me everything he didn't get chance to before we left.

The others barely even said goodbye, and I get it. This is not goodbye. I don't accept that. None of us do. And so, there was no need. I'll see them all again soon.

I lose track of time as I follow Nevin. We rise above the clouds to avoid anyone spotting us since it's still early in the day.

"We'll need to land soon and move in on foot," Fallon calls out. Thank god for her magical map, because I have no fucking clue where we are at this point.

I follow Nevin as he starts to descend. The large green forest in the distance must be the forest Levi told us about. It doesn't take long until we land, and Fallon wobbles a little as she finds her feet. Nevin shakes out his arms from carrying her for so long while I stretch out my wings before putting them away. We might be pretty far from anyone and anything here, but there's no point in risking anyone seeing me. Plus, walking through this forest with them out would be more than a little difficult.

"We need to go this way," Fallon says, looking at her map and pointing into the distance.

"I'll go first, Fallon, you stay in the middle, just keep on top of where we're going. Remy you bring up the back," Nevin says, and I agree. He's been scouting the area, so it's better for him to go up front, though I always did hate taking up the back.

We walk for an age, but it doesn't feel like we get very

far because the foliage is so thick where we are. I try not to get pissy about it, because I love being outdoors, but still. Tripping on the undergrowth wasn't something I exactly planned for today.

Fallon stops in front of me, her hands clutching her head. "Wards," she groans as she falls to her knees.

I rush towards her, but fall to my knees when the overwhelming pain slices through my mind too.

"Fuck!" Nevin roars. "Fallon, you need to overpower them!"

She looks at me with a tear rolling down her eye, but nods and she starts to glow as she shakes. It hurts to keep my eyes open, but I don't lose eye contact with her. As her power builds, the pain starts to subside in my mind and I take her hand, hoping that my conduit can work with her too. It only takes a second after I touch her that a pop sounds and my ears ring, but Nevin is on us and pulling us backwards.

When the ringing pulls back, the sounds of fighting intrude. So much for our stealthy approach. My heart jumps to my throat. How many of the others were trapped in wards? Did Fallon break all of them or just ours?

"Fuck, fuck, fuck!" Nevin creases the map in his hand. "Amelia is gone."

Fallon's phone starts to sound in her pocket, and her eyes clear a little as she brings the phone to her ear. "Okay.

Yeah I got it," is all that she says.

"Mama tracked her. I have the location, but we need to go. I'll text the others with the update incase Mama can't reach them."

"Should we really leave without them knowing?" Nevin asks, looking nervous.

"Yes, there is no fucking way I'm letting her escape us again. If she's on the run, she won't have as many people with her, and it's likely she won't have time to set any wards. She might have a Witch with her, but so do we. I am not giving up, not when we're this close to putting an end to this bullshit."

"I don't know…" Nevin shifts, biting his lip in nervousness. "Levi is going to have my fucking hide."

"You don't have to come with us. I can go with Fallon, she can portal us, you can stay here and find the others."

"Are you kidding me? Levi might kill me for leaving here, but if I let you go alone he'll skin me alive, wait till I heal, and then do it all over a-fucking-gain. I think not." He turns to Fallon, whose eyes are still cloudy while she glows. "Can you portal us to where we need to go?"

"I can," she tells him, nodding. My gut twists, because she obviously used a lot of power already and I don't want to push her, not when she looks so off already.

"Are you sure? If you don't have enough juice left, we can fly. You just need to adjust the map."

"No, I can do this," she says, sighing as she gets back to her feet. She sways a little, but Nevin steadies her, eyeing me warily.

"Are you sure this is a good idea?" he asks me, as the shouts continue in the distance.

"No, but it's our only shot. If we don't go soon, the guards we were here to find will find us, and that could give Amelia too much fucking time. I'm not risking it."

"Okay, then let's do this." He nods. I turn to Fallon, worrying about if she can do this, but if my friend says she can, I trust her.

"Open this portal."

We step out of the portal into another forest, but the humidity here is almost suffocating. I'm currently severely regretting my wardrobe options. I push it to the back of my mind as I take in our surroundings.

"Are you sure this is the right place?" I ask Fallon as the portal closes behind her and Nevin.

"Yes, there's a building not far from here." She shows me the new map, it looks totally different from the one I saw before. She spelled the parchment before we walked through the portal, to set a new course once she got us to where we needed to go.

"Okay, well let's get moving, because I don't want to

give them any more advantage than they already have on us." Nevin nods at my words and takes up the front again, pushing his way through the greenery. Fallon stumbles along behind him, her glow from before dimmer, but her eyes still cloudy.

"Are you okay, Fallon?" I ask quietly as we move closer to our target.

"I'm fine," she says, but she doesn't even really sound like herself. Worry crawls up my throat threatening to choke me, but I'll just need to keep her guarded too. She's obviously used too much of that unknown power of hers. I know she said she was getting closer to mastering it, but she obviously hasn't.

I try not to sigh as I follow behind them, keeping my eyes and ears open for anyone in the forest around us.

It doesn't take long for us to find the building Fallon mentioned. What she failed to state, however, was that the building is a fucking fortress. "How the fuck do we get in there?"

"I have an idea," Nevin says, looking as pissed off as I feel about this situation. It's not the first shitty position we've found ourselves in together, but even so. I knew this wouldn't be easy, but fuck.

Nevin motions that he's going to scout, and I nod, staying with Fallon, who's sitting on the floor with her eyes closed. I leave her to rest and keep watch while we wait for Nevin to return.

He's not gone long, but when he returns he looks happy and crouches down to where we're huddled. "I found a bridge. It's not the most inconspicuous of ways in, but it is the quickest. Is she going to be okay?"

"I'll be fine," Fallon grumbles opening her eyes. Her glow is back a little brighter, but her eyes are still clouded.

"Okay, well then, lets head out. It's not far from here," he says, getting to his feet and looking out into the distance. I help Fallon stand, and he takes the lead. I keep Fallon in front of me again, because she doesn't seem steady on her feet.

It doesn't take us long to reach the bridge, which is a fucking rope and wood bridge. Fuck my fucking life. We cross one at a time because it seems old and fragile, like it might snap at the lightest of weights. While I can fly, there's a big fucking drop between where we are and the fortress. If I hit the ground, it's going to fucking hurt.

My heart is in my throat as Fallon crosses, she loses her footing a couple of times, and I hold my breath each fucking time. If anything happens to her, I won't forgive myself. Especially not after everything she's already been through because of all of this. Because of me.

We reach the door, solid wood nestled amongst the sandstone, and Nevin breaches it as quietly as he can. While the map led us here, this place, is well, a fortress.

They could be anywhere. I check Fallon's map, and it still shows that they're here, so we head inside into the dark corridor.

"You need to rein in your power," Nevin tells her. "Just until we reach them. Your glow is going to give us away." She nods, and slowly her glow dims. She still seems a little out of it, but considering the amount of power she's been using between the wards, the map and the portal, it's not that surprising.

We move forward through the dark, damp hall, and I've never been more thankful to be at one with the shadows, because I can see, maybe not super well, but well enough that I don't trip. I keep one hand on Fallon's shoulder to keep her heading in the right direction, since her eyesight won't be any good in here.

We reach the end of the corridor, and it splits in two directions. "Which way?" I whisper.

Nevin shrugs, but heads to the right. We follow him until the corridor opens out to a huge, high ceilinged room, light filters in through windows close to the roof.

I move with Nevin and Fallon towards the middle of the room, trying to work out where to go from here, when a wave of dizziness washes over me.

"Fallon," I gasp, reaching out to her, but I miss and fall to my knees. "Something is wrong."

I open my eyes, they feel dry, and my lashes are stuck together. It takes me a minute to remember where I am.

What the ever-loving fuck is happening?

I blink again and my vision starts to focus. I'm on the floor, face down, the cold seeping into my numb bones. I move to sit up, and the sound of metal dragging on stone pulls my attention. That's when I feel the burning at my wrists.

I look down and see the iron cuffs, attached to what looks like iron chains.

Fuck.

Amelia must have known we were here after all.

I push myself up so I'm sitting, when I spot Fallon standing in the corner of the room, her eyes still cloudy, her glow back. In front of her, Nevin is sitting on a chair watching me, a smile on his face.

"What's going on?" I ask, my voice hoarse, and Nevin belts out a laugh.

"You should've known better by now, who to trust."

To be continued…

ABOUT THE AUTHOR

Sloane Murphy is the author of the international bestselling series, The Immortal Chronicles, as well as a range of other paranormal and contemporary romance. Sloane lives in Peterborough, England, with her husband & fur baby and over the years, she has developed an unhealthy appreciation for cheesy YA Films, cupcakes and bad pop music. She adores fairy tales, ballet and all things supernatural, drinks far too much coffee, and watches an ungodly amount of Netflix. When she's not busy writing, she can be found exploring the world with her husband and chocolate Labrador.

If you would like to send Sloane an email, you can reach her at sloane@authorsloanemurphy.com

Want to sign up for her mailing list? You can sign up on her website - www.authorsloanemuphy.com

Or come join her reader group on Facebook, The Shadow Realm

facebook.com/sloanemurphybooks

twitter.com/SloaneMurphyBks

instagram.com/sloanemurphybooks

bookbub.com/authors/sloane-murphy

ACKNOWLEDGEMENTS

There are too many people to thank for this book, so I know I'm going to forget someone somewhere, but here goes…

To Jenna and Cassie, my thruple, my musketeers, thank you for dealing with my whining and bitching, and making me do all the words. I love you guys.

Sarah, as always, thank you for just putting up with me, just because your family doesn't mean you have to put up with my shit, but you do, and you do more for me than I have words for here, but thank you, for everything.

Claire, thank you for dealing with my shit, for picking me up when I couldn't, and for loving these guys so freaking much.

Heather, you're a freaking rockstar. You know it, I know it, the whole world knows it. But still, thank you so much for everything!

To everyone at HII for believing in me. Steph, Blake, thank you guys. For all of it!

To my husband, thank for you accepting that sometimes I write on fucked up timezones (I'm looking at you Jenna aha), thank you for not complaining when we're mid conversation and I space out because plot lines reveal themselves in the weirdest of ways. I love you more than words can say.

Finally, thank you to all of my readers, without you I wouldn't be here. I'm so very thankful that you've stuck with me, even when I took a huge hiatus. For reading and loving Remy and her guys, and her friends, and just this entire world inside of my head.

Thank you all from the bottom of my twisted little heart <3

ALSO BY SLOANE MURPHY

THE SEVEN REALMS SAGA

The Shadow Walkers Saga

(Reverse Harem Paranormal Romance)

A Crown of Blood and Bone

A Crown of Smoke and Ash

A Crown of Shadows and Secrets

A Crown of Thorns and Lies

A Crown of Fire and Wrath

A Crown of Pride and Ruin

The Shadow Weaver Series

(Menage Paranormal Romance)

Witch's Curse

Hunter's Heart

Demon's Blessing

The Shadow Queen Series

(Reverse Harem Paranormal Romance)

The Shadow Queen

The Shadow Legacies Series

(Rejected Mates Romance)

Luna Rising

THE IMMORTAL CHRONICLES SERIES

(YA Paranormal Romance. Complete Series)

Descent

Crash

Soar

Rapture

BLACK WATER ACADEMY SERIES

(Upper YA/NA Paranormal Romance. Reverse Harem)

Marked

Chosen

Hunted

DARK FAE DUET

(Paranormal Romance. Dark Fantasy)

Summer Princess

Winter King

OTHER AUTHORS AT HUDSON INDIE INK

Paranormal Romance/Urban Fantasy

Stephanie Hudson

Xen Randell

C. L. Monaghan

Sorcha Dawn

Sci-fi/Fantasy

Devin Hanson

Crime/Action

Blake Hudson

Mike Gomes

Contemporary Romance

Gemma Weir

Elodie Colt

Ann B. Harrison

Printed in Great Britain
by Amazon

78840119R00228